TEA TIME

TALES FOR PALE OLD LADIES

Patricia Ann Hanly Wood

Tea Time Tales for Pale Old Ladies

tellwell

Tellwell Talent
www.tellwell.ca

ISBN
978-0-2288-7161-3 (Hardcover)
978-0-2288-7160-6 (Paperback)

Table of Contents

To Amanda Ellis who got me started on very short fiction,

To Carole Bailey, Daisy Soderstrom and Suzanne Kranz
who listened to readings and encouraged me,

To everyone who has helped or hurt me
in my time on this earth,
for the courage and sensitivity gleaned
from just living among you,

To the Australian Writers' Centre who published over
a year of monthly prompts for flash fiction writers
during the pandemic, I thank you. I never entered
your contests but they did teach me to write to a
deadline and to enjoy sharing telephone readings
with friend and published writer, Amanda,

I dedicate this volume.

A book begins as a lone venture.

It does not finish as one.

I send my sincerest gratitude to
Lara Hyde, my editor, who guided me, taught me
and alerted me to mistakes - which I endeavoured to correct
and idiosyncrasies - which I sometimes did not.
Any errors that remain are mine.

Reggie Labay, my project manager,
deserves my appreciation for patience
and understanding through the long and eventful
period while this volume has been in progress.

Finally, thanks to all the team at Tellwell Talent.

Introduction

The *Pale Old Ladies* idea comes from my isolated journey through the COVID-19 pandemic. I spent rather more time indoors than was healthy, leaving me with an alabaster complexion. I began to look and feel my age. I had never consciously observed that I was aging until the passing of my dear father and had always recognized myself in the mirror as a youthful person until encountering the vicissitudes of these *interesting* times. I know that if I do not find the courage to send my stories out into your hands now, I may, indeed, run out of time.

The eleven VSS (very short stories) - or flash fiction pieces, as some call the genre - were inspired by the Australian Writers' Centre which published over a year of monthly prompts for flash fiction writers during the pandemic. At the time of writing, I brutally edited these stories to meet the Centre's length requirements of five hundred words, for most, and six hundred words for two. If you count words now, you will find that some are over by a few words. I have re-edited them for clarity and flow. I was thankful for what the parameters taught me about economy of words but I do not wish to inflict upon my readers what sometimes amounts to skimping. If you are interested, I have kept a copy of the length-compliant edit and the details of the prompt for each VSS. Otherwise, enjoy these as they stand.

Of the longer short stories, one started out to be a VSS but veered completely off the pavement in terms of length. I liked the characters and did not want to just toss the effort out so I wrote the story to the length that it wanted to be. Another was never intended to be a VSS. I awoke one morning with a character in mind and he was insistent upon being given his due attention. If I live long enough, his story may form part of a novella or novel. Viktor is relentless and unwilling to let me go just yet.

Charles Dickens' Christmas books were written as gifts for his friends. I have a beautifully illustrated first edition of *The Battle of Life*, one of his lesser-known yule stories. That slim volume, given to me by my aunt Loulou Gwendolyn Ruth Thomson, inspired me to follow Dickens' example. The book you hold now was meant as a Christmas gift for my friends. I certainly do not imagine myself in the same league with Dickens. However, millions of brides wear white when they marry because Queen Victoria chose white for her wedding gown. Imagine that I am to Dickens as a modern bride is to Queen Victoria. I hope that these stories will leave you amused and reflective - but more than that, I hope they will make you certain that I hold you in my heart.

Please Note: You certainly do not need to *be* a pale old lady to enjoy these stories but I heartily recommend that you take time for a cup of tea as you read.

"Teatime brings a whisper of grace to our otherwise hectic lives." - Anonymous

Something Special

The coat was perfect. The price was right, too. At ninety-nine dollars, it cost less than half the original amount. The saleswoman had helped Alice on with the coat, settling it just so over her dowdy shift and arranging the hood around her face in the most flattering way. Falling to mid-calf, the coat was black faux-fur but so luxuriant that it appeared genuine. There was one only.

Alice could scarcely believe her luck. She drank in her image in the mirror. She looked and felt elegant – transformed from just plain Alice to sophisticated Alicia. Her eyes twinkled as she nodded in response to the saleswoman's questioning expression.

But for the fact that her old cloth coat was much heavier, Alice would have worn the new coat and carried the old one. She handed over the cash and accepted the treasure with quivering fingers.

The very act of holding the new coat in the store's refined bag gave a lift to Alice's posture, an energy to her step and an enigmatic smile to her lips. Normally ignored and almost invisible, Alice went about her errands that day attracting smiles and admiring double-takes from passers-by. A policeman controlling traffic at a malfunctioning Walk / Don't Walk sign stopped the cars and waved her across the street with a courtly gesture. A man removing the paint from last month's Christmas display window stopped in mid-scrape to beam at her. An older lady met Alice's eyes with a merry gaze.

"Come in, dear," Gran welcomed as she opened her apartment door to admit Alice. Setting all the shopping bags on the bench inside, Alice slipped off her winter boots and noted the aroma of toast.

"Toast isn't dinner, Gran!" Alice admonished as they shared a long but gentle hug. They were almost the same size but Gran was fragile. Alice put the groceries away, worrying about the tea-and-toast anemia she knew was common in elders who lived alone. She decided to fix a nutritious meal and dine with Gran before leaving.

"What else have you been up to?" asked Gran with anticipation.

"Shopping the sales," replied Alice, who always brought something extra with Gran's grocery order.

A ruby-red glove, scarf and hat set, picked up for next to nothing, a remaindered mystery novel and some fancy Christmas-themed chocolates emerged from bags and were grasped by Gran's eager, trembling hands.

"What's in the big bag?" mused Gran curiously.

"Something special!" announced Alice, pulling the coat triumphantly from the wrapping. Before Alice could explain that she had treated herself, Gran gushed thank-you's and raved about Alice's generosity.

After Alice had settled the coat just so on Gran's shoulders and arranged the hood flatteringly around her face, Gran sparkled and preened before the mirror. Though Alice worked hard to share her grandmother's pleasure, inside she felt diminished. She realized that she was never meant to be anything but just plain Alice – nothing special.

Shadows and Echoes

Her "ex" had often joked that she was part rooster. She reflected that this was inaccurate in both gender and volume level. She liked silence at dawn - before others arose. Now at forty, divorced, childless and orphaned, Almiretta Hendry found that quiet was easily achieved. Still, today, as everyday, she had awakened naturally at sunrise.

First, she released her hair from the loose braid that prevented over-night tangles. She brushed, twisted up and fastened - with antique Bakelite hairpins - her long locks into a soft bun atop her head. Clearing the brush, she popped the shedded strands into a silver hair-receiver.

Over her undershirt went, first, the restrictive corset and next other unmentionables. These were followed by an azure ankle-length skirt and a white puff-sleeved blouse which was topped off with an azure jacket, cut to a point at the waist. The final touch was a straw boater which she secured with blue enameled hat pins. Her comfort in 19th century clothing and her assortment of old-fashioned skills made her a valued interpreter at the local living history museum but left her out of step with her own times.

A thermos of tea and a half dozen of her home baked scones were placed carefully into her basket. These were to be enjoyed along the way. Before bouncing out to greet the friend who would drive them to the ephemera show in a distant city, Almiretta checked that she had moved her cash to the tiny blue reticule with the silver ring closure.

They chatted intermittently, enjoying the snack and agreeing to dine at the historic grand hotel near the exhibition hall. Almiretta's mouth watered at the thought of the seafood chowder, the hotel's signature dish since the last decade of the 1800's.

Show admission paid, the two split up - he to find dealers in colourful mid-century modern adverts and she to seek Victoriana. The first dealer, smiling at her outfit, directed Almiretta's attention to a framed print of a Gibson girl confidently pedaling a bicycle, her hairstyle a prototype for Almiretta's. She loved it. It was in excellent condition - but the price! Almiretta pointed to an embroidery pattern, which declared in ornate Victorian script, "Patience is a Virtue." At a fraction of the print's price, the pattern was a better value. *Print or pattern – print or pattern?* Almiretta dithered. Her thrifty side winning out, she chose the pattern and opened her antique purse to count out the payment.

"Almiretta!" her friend called from a kiosk specializing in vintage illustrated certificates - Sunday school, birth, membership and marriage. "Look, it's your name!" he said.

The certificate, with a softly tinted image of a Victorian bride and groom in a lemony sunrise, recorded the union of a Nicolas Hendry and a Helga Svensdottir on June 15, 1892. The witnesses had signed Delbert Allan Townrow with a flourish and Almiretta Hendry Townrow in a careful but unflowery hand. Names, however rare, might be shared but there could be no mistaking the handwriting. Almiretta recognized it as her own.

Last Rodeo

Part the First: The Worst Drink on God's Green Earth

The flashing numbers on the traffic signal were urging Peridot and the other pedestrians to move smartly to the opposite sidewalk when she realized that a man standing - well, that was a generous thought - at her destination was watching her. She might have turned around and walked the other way had the crossing light not been flashing, hurrying her along and suggesting in its urgency that there would be no time for a safe return. The man was the tallest of the group of four. They wore cowboy hats and western string ties. She could tell that he was on his way to winning a hangover for the following day. His friends or acquaintances - she was uncertain which - were rather past the point of no return for that dubious prize. Draping themselves around the light standard for support, they were, not at all discreetly, checking out the other women who were crossing at the light. The tall one stood unassisted but not quite straight. He removed his hat as she approached.

Crap! Peridot thought as her feet secured the sidewalk and his eyes met hers. *I thought I was past that sort of thing. What is there about the way I look that could suggest that I would invite this kind of attention?*

During her youthful years she had been convinced that stenciled to her forehead, in an ink that only males could see, was a message saying: "Assault, abuse or otherwise annoy this woman." She had been certain that it must have faded as she embarked on middle age. Surely it could not have been renewed recently.

Her bright aqua cotton suit was buttoned up to the collarbone, the jacket covered her elbows and her skirt grazed her ankles - just above her sensible shoes. Her hair was twisted up into a tight no-nonsense schoolmarm bun. Dorothy Parker clearly had not run in the same circles as Peridot who, having worn glasses since high school, had found that they provided no defence at all from unwanted attention.

Calgary post-Stampede was enjoying cool evenings, cold nights and chilly mornings, though the days tended to turn hot by afternoon. The 1999 Stampede had been memorable for its low temperatures and foul weather. Storms with rain, hail and - some even claimed - snow had greeted the competitors and visitors. Still, the city's population had swelled, hotels had filled to capacity and the festivities, though literally dampened, had carried on with enthusiasm.

A calm something like a gentle exhale followed the busy, frantic days of the world-renowned celebration of ranch skills and cattle culture. Still, in the same way that the light lingered late into the summer evenings, a few cowpokes continued to loiter in the city.

He was speaking to her now. He held his hat self-consciously in both hands. This suggested to her that he had some manners and was not so drunk that he was unable to remember to use them. (To be fair, she had to give him credit for varying his gaze between her eyes and his hat and for refraining from scanning her body up and down. She would have found that action vile; his friends seemed to have no such discernment.)

"Darlin', got paid t'othuh day an' Ah'd be real pleased 'f you'd agree tuh let me take yuh out an' show yuh uh good tahm," he said in a gentle but resonant voice.

She could hear that the other fellows were saying something similar to other women in the collection of pedestrians. Most of the women walked on as if no one were there. One strident woman with a short blunt haircut shouted, "P*** off, creep."

Peridot's memory flashed back to the voice of The Friendly Giant, a popular children's show host from her childhood, reading aloud from a book called *Never Talk to Strangers*, and then to her grandmother's admonishment that a lady did not speak to a gentleman unless they had been properly introduced.

By this time the other men had found their strategies unsuccessful and were focussed on their tall friend's efforts with Peridot. The men were hooting and hollering to release their indignation at being either ignored or sworn at.

Since the tall, blue-eyed man with the gentle voice seemed sincere, Peridot felt that it was not quite right - not polite - to ignore him entirely. However, she certainly did not intend to let him think that she endorsed this type of forwardness. Although she knew enough words to swear fluently at unco-operative computers and printers, she also had no intention of spouting profanities at a person - even a forward one. He was waiting quietly for an answer. She was close enough that she could see a cigarette package in his shirt pocket. Her allergies were already becoming irritated by the cloud of tobacco smoke hovering around his cohort.

"Well, sir, there wouldn't be any point in that. I'm not a party girl and I would never marry a man who smokes and abuses alcohol ... but thank you for your kind offer," she told him firmly but politely and punctuated the statement with a pleasant (but not inviting) smile.

She realized that he was offering something that *he* considered generous and attractive even if she did not share his view. She mentioned marriage not because she was interested in doing *that* again - once had been horrible and more than enough - but because it generally sent men scurrying in the way that the first sign of a dish rag after any meal had dispatched Peridot's brother to the sanctuary of the washroom. (The last dish had always emerged from the water before his return.) While religious fundamentalists were less likely to be chased off by mentions of marriage, she was confident that this man did not fall into the category of the devout in any religion. She felt the victory of an escape within her grasp and made an effort to restrain the beginnings of a gloat.

The man stared back at her as though he would have scratched his head in bafflement if both hands had not been occupied by slowly rotating his hat. He was uncertain whether he was more fascinated or more aggravated.

"Well, don't that beat all!" he replied after seeming to come to some resolution or epiphany.

"Ma'am, Ah'm goin' out with muh friends tuh gyit stinkin' drunk fuh the last tahm an' Ah'm fixin' tuh smoke muh last pack uh cigarettes. Ah mean tuh enjoy muhse'f. Ah'd be honoured if you'd meet me fuh aftuhnoon tea at The Palliser at two uh clock the day aftuh tomorruh. If yuh'd do that, yuh have muh promise that you'll nevah need tuh worry 'bout me touchin' drink or smokes again … an Ah'm uh man uh muh word," he explained deliberately.

"The Palliser … at two o' clock … on Sunday … for tea," she repeated slowly as if unsure that she had heard him right. She paused before adding what they both understood was the definite "yes" he was waiting to hear. "And no cologne or aftershave, please. I have allergies."

She had been unprepared for this turn of events. Had the sense she'd been born with evaporated into those earnest blue eyes? Except for the eyes and the fact that he was clean-shaven, he appeared more than a bit rough around the edges. His face was scarred in several places, his nose showed evidence of a long-healed fracture and his hair was wild and in want of a comb. She felt that she should have been frightened. The Palliser tearoom, she reassured herself, should be a safe place for a woman. She resolved to arrive very early so that he could not glean any clue to where she was staying. A mild complaint formed in her mind for the mother who had programmed her to be polite but had failed to teach her how to defend herself from people who were forward.

She was more than halfway up the next block before she realized that she did not know the man's name … and that he could not know hers. When she looked back, all she could see was a display of back-slapping and shoulder-punching by his friends. She was too far away to hear the words but she could tell from the hoots and whistles that he was taking a ribbing. Peridot turned back and hurried on her way.

When his friends settled down a little, Stuart pulled out his wallet and moved the amount he imagined it would cost to take a lady to tea at The Palliser - plus fifty dollars more - to a hidden section where he kept his savings. He had no account in a bank. He drifted from job to job and quickly spent whatever he was paid. Money could not be stolen if it had been spent. Being robbed enraged him. He had been "relieved" of his military medals and his ready cash in a dark alley one night long ago. The thought of this incident still raised his hackles. There had been too many in the heavily armed gang and he had been too drunk for a happier outcome - happier for him, at least. He shook off the memory and calmed himself.

*****

The next morning - it was technically morning as the clock read 11:50 - Stuart felt more miserable than he should have, given what remained in his wallet. Checking the contents, he was relieved to find that the savings section had not been touched. There was still money in the spending part, too. He sat staring into space and puzzling about that fortunate but unexpected circumstance until he happened upon a vague memory of winning at cards.

There ain't no sech thing as uh friendly game uh poker, he thought to himself with a sly smile.

The sour smell of vomit hovered over the base notes of stale smoke and sweat. He checked the-day-before's clothes, which he was still wearing, and reached to the floor to find his boots. He saw no evidence of a stomach "evac" there so he assumed that one of the other fellahs must have brought that particular aroma into the room. He pulled on his footwear, levered himself upright and glanced around the room. There were four bunks, three with saddles over the foot of the bed frame. Unlike his shorter roommates, Stuart's height required that his feet extend beyond the bed frame. For this reason, his own saddle was on the desk with his guitar case. He looked more carefully at the occupants of the other three beds. There was no sign of wakefulness from his chums but they all seemed to be breathing - a definite plus, he considered.

He tried to figure out whether or not breakfast would improve his condition. He knew of an all-day breakfast place a couple of blocks away. His brain was crying out for coffee but he knew that water was what his body really needed - in quantity. Fog in his brain made it difficult to co-ordinate shedding yesterday's clothing, washing himself and finding fresh - if smoke-drenched clothes could be called "fresh" - trousers, shirt, socks and underwear. The thought of lying down again was deeply tempting. Only the certainty that he had a mission kept him in motion. He had completed missions with injuries, gunshot wounds and other complications. A hangover, he was determined, would not defeat him now. Checking his face in the mirror, he felt that he could not trust himself to shave. He was sure that any attempt would mean adding new scars to his already "not purty" face. He returned the shaving soap and razor to his kit, found his hat and room key and left quietly.

At the diner, he requested a double order of toast plus three poached eggs with runny yolks before asking the waitress to keep the ice water and coffee coming. For some, the headache might have been almost debilitating but he was determined to press on through it. He remembered promising that this would be the last time and he was thankful for the poker win. It had allowed him to drink enough to feel so miserable that he never wanted to be hung-over again. He still stank of cigarette smoke. Although he craved nicotine, he was motivated not to give in to that temptation, either. The waitress was helpful with directions to all the places on his list. He left her an unusually generous tip (with silent gratitude to all the losing poker players), thanking her politely for the information. As with any mission, he had reconnaissance to do, information to analyze and equipment to assemble - all on a tight schedule and without the support of the military from which he had retired years before. This was, after all, a personal mission.

*****

Peridot had risen early, bathed at leisure, dressed in a white linen dress, put on a blue cotton jacket and hurried down for breakfast. (Though she did not consciously grasp this, the blue of the jacket was the shade of the man's eyes.) She had arranged a tour to Banff for that day. The itinerary included lunch at the Banff Springs Hotel, a stop for taking photos of the Hoodoos and a visit to the Whyte Gallery of the Canadian Rockies. Free time would be allocated for dinner. Some tours included the hot springs. She preferred the Hoodoos – tall abstract natural formations carved over time by wind and water.

Fortified with herbal tea, a soft-boiled egg, toast, fruit and yoghourt, all of which she had thoroughly enjoyed, she found the tour pick-up point with plenty of time to spare. Among the people waiting for the tour bus was an older lady who was also unaccompanied. Peridot began chatting with her. They discussed their anticipation of the tour and the circumstances of their previous visits to Banff. A quarter century before, the lady had passed through when cycling across Canada with a group of women. Peridot had attended a museum management course at the Banff Centre almost fifteen years earlier and was eager to catch a view of Mount Norquay again. She was also looking forward to dining with Fred who had been a fellow student in that program and who continued to work in the local museum.

Somehow the topic turned to tea at The Palliser and Peridot found herself describing the circumstances of her invitation and her concerns about personal safety. The older lady, who insisted that Peridot call her Millicent, seemed to draw out Peridot's entire miserable relationship history in condensed form. This transpired without Peridot's making a conscious decision to reveal it and without her even noticing.

"Give him a fair chance, dear. He might be a kind person. It can be a long and lonely life if you live in fear of every romantic overture. Be cautious and vigilant but don't write off all men just because you married one bad one," Millicent advised.

"I am not sure that I class having someone try to pick me up on the street as a romantic overture!" Peridot objected.

"It wasn't ... but the invitation to tea certainly was," Millicent clarified. "Whatever did you say to him?"

Peridot was able to repeat, verbatim, her words to the man and his response to her. Millicent laughed: it was a high-pitched tinkling sound.

"I intended to scare him off," Peridot lamented, "but it didn't work out that way."

"You must have put the fear of God into him if he has offered - more than offered, promised - to give up both drinking and smoking and has invited you to afternoon tea," Millicent assured.

"I'm very fearful - in fact, I'm terrified - of being touched after my experiences with my ex and ..."

"Don't you have any positive memories to draw on?"

"None!" Peridot replied. "I was assaulted by my first boyfriend - I threw him off me before the worst happened. Where the strength came from, I'll never know. Some time later, I went to an outdoor concert with my mother and some friends and, while we were walking to the gate, a man grabbed my arm and tried to pull me toward him. I was like a deer in the headlights, frozen and unable to speak. My mother had to tell the man, 'I'm her mother and I think you should move along now.' A guy in the subway stopped me to ask for directions and while I was tying to help him, he put his hand up my skirt. A man in the aisle seat of a train crowded me right to the window and put his hand on my leg. A strange drunk impeded me and tried to kiss me - all the while describing in merciless detail how he had beaten his wife half to death when she tried to run away while he was talking to her. In another case, a boyfriend came to take care of me when I put my back out and did most of what he wanted when he discovered that I could not make a move to defend myself ... and then there was the engaged friend who had had a row with his intended and asked if he could pour out his sorrows and get some useful female advice. He did his best impression of an octopus - all hands, I mean. This just scratches the surface and I don't do anything to invite this kind of thing. I thought getting married would save me - and Chuck was a perfect gentleman *before* we were married but he didn't protect me from the man sitting beside me at a colleague's wedding. The man - the one beside me, I mean - had creeping hands under the table. I just kept pushing them away because I didn't want to make a scene at Deidre's wedding. I was almost apoplectic by the time the dinner was over and Chuck yelled at me for being 'crazy' and ungracious. After Chuck and I were married - well, there was no one to save me then and my vote didn't count."

"Did you not know what to expect from marriage, dear?" Millicent probed. People, she knew from experience, were more likely to talk openly with a stranger whom they expected never to see again.

"I knew. I had the Boston Women's Collective book *Our Bodies, Ourselves* but I didn't anticipate that my physical pain and my personal preferences would be irrelevant to the husband who was supposed to love and care for me. I expected that there would be ... tenderness. Silly me! He was truly mean only when he was sober, Mondays to Thursdays. He never let the drinking interfere with his work. I guess some women would consider themselves lucky in that. On the weekends, he was maudlin and apologetic before he passed out. I became a little tougher after the divorce. If I had the wedding guest thing happen to me now, I would smile very innocently, take the cretin's hand, break his wrist and let him explain that to his wife who was sitting across from him. It makes me so very angry that the louse plagued me because he knew I was too polite to make a fuss."

"I'm sorry, dear ... but they're not all like that. As difficult as it seems, I'd like you to try to stop thinking that you can't stand to be touched at all and think only that you hate to be touched by anyone who hasn't your best interests at heart. There is tenderness out there and an embrace, a kiss, a caress … and more can be beautiful."

"Perhaps. But that just seems to be a fairy tale to me," Peridot replied as the bus pulled up and began loading.

*****

Stuart began with "recon" at The Palliser. He observed carefully the clothing of the people who entered the tearoom. He went to the lobby phone and called to make a reservation for Sunday at 2:00. He explained to the young woman who answered that he had no experience with afternoon tea and would she please explain how it worked - "lahk yuh talkin' tuh uh Martian." She laughed a kindly little laugh and told him in detail. He made precise notes.

Stuart knew that The Palliser welcomed western garb but he was equally sure that that type of wardrobe was not right for this lady. He went to the second-hand stores next and equipped himself with appropriate clothing - except for a short-sleeved white dress shirt and appropriate socks ("gentlemen's hosiery", the salesclerk called them), which he had to buy new at Eaton's department store. The second-hand store offerings of shirts and socks were either too shabby or the wrong colour. He also bought brand-new underwear to help him feel empowered to turn up for tea with The Palliser's up-scale clientele. No one would be seeing it, he knew, but a little psychological advantage was welcome on any mission.

While he was looking for a blue business tie, one of the second-hand shop ladies suggested a bright blue bow tie which would compliment the navy jacket he had selected (not to mention highlight his "fine eyes"). The jacket-and-tie combination worked with the "candlelight" (he would have called the shade "bone" or "buff") cotton slacks. She taught him how to tie the bow properly and assured him that his "lady friend" would be impressed.

Though a bolo tie with a silver slide was what he normally wore for an evening out, he knew how to do a four-in-hand and both a full and a half Windsor knot for a regular necktie. The bow tie had been outside his repertoire before the sales lady's kind instruction.

Next on his list was a "propah" haircut. He slipped in just before the barber's early closing time. Stuart was certain that he would be capable of shaving himself by the next day. A "propah" shave was much more expensive than he recalled and the shop was not open on a Sunday, said the little card in the window.

Stuart walked back toward the hostel - or flophouse, as he called it - feeling pleased with his purchases. He began to wonder why, even after showering and changing into fresh clothes, he still carried the aroma that an ashtray acquires after an all-night poker game. He concluded that staying in a room with four smokers - now three - was to blame. Nothing that sat in that room for any length of time could escape picking up the odour of cigarette smoke. He would need a better strategy if he meant to keep his new clothes smoke-free for the allergic lady. It was a good thing that she had spoken up. Otherwise, he might have tried to mask the stale smoke with a strong aftershave.

He went back to the diner, ordered an open-faced hot beef sandwich, and, while eating, considered the problem. He reasoned that he would require a secure smoke-free place to store the clothing overnight. He would also need a place to shower and change - somewhere other than his shared room. Reflecting on the other costs related to the outing, he decided that the place would need to be inexpensive in addition to being free of tobacco fumes.

The diner was slow. The lunch rush was over and the supper crowd was not expected for an hour. The same waitress was still on her shift. When she came over to refill his coffee and water, he outlined the problem. He figured that he could shower and change at a public swimming pool or athletic centre for the price of admission. The problem remaining was the need for a safe place to leave his "new" clothes overnight.

"Ah'm not fixin' tuh use thuh pool, jus' showah an' dress," he explained to the waitress.

She compressed her lips and a crease formed between her brows.

"I'm real sorry, mister. I don't know you well enough to have you 'round to the house," she told him slowly.

"No, ma'am, not propah, but maybe yuh maht take muh clothes - if yuh got no smokers at yuh house - and bring 'em back tuhmorrah. Thuh clothes, Ah mean."

"Sure thing, mister. You come in for breakfast about noon an' pick 'em up," she agreed. "I start later on Sunday so I can go to church with my family. Pool's just up that way," she told him, waving a hand to indicate north, and continued, "I'll draw you a map to The Palliser. Tea, you say? That's real fancy - too rich for my purse!" she laughed.

"Mahn, too!" he affirmed. "But Ah invahted thuh lady an' she accepted."

"Must be something special," she mused aloud.

"Ah nevah bin so aggravated an' so fascinated with one woman in mah lahf. Nevah felt thuh need tuh change muh ways b'fore neithuh. Ah guess she *is* sumpthin' special."

"Beautiful?" the waitress asked.

"Not so's yuh'd notice. Not thuh kahnd tuh stop traffic but not hard on muh eyes neithuh. She's got these tahny hands and real inter'stin' eyes an' she's surely got me all cattywampus - that means confused, ma'am," he explained.

The waitress glanced at his hands - unusually large compared to his wiry physique - and thought that his appraisal of "tahny hands" might not conform to popular opinion.

"She rich?" the waitress asked instead of voicing her evaluation.

"Ah wouldn't say so – not real p'or neithuh."

"Then why is this lady different?" the waitress probed.

"Onee three kahnds uh woman Ah meet on thuh street. One kahnd ignores me lahk Ah'm not theyah. Second kahnd tells me tuh gyit lost ... an' sometahms thuh language, well, Ah'd nevah be sayin' that in thuh presence ovah lady nahs as you. Third kahnd tells me, 'Sure, let's go'."

"But not this lady?"

"Not this lady! Declahned muh offuh uvah naht on thuh town ... said it be uh waste uh huh tahm – huh tahm! 'Cuz she'd nevah marry uh fellah drinks an' smokes. First Ah took it tuh mean she thought Ah ain't no good ... but she cawled me 'suh' ... an' Ah realahzed Ah could be uh fellah 'don't drink an' don't smoke' ... an' Ah am startin' this mornin'. An' she's meetin' me fuh aftuhnoon tea tuhmorruh!" he declared triumphantly.

"Surely you're not looking to get married," the waitress challenged.

"Nevuh figyuhd Ah was. Guess Ah jes' changed muh mahnd. Won't be anytahm soon. Ah know this lady's goin' tuh need tuh be courted raht and propah. Ah gottuh be lahk thuh tortoise in thuh story – slow an' steady wins thuh race. She'll want gentle an' cahm. No rushin' 'round fuh huh."

"Where's she come from?"

"East, Ah'd say."

"Old cowpoke like you willing to go east?" the waitress asked with a large measure of skepticism in her tone.

"She says the word, Ah'd go tuh Timbuktu. 'Tween muh military days an' muh work on thuh oil rigs, Ah got 'round this world some. Ah lahk thuh smell uh horses an' cattle bettah 'n' oil so ah bin driftin' 'round cattle country an' thuh rodeo circuit gettin' work as Ah can, ma'am. Even worked some uh them greenhorn rahdin' tours."

"They can take the man out of Texas but they can't take Texas out of the man?" the waitress joked.

"Sumpthin' lahk!" he chuckled. "Guess that part uh muh lahf's ovah, too."

"What's her name?"

"Lady!" he replied with a silly grin and a feeling of heat and colour overtaking his cheeks.

"You're havin' me on!" she exclaimed, grinning.

"Truth is Ah don't rahtly know," he admitted.

"She didn't give you her name?"

"Ah nevah give huh mahn neithuh … makes us even," he replied with a laugh. Then realizing that once again he had failed to introduce himself, he inclined his head in a manner suggestive of a polite bow and told her, "Ma'am, Ah'm Stuart Cowton an' Ah'm pleased tuh meet yuh an' real grateful fuh awl yuh help."

"I'm Naomi Brownwell, Mr. Cowton," she replied with an echoing gesture.

"You best cawl me Stuart," he suggested.

"I'm fine with Naomi, then. How will you find her if you don't even know her name?"

"Ah 'xspect she'll be there uhwaitin' fuh me. Ah got huh figyuhed fuh thuh punctual kahnd – jus' muh feelin', y'unnerstand," Stuart explained.

"You really believe she'll turn up?"

"Don't know fuh hundert puhcent but Ah'm bettin' she'd jus' say no thanks, not stand me up. Seemed too mannuhly tuh do that," he concluded.

"So you think you've fallen in love then?" she asked with an edge of disbelief.

"No, ma'am. Ah nevah b'lieved in love at first saht. Ah seen plenty uh lust at first saht in mah tahm but real love don't come that cheap. Kinduh lahk uh garden – put in some seed an' cyeh an' tahm an' watuh an' sunshahn an' it otta grow - but instant an' effortless, nevah!"

Naomi had looked through his "fashion finds", as she called them. In the back office, she found a hanger and some plastic film from a laundry delivery. Stuart arranged his "new" trousers and jacket on the hanger and covered them with the film. He began placing all the smaller items in one plastic shopping bag. This he settled over the hook when the task was complete. Naomi fixed her gaze on the packaged white shirt and told him that it would need to be ironed for the Palliser.

"Ah know how tuh ahrn - anyone bin military knows that - but Ah got no ahrn an' no place tuh use it, 'f Ah did," he lamented.

She noticed that he pronounced iron as one syllable rather than the two used on the national broadcasting system which set the standard for Canadian pronunciation.

"Don't worry, mister ... I mean Stuart. I'm ironing my family's church clothes tonight and one more shirt won't be a burden," she insisted.

He told her that he was grateful for her kindness.

*****

Stuart's friends did their best to persuade him to go along with them for another evening of drinking and carrying on. They urged, cajoled, teased and bargained with him but he declined. Then they ribbed him about having a lady who was too fancy to spend time with the likes of them. He remained immovable. Finally, they just filled the room with smoke while they readied themselves for a night of carousing. As painful as the tobacco fumes were for Stuart, he felt disinclined to ask them to stop. The rules could not be changed to accommodate the new Stuart. After he had suffered the ebb and flow of waves of "nic fits", he decided that some fresh air might help.

He went to the nearest newspaper vendor. In a symbolic nod to the lady from the East, he bought a *Toronto Star.* He sat down on a bench and turned to the entry of the famous advice columnist. The first letter was from a widowed mother who had noticed that her recently married daughter had suddenly become "clumsy". The columnist's response explained that, while such sudden changes *could* signal health problems, most often they were a sign of spousal abuse. A list of contacts and resources for escaping abusive relationships was provided at the end of the column.

It enraged Stuart to think of a man treating his wife - or any woman - cruelly. Stuart's mind wandered and he imagined meeting this new husband on a dark night in an isolated spot where it would be possible to correct the man's manners with impunity. Perhaps it was the nicotine withdrawal that was disturbing the calm which Stuart knew he needed for the mission ahead of him. He brought himself back into focus by thinking of the tiny hands and the green eyes with golden halos around the pupils of the lady he had invited to tea. He remembered the cautious smile she had given him when she had accepted his second invitation. He re-examined every aspect of their first meeting. He felt, once again, the crushing feeling he had experienced when he had thought she was telling him that he was beneath her. He replayed the moment when he knew that she was being clear on what she would and would not accept. That had impressed him. No woman had ever spoken to him in that manner before ... and she had called him "sir". He drifted to her severe hair style and wondered how long her hair might be and whether he would ever have a chance to see her wear it down.

He recalled the little trace of a gloat which had flickered across her face when she had thought she had put him in his place. He appreciated the fact that she liked to win a contest of words. Good manners were important but some spirit along with them was more than appealing to him. He hummed "I'm Looking for a Hard-headed Woman." It made him smile inside and out.

He had not realized that he was looking for anything except a paying job, a place to sleep, palatable meals and occasional female companionship that ended at or before dawn. If it ended before bedding down, that had always been fine, too. What he could not abide was having any part in causing the misery of a regretful woman.

He thought about how he had lost a good female friend that way once. They had been young - high-school age - and were joking around when the situation had gotten out of hand. He had not considered it to be anything serious - a couple of kisses and an embrace that was closer than was decently chaste. However, Lillianna had been so embarrassed that she had never spoken to him again as a friend. They had greeted each other in passing for the sake of appearances but a friendship he had valued had been destroyed by carelessness. Because of that, there had been no carelessness even in his worst days of "tomcattin around", as he called.

"Eithuh yuh want tuh, darlin' or yuh don't. Jus' tell me what yuh prefer an' Ah'll b'have uhccordin'ly," he would say to make sure that there was always a conscious choice.

A wave of anxiety from nicotine withdrawal broke his recollection. This was the longest he had gone without a cigarette since his last military mission. Giving up drinking was not, he figured, likely to be difficult as he always remained sober during periods of work, sometimes weeks or months at a time. Smoking was different: it was his daily companion - a pack to a pack-and-a-half most days. He wondered if it would be necessary to give up poker, too. Smoking and drinking were so much a part of the card-playing environment that it might feel like torture to be around it.

*****

As the light faded, Peridot sat next to Millicent on the tour bus. They had had a full day crowned by a spectacular sunset. Fred, Peridot's acquaintance from long-ago seminars and conferences, was now the man in charge of the museum, with a salary that allowed him to invite both women – ladies? (he was no longer sure which to use) – to dinner at one of the nicer places in town. It had been a great chance to catch up on all the news in the Alberta museum community and to hear about Peridot's career change to ESL instructor.

Fred had a stable relationship which he was sure was not headed toward matrimony. There had been so many years when marriage was not a legal possibility that it was now unimaginable that a certificate could improve on their life together. He was confident that gay marriage was on the horizon but he figured that it would be a few years yet before the government figured out how to slip the legislation through.

Fred knew that Peridot had divorced but it always surprised him that it had taken another five years after he had met her that first time for her to leave what had clearly been an abusive situation. He remembered her as an emerging butterfly who had been startled to discover that flight was among her capabilities. She had begun every challenge in the course without confidence until, finding her strength, she had soared. He had imagined that the husband back home had kept her in a box, figuratively speaking. Fred had doubted that she could return from the inspiring experiences in Banff to fit back into any box. He was now cheered to see that Peridot was excited about her life – that she had shed so much of what had limited her during the marriage.

Millicent encouraged Peridot to tell Fred about the invitation to tea. When Peridot had begun describing the situation - that she had been walking back to her hotel in the evening - Fred had told her how delighted he was that she was able to be out in the evening alone.

"Remember how you always walked into town from the Banff Centre with an entourage of five gay guys who closed ranks around you to protect you? Did you know, three of the five have died of AIDS? They thought that they were in exclusive relationships but each of their partners brought home the disease from someone else," Fred told the ladies, withholding from Millicent that he had been one of the original five - now one of two survivors.

There was a moment of silence for those lost before Fred turned back to the present.

"Tea at The Palliser is something special. You definitely should go."

"I just don't need any man trouble now. I've been happier and healthier since I've been on my own," Peridot declared with a firm set of her jaw. "And besides, we live in dangerous times. You must have read in the news about that villain who was deliberately going around spreading AIDS to women ... and I'm allergic to penicillin, the treatment of choice for gonorrhea and syphilis. I'm sorry ... table-time topics!"

"You've agreed to go to tea not an orgy! You must be ready for a change or you would have said no thanks!" Fred insisted.

"It just seemed wrong to say no to two invitations - especially since he actually listened to what I said about drinking and smoking," Peridot explained defensively.

"All my women friends complain that straight men don't listen. You've met one who does. Aren't you just a little bit curious to know more about him?" Fred urged.

While Millicent made encouraging noises, Peridot said, "I guess," without conviction.

"My next problem is what to do about who pays. He didn't look like he was flush with money and in southern Ontario, women pay their own way to keep from handing over power to the man," Peridot objected.

"I may be able to help with that. Tell me what this fellow and his friends were wearing," Fred elicited.

"String ties, western boots and hats, jeans - definitely not designer - with collared shirts ..." Peridot furnished from the picture in her memory.

"You can stop there. I know the type. If you try to pay your own way, you will deeply insult this man. Women's lib hasn't really hit the rodeo circuit yet - though there are women barrel racers. *He* invited *you* so he pays," Fred explained.

"So what do I do to even up the obligation? I want to show my independence."

"Normally you would cook for him but since you don't have kitchen privileges here, invite him on a picnic and assemble the feast yourself - assuming you decide to see him again, of course," Fred recommended.

"That sounds very domestic when what I'm aiming for is strong and self-sufficient."

"You asserted your independence when you rejected his first offer. Think of that ... and what's the worst that could happen?" Fred demanded.

"I could end up violated, murdered and thrown in a ditch!"

"You watch too much TV," Fred argued.

"The statistics are -" Peridot started.

"- worse for gay men," Fred countered.

"Even if that's true, it doesn't give me comfort."

"Listen, he's chosen a public place - a safe place - and an event with a fixed duration. Tea doesn't go on indefinitely. It ends while it's still daylight. He wants you to feel safe and comfortable ..."

"'Won't you come into my parlour?' said the spider to the fly ..." Peridot quoted, voicing the words of an old rhyme that Victorians had used to warn young ladies against risky behaviour.

"Perri, give him the benefit of the doubt. I'm willing to bet that *you* have had afternoon tea once or twice," Fred countered.

"Several times. Once at Fortnum and Mason in London ... lovely," Peridot recalled.

"And I think it is unlikely that ... what is his name, anyway?" Fred inquired.

"I don't actually know. Somehow that was missed in the ... umm ... encounter," Peridot admitted.

"Well, what is his most memorable feature?" Fred continued.

"You mean besides the previously broken nose?" Peridot began but Fred scowled at her.

"All right, I'm sorry," she relented. "He has incredibly blue eyes."

"I think it is very unlikely that Mr. Blue Eyes has ever ... um ..."

"Taken! The verb for afternoon tea is 'taken' unless you want to use 'enjoyed' to describe the sensation," Peridot supplied in a teacherly fashion.

"So, it's unlikely he's ever *taken* afternoon tea. He chose that for *you*. He's willing to give up his comfort for yours. How long has it been since you and Chuck separated? It's got to be at least ten years."

"Yes, the divorce has been final for just over ten years," Peridot affirmed.

"And you haven't had anyone … umm … in your life since then?" Fred asked suggestively.

"No! And don't be vulgar!"

"It's time, Peridot!" Fred insisted. "Look, I don't want to push you but I want you to be open to something new."

"I'm not sure I can go. I don't know what to wear," she teased.

"What were you wearing when you first met him, dear?" Millicent asked.

"A cotton suit - jacket and skirt - in a bright aqua, with a white linen shell," Peridot responded.

"Wear something blue to match his eyes - or pink, if you want to pretend you weren't mesmerized by them," Fred recommended. "Just don't wear white. You're too pale and it looks too … matrimonial. Not yellow either - that has never been a good colour for you."

They persuaded her to describe every clean outfit that remained in her travel wardrobe, commenting on the impression that each would make. They came to no consensus but the time glided by so quickly that Fred had found it necessary to drive them to the pick-up point to catch their bus. Fred encouraged her to go to tea and she promised that she would. Peridot and Millicent thanked him for dinner and for the ride. By way of goodbye, he performed the little bussing, which was becoming popular in the media, on each of the ladies' cheeks.

"It was a pleasure to meet you, Millicent … and Perri, let me know how it turns out!" Fred called out as they boarded the bus.

Peridot mulled over all the details of the discussion of appropriate tea clothes as Millicent dozed on and off. Later, in her hotel room, Peridot set out three different outfits and two possible hats. She decided that she would just dress in the ensemble that most appealed to her when the time came.

She made two phone calls, first to the front desk to request a wake-up call and then to the kitchen to arrange a full room service breakfast. This indulgence ensured that she would not be tempted to go anywhere in the morning. She wanted to avoid ending up in a panic for time. She planned to be sedately writing postcards in the lobby when the man walked through the revolving door. She preferred, for reasons of safety, that he should have no hint that she was staying at The Palliser.

She was not as well off as her accommodations implied. In the original plan, she and Minette, an old friend, would have shared a room with twin beds. The luxury of staying at The Palliser was made possible by a post-Stampede promotional price. In the end, Minette had had to cancel when one of her daughters developed pregnancy complications. The hotel staff had been delighted to exchange the originally booked twin room for an upgraded queen. This enabled the hotel to accommodate a family who wanted a room adjoining theirs for their two teenaged daughters. Peridot was more than satisfied, making it a three-way win.

*****

Stuart arose Sunday morning and checked his kit for razor, shaving soap, toothbrush, toothpaste, comb, nail file and deodorant. He knew that it was unlikely that his friends had disturbed his possessions but, on a mission, unsecured equipment had to be checked and re-checked. He smoothed his hair into place and looked in his wallet. All the money he would need plus some extra was there in the savings section.

He wondered whether the little tremor just south of his ribs was due to excitement, anxiety, or tobacco cravings. Which of these it was did not much matter. The mission was on. There would be no time for distractions. As he walked to the diner, he reviewed what he had learned about afternoon tea. First would come the decision on the choice of tea. They could select one variety - served in a large pot - to share or they could each have "their individual preference" (as the lady on the phone had termed it) served in smaller pots. A three-tiered serving plate would be brought to the table soon after the tea arrived. The little sandwiches and "savouries" were to be enjoyed first in small nibbles - even if the whole would fit into the mouth. The event was to be slow and stately, as though no one felt truly hungry but was just eating to be polite. The scones were next - small pieces to be broken off and dressed with butter, jam, and whipped cream as desired. There would be two scones - one plain and one fruit - for each person. Finally, the fancy sweets would be enjoyed. He had been warned to take his cue from the lady, who would know whether these were bite-sized or would need to be eaten with a fork or spoon.

There was to be no rattling of saucers when replacing the cup and never anything but the most gentle stirring if milk and sugar were added. The last point was familiar from his memories of his mother. No one needed to tell Stuart to ensure that the lady was to be comfortably seated before he seated himself. That also had stuck from childhood.

"It is acceptable to linger over a final cup of tea after the last sweet has been consumed," Stuart had been told. The presentation of the bill soon after would signal the time to leave. If he wanted to "protect the lady from the coarseness of money at the table," the gentleman would be welcome to take the bill to the cashier so that he could pay it out of the lady's sight. Stuart had told his instructor that he did, indeed, prefer to settle accounts in that way.

*****

Peridot was well aware of the set price for taking afternoon tea at The Palliser. Before Minette had had to cancel, they had planned on this precious extravagance. Without Minette, however, Peridot had considered it unnecessary and, perhaps, a little lonely. She had tried unsuccessfully to suppress the delight that she had felt in the man's serendipitous selection of something so completely to her taste.

She worried about whether the cost of tea for two would be a hardship for the stranger. Then she wondered how the cost of tea would compare to the expenditure required for his first offer. She could count on the fingers of one hand the number of times that she had been in a drinking establishment. Those occasions had been office-related and not optional. The price of a glass of ginger ale or a cup of tea on those occasions had, she thought, been extortionate. This was in the days before designated driver campaigns had ensured that anyone staying sober to chauffeur drinking friends would be offered a variety of inexpensive alcohol-free beverages. She remembered vaguely her last time in a pub. Draft beer had been significantly cheaper than the non-alcoholic choices. A little smile slipped over her face when she considered how much the stranger would save if, true to his word, he stopped buying cigarettes and alcohol. This thought reduced the guilt she felt regarding the cost of the set tea.

She returned to the closet all the outfits she had set out the night before, pulling out instead a white organza-and-lace two-piece dress with a high collar. She pulled out the blue jacket – the one she now recognized was the colour of the man's eyes. After being worn for the very full previous day, it looked a bit less than fresh. She phoned housekeeping for an iron and an ironing board. She washed the jacket in the bathroom basin using the travellers' laundry powder that she always carried but had never before tried. After multiple rinses, she squeezed out the dripping item, rolled it in a towel and, using her whole weight, stepped carefully up and down the length to squeeze out as much moisture as possible. A knock at the door signalled the timely arrival of the ironing equipment.

At half past one Peridot, properly turned out, sat sedately on a chair that commanded a view of the hotel's main door. When she had checked herself in the mirror, she had found that the white organza and lace and the slightly softer twist-up of her hair made her look "sweet". She expected that this would please the man but it was not the effect that she was striving for. She had rather hoped, with the moderating influence of the blue jacket, that the look would say "prim and proper".

The full-brimmed, organza-trimmed white straw hat, affixed to her hair with a blue-enamelled butterfly hatpin, looked sweetly old-fashioned. Peridot did not care what other people might be doing in the late 1990's. She would not be taking tea without a proper hat.

There's something charming about a man who gives an invitation to tea, she bolstered herself, as she lifted her pen from a postcard. *Also, how adorable is it that he told me he's a man of his word?*

A shiver ran over her as she considered that psychopaths were believable because they felt no guilt about lying. She shivered a second time at the mental image of herself being dragged from the lobby by the throat in the jaws of a creature half-man and half-lynx while no one lifted a finger to help her.

"Stop that!" she startled herself by saying aloud. She looked around but no one seemed to have noticed. She worked at being inconspicuous, pulling her knees even closer together and folding her hands humbly in her lap on top of the array of postcard mountain views.

*****

Stuart approached The Palliser, passing under one of Calgary's many overhead pedestrian bridges. He noticed several men in business suits and neckties but none of them wore bow ties. An anxious little flicker in his stomach unsettled him until he recognized approval in the smiles of the women who looked at him. He straightened himself a bit and walked a little more confidently. He decided that he needed to treat this more like a parade than a stealth mission. He did some breath control exercises, letting his tension drain out as he exhaled.

Stuart, he said silently to himself, *where yuh headed if thuh lady don't want tuh see yuh agyin? Yuh fixin tuh keep yuhse'f on thuh road tuh bettah things or yuh plannin' tuh drown yuh sorrows in drink?*

He pondered that for a few moments. Then he decided that he was made of "stronger stuff" than that. He realized that the promise he had made to the lady was also a commitment to himself.

Muzak was playing in the lobby. Peridot recognized the faint instrumental as "Ghost Riders in the Sky", a once-popular crossover hit from the country-and-western repertoire into mainstream pop. She thought of the last stanza's warning to the cowboy to reform and she smiled.

At just that moment, Stuart stepped through the doors. He returned the smile, thinking it had been intended for him. Peridot stood as he walked toward her but did not extend her hand, clasping her purse and the postcards instead. Stuart, knowing that hand-shaking was at the lady's option, made a half bow.

"Stuart Cowton at your service, ma'am. T'suh pleazuh tuh see yuh ahgyin," he declared.

"Peridot Stone! I'm delighted to see you again, too," she greeted him, adding a movement that suggested a curtsey without the showiness of the full formal execution.

"Ah don't mean tuh offend yuh bah bein' forward, ma'am, but Ah want yuh tuh know yuh look real fahn. That dress is jus' what Ah 'magined uh propah lady maht wear tuh tea," he told her hesitantly but sincerely.

"You're very nicely turned out, too, Mr. Cowton. I'm especially fond of the bow tie," she revealed softly, giving him a conspiratorial smile.

He bent his arm at the elbow, turned his fingers into a gentle curl and moved to stand beside her as he eased his arm fractionally toward her. He waited but she did not take the offered arm. He wondered why. He was sure that he had done it correctly. A look at her face told him that she was pleased by the gesture but her stance clearly indicated that she would not accept. A brief wave of irritation passed through his mind before he focused on the delight in her eyes.

He restored his arm smoothly to his side and almost crooned, "Well then, aftah you, ma'am." The open palm of his other arm discreetly indicated the direction of the tearoom.

"Thank you, sir," she replied, setting off with a graceful but purposeful stride.

Nothin's goin' tuh be simple with this lady, he thought silently and appended the thought with, *an' that ain't uh bad thang … just uh maht confusin'.*

"Reservation fuh Cowton!" he responded when welcomed by the uniformed woman at reception.

"Yes, Mr. Cowton, your table is by the pillar to the right. I hope that will be satisfactory," she explained.

"Yes, ma'am," Stuart agreed before turning to his tea date and asking, "s'long as that suits you, Miss Peridot?"

"That will be lovely," she assured, smiling at each of them in turn.

When Stuart and Peridot were seated, they discussed the selection of their tea immediately. Stuart agreed that a shared pot would be best but deferred to her clearly superior knowledge for the choice. She selected a rose-scented green tea. The white-aproned waitress conveyed their choice to the kitchen. When she was out of earshot, Peridot instructed Stuart on names.

"You may call me Ms. Stone or you may call me Peridot but not Miss Peridot. I do not consider that all listeners have the right to know whether or not I am married."

"Ah meant no offence, ma'am," he apologized.

"None taken," she assured.

"It's jus' uh little bit uh Texas 'as followed me awl ovuh fuh more 'n twenty years ... an Ah know this ain't Texas, Ms. Stone," he explained.

"And what do they call you?" she asked.

"Stretch, sometahms. An' Stu - Ah don't cyeh fuh that none - an' Cowton an' uh whole lotta othuh things Ah nevah say in front ovuh lady," he told her with a mischievous grin.

She laughed, a light effervescent laugh.

"What do you *prefer* to be called?" she probed.

"Stuart, ma'am, thuh name muh mamma give me ... but Ah'd lahk yuh tuh know Ah bin real pleased tuh heah *you* cawl me 'sir' as Ah don't gyit much uh that now ... though Ah once did."

"Well, sir, I'm glad you're pleased," she bantered playfully. "If I'm to call you Stuart, I think it best that you call me Peridot ... and since I don't class you in with 'all listeners' I think it's fair to tell you that I was married for eight years and I've been free of Chuck Stone for longer than that - more than ten now," she confided.

"Not uh happy union?" he asked. When she shook her head, the trim on her hat shimmied in a manner that almost took his breath away. It suggested dappled sun on slowly moving water or moonbeams twinkling on snow - elegance and grace with a bit of mystery.

"Ah ain't nevah bin married. Nevah bin close neithuh," he told her when he recovered. "Ah bin driftin' job tuh job since Ah left thuh military. Ah bin rootless but Ah'm not homeless. Most uh muh jobs got uh bunkhouse, uh cabin or some-such ... or he'p fahndin uh place tuh lay muh head."

They talked easily about their travels and their taste in music. Stuart described the points of most interest from the just-finished Stampede. Peridot recounted the details of her visit to Banff the previous day - editing out the discussions of his invitation to tea.

He remembered all he had been told about taking tea. Where he had any doubts, he let her take the lead, which she did smoothly and without calling attention to his uncertainty. With concentration and observation, he managed not to embarrass himself during this new-to-him experience where, he noted, she was clearly at ease.

Of her choice of tea, he managed to compliment the scent. He knew that he would forever remember her when the fragrance of rose touched his mind. However, he thought silently, *tea must be the worst drink on God's green earth.* As they finished the last dainty sweets, he excused himself.

"Tuh warsh muh hands, ma'am," he said.

His 'mamma' had told him that handwashing was the only use for a washroom that could properly be mentioned in polite company. Instead, he went to the cashier to pay the bill so that Peridot would not be confronted with the vulgar truth of the cost of their entirely enjoyable afternoon.

They had lingered over the last cup of tea, which she had poured when he returned from his "errand". When he set the cup gently in the saucer for the last time, he was relieved that his big, rough hands had been equal to the task of manoeuvring the fragile bone china without damage.

She thanked him graciously for a wonderful afternoon as they left the tearoom. In the lobby, he spoke of the next day.

"If you'd allow me, ma'am, Ah'd lahk tuh take yuh tuh see uh movin' pitchuh tuhmorruh aftuhnoon. Ah bin askin' 'round an' they say *Thuh Thomas Crown Affair* an' *Thuh Sixth Sense* ahr both good," he suggested.

"Oh, Mr. Cowton, I don't know you well enough to spend two or three hours sitting in the dark with you ..."

"Well, darlin', we wouldn't wantah rush things none," he interrupted, striking just the right balance of ambiguousness so that she would be unable to tell whether or not there was a small measure of sarcasm.

"... but, if you would permit me," she resumed, "there's an urban park - Olympic Plaza - not far from here and I'd be pleased to take you on a luncheon picnic tomorrow, weather permitting, of course."

He had felt aggravated (or was it hurt?) by her first response but then, there she was, turning him "awl cattywampus" again with a counter offer. He smiled and accepted readily.

Ain't nothin' evuh gonnah be simple with this lady! he thought to himself. *But what is lahf without uh challenge? Ah jus' hope there's cawffee er lemonade er anythin' 'stead uh tea tuh drink at this picnic. Really mus' be thuh worst drink on God's green earth.*

Snap Shots

Three o'clock said the cafeteria clock when Polly looked up from her newspaper. Having a spare in the last period every Thursday allowed her to catch up on all the bad news: violence in Northern Ireland, arrests and claims of police brutality during bath house raids in Toronto, suppression of student protests in the U.S. and public outcries for dress codes in Canadian high schools. It was just another average day in the news cycle at the close of the 1960's.

In five minutes, the bell would sound to signal the end of classes. Polly folded the newspaper and pulled out the magnetic photo album she carried everywhere. No magnets, but adhesive on both the backing and the transparent overlay, held the treasured photographs in place. Davey in uniform smiled lovingly from the first image. Wearing a fashionable flowery shirt, he laughed in the next. The third showed him embracing Polly. An Irish Republican Army sniper had ensured that he would never do any of those again.

Polly had stopped wearing her wedding ring after moving to Canada. It was not that she loved Davey's memory less. It just would have generated too many painful questions. Being older at twenty-six and obviously English made her enough of a misfit among the other secondary school students.

"Brit!" voices had accused her in the halls between classes. Her locker had been vandalized. Only crumbs remained of the McVittie's biscuits her sister had sent her as a treat from *over 'ome.*

Polly's suspicions about those responsible were strengthened but still unprovable when a bold band of the sons of I.R.A. supporters had pulled down the official portrait of the Queen. Horst had seen them.

Horst was artistic, cultured, and old-world-charm-personified. Seeming to know that a fellow could safely adore all women or one woman but not any number in between, he called all the female students *Liebling* or *Liebchen.* He offered them sincere compliments and pleasant comments.

"*Blau* iss zuch a goot colour for you, Elizabet. It highlights your eyes, *Liebling.*"

"Cheryl, the shoes are *wunderbar, aber, Liebchen,* they take attention from your luffly smile."

At the sound of a commotion at the "caf" doors, Polly tucked her album safely into her shoulder bag, away from unsympathetic eyes. Turning, she observed Horst being surrounded by a group of male students. She recognized the O'Toole brothers and one of the Feheely kids. Not all of Irish descent, this apparent league of nations included Yuri, Angelo, a Vanderhalter, one of the Machado kids and Bart Abbotson.

"Fag!" one of them spat at Horst. Polly knew that this did not mean "cigarette" as it did back *'ome,* but something insulting … menacing. She stomped into the centre of the circle, draped herself around Horst and kissed him suggestively. Thanks to theatre arts class, he managed not to look as stunned by this as he felt.

"Tell your li'le chums to buzz off, love. You're busy!" she declared, pulling him from the circle and through the doors to safety.

Fixtures and Chattels

Veracity aligned her finger with the windowsill, allowing the ladybug to crawl aboard. The tiny window was sealed with more than a half century of paint layers. How had the delicate creature come to penetrate the dusty, lifeless attic? She moved carefully out of the room, down the stairs, through the kitchen and, shouldering the screen door, onto the back porch. At the railing, she spoke to the cheerfully coloured beetle ("Entomologically correct?" she wondered):

"Ladybug, Ladybug, fly away home.
Your house is on fire, your children alone."

At the last word, she launched the bug into the air.

Odd, she reflected, *what rhymes people had once taught children and how these rhymes come back later in life.*

As a child, she had thought that this couplet was meant to keep her in her place through fear of fire. Now she was certain that it was about responsibility. The very moment you were not where you were supposed to be was when the worst would happen.

She circled the house, sold by her parents to strangers while she vacationed in Europe. In the large flat area that had been Grannie's vegetable garden, she picked up a clump of earth and squeezed it until a shower of dust slipped through her fingers. Next, she lifted the lid of the rain barrel. Still hanging inside on an S-hook was the battered aluminum pot that had always served as a dipper. Grannie had preferred rainwater for hair washing, believing in its softening qualities. That was before anyone had heard of acid rain. Veracity ladled a half pan of the cool water over her head. The miniature cascade flowed down her tresses and dripped from the tips of her locks. A small breeze, hardly a wind, whispered in her ear about life and loss. The dry air carried the moisture away as she visited the little gate in the front yard, the decaying apple tree by the bedroom window, and, next to the side door, the snowball bush, the bleeding hearts and the high bush cranberry.

Back in the attic, her fingers lingered on the vise Gramps had used to make furniture for her dolls. Grannie, she remembered, had finished each piece with glossy coats of orange shellac while Veracity had watched in wonder that such beauty could come from a few cast-off sticks and a can of "smelly gunk" worth pennies. The vise was a fixture. Attached to the built-in workbench, it belonged to the new owners.

There are no ceremonies for saying goodbye to a house. No music, no congregation of friends, nor commissioning of clergy eases the passage. She did a final walk through the empty main floor, taking the wallpaper and room colours with her in her mind's eye.

The dipper from the rain barrel sat on the seat beside her when she dropped the house keys off at the lawyer's office. Back in the car, Veracity wondered if the ladybug had arrived home in time. Then she began to weep.

Mistaken Identities

She stood alone in the disorderly queue waiting to speak with the young woman at Mall Information. The "You Are Here" map had been worse than useless, adding many steps to her day without yielding results.

Why could people not line up properly? she wondered. She was sure it must be her turn but how could anyone tell in the chaos?

The *stupid girl* had put the crystal into the cupboard rim down. This was the result. The dessert cups and the water goblets exhibited tiny chips or rough spots on their rims. The pattern was no longer kept in open stock. She doubted it was from one of the famous makers such as Steuben or Waterford. Still, the crystal pieces had been passed down to Delia from her great-aunt and, therefore, Delia treasured them. Now they needed professional help.

All this, and Delia's son was planning to marry this … this - a number of much-too-rude or vulgar terms came to Delia's mind until she settled on *snip.* She was a snip of a girl who "just did not know" - a strong and wide-ranging complaint which meant that the girl had been improperly or insufficiently socialized. The girl had a ridiculous and pretentious name: Tiffany. Had her parents not known the difference between a shop and a child? It was clearly just too much; her son called the girl "Tiff" – as in a little fight. There was going to be more than a *little* fight, Delia was certain.

While his mother ran her errands, Ryan was at home looking his girl over and wondering why his mother did not like Tiff. The girl was friendly, pretty, shapely and sexy. He smiled a wry half smile. Maybe that was it – *sexy* was not a positive quality in his mother's mind. Actually, he was not sure what his mother thought about being sexy but looking sexy was certainly objectionable to her.

Ryan was enjoying the view. Tiff was appealing in a fluffy pink angora top with a plunging V-neckline, black satin slacks which clung to her form, and white ankle boots with quivering leather tassels on zippers above stiletto heels. She resembled a lucky rabbit's foot.

Didn't you have to rub a rabbit's foot for luck? he mused with an evil grin. He could barely wait.

Tiffany saw the grin and thought about how tiresome it was to have a boyfriend who leered at her so much of the time or trotted her around to his friends to be leered at by them. She wanted to be treated as a person. Being treated as an object was not what she had had in mind when she had asked for her older sister's help the previous year. Tiffany had known that she needed a change but she had not expected it would have to go on and on.

Sitting home every Friday and Saturday night while her popular sister never wanted for admirers or frantically fun evenings out, shy Tiffany had felt miserable and alone. Mercedes had known all the necessary treatments. She counselled a new hairstyle and magnetic clothes; gave Tiff lessons on manicuring her own hands, applying alluring makeup and plucking her eyebrows; and (the final touch) taught her sister about tipping her chin just so and fluttering her eyelashes in a flirty fashion.

Tiffany's studies of the animal world had suggested that she would need the equivalent of shaking a few colourful feathers to attract attention in the courtship dance. She hoped that, after she was noticed, the relationship would become human and companionable. Then she could drop the façade. However, that was not what she felt was happening. It was all very confusing. Ryan was not her first mistake but at least he had not become violent, as the others had when she refused to submit to their sexual demands.

She admired Ryan's mother whom Tiffany considered poised and gracious. When invited for dinner, Tiffany had done her best to please this lady. Etiquette books borrowed from the library had taught Tiffany what she knew about table manners and agreeable topics for conversation. Tiffany felt afterwards that she had performed acceptably on the occasion.

Tiffany and Mercedes' parents worked opposite shifts. For this reason, there were no family dinners. If there was fine china in their house, Tiffany had never seen it. They ate individually at each person's convenience. The rule was that, after use, the earthenware dishes were to be rinsed before being placed in the dishwasher. Unless Tiffany talked to herself, there was no table-time conversation.

Delia headed home with the repaired crystal. It looked as good as new. *Maybe the girl might be trainable,* Delia hoped. She remembered that Tiffany had offered to help with the clean-up after the meal. The girl knew enough for that, at least, but nothing about the careful individual washing and hand drying of the delicate pieces that made up the Wedgewood dinner set. *Thank heaven,* Delia thought as she considered that she might have brought out the more valuable Minton china. Reconsidering, she decided that such a "sexy Sally" would have no interest in the refinements Delia valued. Ryan, like his roving-eyed father, would not stay long with anyone who had even a modicum of refined taste and higher standards.

Mean-ings

Elizabeth waited in line (a "queue" to Allister) at the postal station to dispatch a letter signed with lots of x's and o's. (Allister called them naughts and crosses.) Both knew that these represented all the hugs and kisses they could not share due to pandemic travel restrictions. They sequestered - Allister in England, Elizabeth in Canada - not happily but responsibly.

He called it a "sunset romance" while she, coming from a country where the season of ice and snow was long and beautiful, termed it a "winter-of-life relationship". They had moved slowly, cautiously - perhaps suspiciously at first - toward commitment. Citing recent statistics on romantic fraud, she described herself as paranoid.

"Not paranoid if they really are out to get us - and the numbers show that they are," he affirmed, accepting her concerns where many would have ridiculed them.

She recalled the delightful, though small, extravagance of taking lemonade and dumplings at Raffles in Singapore. Allister had quoted a song from *Gigi* to remind her that their remaining time on earth was uncertain and, therefore, precious. He suggested that if their two years of courtship had allayed her fears, he wanted to lose no more time than it took to put their affairs in order and plan a wedding.

The memory was interrupted when the man ahead of her dropped his pandemic-mandated mask and began an intense excavation of his dripping nose. Elizabeth fled the line. She feared her happiness might be snatched away by the deadly virus.

Having visited Allister's simple pied-à-terre in London the year before, she believed that his lifestyle and assets were not dissimilar to her own, the results of careful management during a hardworking career. This put her at ease. Allister had never corrected this impression.

After his return from Singapore and the implementation of travel bans, Allister's two younger sisters had quarrelled with him about his decision to marry. They accused Elizabeth of being what the Americans called a "gold-digger" who would take Allister's estate in Scotland, his country house in Wales and the over £2 million on deposit, all of which the sisters anticipated inheriting - unless Allister married. Furious, he had written each a cheque for £500,000, telling them to expect nothing further from him and to stay away unless they could be joyful about his marriage.

Later, the sisters concluded that Lydia must have unknowingly infected him then. She was already recovering in hospital when Edna found Allister and called an ambulance.

"Everything to Elizabeth!" he had wheezed before the oxygen mask covered his face.

The small couriered package arrived just as Elizabeth started up the verandah stairs. Allister's sisters, knowing that there was no written record of his wishes, had enclosed only a black-bordered death notice, a cemetery map with the grave site highlighted, some photos and a ring. Elizabeth would never know that they might have kept even the ring had they not thought it ugly. Smiling through her tears, Elizabeth understood Allister's meaning immediately:

Diamond
Emerald
Amethyst
Ruby
Emerald
Sapphire
Topaz

- DEAREST! She felt lucky to have known true love, even briefly, so late in life.

The Great Bank Hold-up

She was not sure why, on that frosty January day, she had felt motivated to buy the nationally distributed Toronto business newspaper. News was always depressing and she tried to avoid it. She had taken the paper home, scanned the front page, turned to the horoscopes which forecasted bad consequences due to the alignment of the planets, read the advice column - more strife - and, finally, studied the obituaries. She had not expected to see any names she recognized. She had lived away from "the city" for a number of years. Most people she knew either placed no death notices at all or used small local papers. The funeral home websites shared such information but she did not have Internet access at home.

Forrester, Josef, it said, with the original - and, for her, unpronounceable - Slavic name in brackets. Forrester, she remembered, was a translation. She felt sad that she would not be able to go to pay her respects. Attendance at any gathering was limited to ten people and Joseph had been the oldest of eleven brothers. The COVID crisis also meant that taking a bus would be risky at what her daughter described as Clara's "advanced" age.

She checked the "survived by" list. Maggie was still living as were all the brothers. However, there were names for younger generations she barely recognized or did not know at all. Clara picked up the telephone handset and called directory assistance. Giving the name as Forrester and the address of the house next to the one where she had grown up yielded no listing. So few people maintained landlines now that she knew that the absence of a listing provided no indication of whether family still resided in the old house. She drifted, remembering the new Chris de Burgh song that had been playing in the bank the day when Josef and his brothers had been there for her.

Josef had nodded to the next brother who joined the line of waiting customers. Three other brothers had already positioned themselves at carefully spaced intervals. It had never been about money. For some it was about loyalty; for some, revenge; and for the youngest brothers, it was just a lark. Whatever their individual reasons, the bank would suffer for its mistreatment of Clara.

The previous Friday, the line had snaked around the roped and stanchioned path and out beyond the glass doors of the bank. In Clara's estimation, there had been at least fifty people waiting to be served as she watched the customer in front of her complete the white deposit slip with the red grid and lettering.

Clients who were unable to fill in the slips were to be assisted but those who were capable were to be reminded that they could save time by doing this before lining up. Such customers were to be politely offered a small number of the blank instruments to take home. There were several reasons for this. Among them was the fact that it was always more reliable for a teller to check something she - it was almost always *she* in those days - had not prepared herself. In addition, bank inspectors preferred to see the client's handwriting and not just the person's signature. A well-trained clientele also equaled a faster moving line.

Clara continued to greet and serve customers pleasantly though she was tired and her body screamed for a washroom visit. On Fridays, when the branch was open until six o'clock in the evening instead of the regular 3:00 p.m., each teller's wicket was closed in turn for twenty minutes to allow processing of the work for that date. This entailed calculating the paperwork and submitting the lists of cheques, deposit forms and withdrawal slips to the proof teller. The fiction was that this should take five minutes, allowing a teller the fifteen-minute break required by law. In truth, this was impossible to do honestly. Clara and most other tellers did not even have the four minutes needed to dash to the washroom and to be back in time for re-opening on schedule so that they could conduct business on the following Monday's date. This accounted for the rampant rate of urinary tract infections among bank employees at her level. While people who worked at desks could slip out for "the necessaries" – as one co-worker termed it, tellers could not leave their stations while customers remained on the banking floor (except for lunch time and, on Fridays, the scheduled pseudo-break times). Hence, the "Double-A" cycle (agony and antibiotics) dogged tellers.

It was over thirty minutes beyond the official closing time when Clara counted out the last cash, warbled a cheery "Thank you and I hope you enjoy your weekend," and, finally, turned the door lock behind her last customer. Although there was still pressure to get on with the many background duties, Clara sprinted to the washroom. She returned to list and send to proof all her remaining items. She went on to help with filing all the signature cards that had been pulled out during business hours and with sorting the seeming mountains of deposit and withdrawal slips into numerical order to speed the savings manager's verification on Monday. All this and preparing their cash drawers for examination and lock-up had to be completed before tellers and the front counter officers could leave. It was sometimes eight o'clock before that happened. Higher level people such as the manager and loans officers could leave as soon as the clients were cleared from the banking floor.

Clara anxiously completed the rough cash count on her blotter. A detailed count was not done every day. On Fridays, especially, a rough count sufficed. She was anxious because the previous day - and in fact, each day that week - there had been a difference between what the paperwork said she should have and what she had actually held in her cash drawer.

The day before, Clara had been out by nine hundred dollars after a detailed balance - where every penny was counted and listed on the "teller's blotter" as the form was called. Both the savings manager and the BAO - branch administration officer - had counted everything in Clara's drawer with the same result. They had had strong words for Clara while she, in a panic, tried to remember the transactions she had processed that day that were large enough to allow such a difference and which might have had "unclear figures" - difficult-to-read numbers. Clara was certain that she had not given out that amount of money by mistake. It was most likely a "reversion of figures" as the amount was divisible by nine. This should have been caught by the proof teller but it was possible for proof to be balanced on a double error while the cash showed an overage or shortage.

Clara had gone back to look at the work she had transferred to the proof teller and had found the error quickly. It was in the listing. The difference between $16,550 and $15,650 was nine hundred dollars. No unauthorized cash had been given out either by mistake or by felonious intent. Still, the superiors had been peeved by the lost time.

Friday's rough count revealed a shortage of two hundred and fifty dollars. The BAO, who had come to lock Clara up (to supervise the return of Clara's cash to a double locked compartment in the vault) rechecked the cash in the drawer, checked the drop drawer in Clara's wicket and peered into the time-locked compartment beneath the drop drawer.

The drop drawer had a panel that fell open when the drawer closed, allowing bundles of paper money - "notes" in teller-speak - to drop into the small time-locked vault at the bottom of a teller's drawer set. There were strict limits concerning the amount of cash a teller could hold in her cash drawer. The drop drawer allowed the teller to secure excess cash without leaving her station. Clara looked at the bundles of cash. She knew that she had made up three bundles of twenties and two bundles of tens, all of which had been fed into the drop drawer. She was certain she remembered making two and a half bundles of fives, as well.

A half bundle was fifty notes. Two half bundles made a full bundle of one hundred notes. A bundle of twenties was two thousand dollars. A bundle of tens yielded one thousand dollars and one hundred fives added five hundred dollars to a teller's count. Tellers took pride not only in the accuracy of their counts but also in the neatness of their bundles. These were tidied and organized so that fifty heads faced up and the other fifty faced down. The bundles were wrapped tightly at one end with paper bands which were hand-initialled by the teller and stamped with her teller's stamp. The other end of every bundle was secured with an elastic band.

A shortage of two hundred and fifty dollars might be a half bundle of fives. Clara looked at the two full bundles of fives and examined her memory. She was sure that she had dropped two and a half bundles through the drop drawer but had recovered only the two full bundles of fives with the bundles of tens and twenties when the time lock opened. Of course, it had been busy. It was possible that she was confused.

To be robbed with an excess of cash in her cash drawer meant immediate dismissal for a teller. However, a teller with an amount of cash over the limit could not close her wicket to remove the excess to the vault while customers were waiting in the line. The drop drawer was the answer to a prayer in that regard. In Clara's previous branch, there had been no drop drawers. More than once, when she had found herself with an excess and a line up of customers snaking out the door, Clara had resolved that, should there be a robbery, she would lock her key in the drawer and tell the robber that he might as well shoot her as she could not afford to lose her job.

*****

Josef and Clara had been friends since childhood. Playing at Clara's house had meant that Josef could enjoy respite from the squabbles among his ten brothers. These contests of will too often turned into physical fights. Josef liked the quiet of Clara's home almost as much as he liked Clara, whom he considered the sister that he wished he could have had. For Clara, who suffered the loneliness of an only child, Josef's almost constant presence was a gift from the angels. Clara's parents welcomed him as the son they had never had because, as the oldest, he was earnest, serious and mannerly when he visited. His strict Roman Catholic parents had impressed upon him that he was to be a model of behaviour for his younger brothers. The threat of an eternity in limbo - or worse, should he lead them astray - figured powerfully in Josef's world view and sense of self.

Although they had thought the friendship fine for the two in childhood, as Clara approached her fourteenth birthday, her Protestant grandparents exploded with all manner of warnings about what pubescent Catholic boys would do to Protestant girls. To Clara's family, however horrifying an unwanted pregnancy might have seemed, it paled next to a possible marriage. In the former case, the infant could be surrendered to the Children's Aid and life could go on. In the latter, they would lose their grandchild and all their future generations to Catholicism. They knew that a Protestant - girl or boy - could never marry a Roman Catholic. The Protestant would be forced to convert. A crisis of months was small when measured against eternity.

Interestingly, and unknown to the parents and grandparents, there had never been a time when Clara and Josef had fancied each other simultaneously. Though the thought might have crossed each mind, it had fled quickly. They were far too familiar - too much like true brother and sister - for the mysteries of romance to take hold.

The tinder was further dampened and the threat extinguished for Clara's family when Josef, at twenty-two, married Mary Margaret, known as Maggie, a proper Irish Catholic girl. Whatever initial suspicions and jealousies there might have been, Maggie wisely accepted Clara in the role of sister-in-law and relied upon her for insight into Josef's character. Maggie was warmly but quietly embraced as family by Clara's parents and grandparents.

Clara and Josef included Maggie in "Perfect Crime" which was their favourite game. As children, they had played detective and criminal, having been inspired by television programs such as *Surfside 6* and *77 Sunset Strip*. This had metamorphosized into Perfect Crime when the players became bored by the fact that the criminal was always caught due to a stupid mistake. Neither Clara nor Josef would agree to being "the stupid one" so Perfect Crime allowed both to be clever. Also, they worked together instead of against each other. With Maggie, they devised ways of stealing beautiful or historical items which they felt were being allowed to deteriorate. Their first "project" was the exquisite art deco lanterns on the facade of a now-defunct department store. It had been bought by developers who clearly had no appreciation for the building's history.

Although the plan might actually have worked, there had never been any intention of carrying it out. The exercise simply allowed the three young people an outlet for the frustration that they felt as they witnessed careless or intentional loss of heritage or beauty.

It was from one such conversation that the great bank hold-up had been planned.

"Something is troubling you, Clara," Josef observed and Maggie concurred.

"It's just work … nothing new. You know that fancy new electronic monitoring system they have in the bank - it *looks* like it's just there to direct the customers to the next open wicket. Well, it does more than that. It counts how much time each teller takes with each customer and calculates an average for each teller. Apparently, I am not processing customers fast enough or I'm serving too few per day or some such."

"But the customers like you. Some even wait for you when another wicket is free. I've seen it. I always wait for you, too," Josef told her.

"That doesn't show up in the statistics that the system reports … and if the customers step off the mats, it confuses the system. Different customers have different needs. This week I had clients who were travelling to several countries and needed travellers' cheques and cash in three or four currencies. One client who always waits for me takes care of all the banking for himself, his wife and his elderly parents. I can't rush him. He's a good customer and a pleasant man. I also served a woman whose husband had left her and had cleaned out all their joint accounts. She certainly needed more time and understanding."

"Surely," agreed Maggie.

"And then there are the problem clients like the man who doesn't have a joint account with his wife but wanted to cash her unendorsed cheque. When I told him that that was against the law, can you imagine what he said?"

"No," replied Josef.

"He said, 'But I'm a doctor!'" Clara told them.

"What did *you* say?" Maggie asked.

"How wonderful for you but I still can't cash that cheque without your wife's signature," Clara quoted herself, adding that the client had started shouting and threatening her.

"What did you do?" Maggie responded.

"I had to refer him to the manager," Clara answered.

"I would have told him where he could shove that cheque," Josef interjected.

"I was shaking. However, the worst we are ever allowed to say to a customer is, 'Thank you and the same to you, sir … or madam.'"

"That is why I will never be in customer service!" Josef declared.

"So true!" agreed Maggie.

"And that isn't the worst. The manager agreed to cash the cheque and brought it back to me and made me count the money out into the customer's hand."

"You can't be serious!" Josef objected.

"Yes … but, of course, the manager put his initials on the cheque so he, not I, will be responsible if the wife ever complains," she concluded with a tone of satisfaction.

"On top of that, I'm so anxious about being monitored that my cash has been out every day this week," Clara continued. "And, of course, all errors but today's have been found. Today, I was short two hundred and fifty dollars - I think it's a half bundle of fives. I've been warned that this can't go on."

"Surely they know that the customers would miss you if you had to leave?" Maggie offered as encouragement.

"I'm not sure that "admin" knows that at all," Clara moaned.

"There is other weird stuff, too, isn't there, Clara?" Josef elicited, knowing that talking about it helped calm her.

"Two weeks ago was the full moon ... never let anyone tell you that that is not a weird time. I had the lady who screams if the computer puts interest in her account and changes her balance. She insists that the balance must be all sixes - to ward off the devil or something - and she blames me if it isn't. She curses me and she demands that I change it back. When I explain that I can't do that, she makes me fill out a withdrawal slip for the amount of the interest and then she argues with me when I ask her to sign it. She says that she is risking her immortal soul. Only after several rounds of explaining that it is for her financial security that I can do nothing without her signature, does she relent.

"Then there's the guy who comes in high on drugs - when there's a full moon only. He never fills out a withdrawal or deposit slip beforehand and he says he doesn't remember his name. The first time it happened, I was entirely confused. It turns out that he writes under two different names and performs stand-up comedy under a third. None of these is his real name - the one we have on file at the bank. Now that I know who he is, I just pull out the signature card when I see him in line."

"Tell Maggie about the chairs," Josef urged.

"There are chairs attached to every wicket but tellers are not allowed to sit in them while there are customers on the banking floor. When I'm in pain with the monthlies or, as now, with a UTI - my sixth this year, by the way - I am not permitted to sit or to leave the counter to use the washroom while the bank is open or while there are still customers in line after closing time. Except for lunch break, that is."

"How do you manage?" Maggie said rhetorically. "Are the administration at all supportive?"

"No. A few months ago, we had a fraudulent operator in the branch pretending to be one of our regular customers.

Since I chat a bit with my customers, I would always recognize the real customer so, instead of cashing the cheque, I went to speak to my supervisor. If I kept to the service time limits, I might not have been sure that the person at my wicket had not been the actual customer. The supervisor called the police. This week, I was served with a subpoena to appear as a witness for the prosecution. Instead of appreciation for being alert and saving the bank money, the manager gleefully told me that the bank will not pay me for the day - or days - I spend in court … and I know that the court witness fee won't even be enough to pay for my transit and lunch!"

"Let's imagine how we could make the bank sorry," Josef urged with an evil smile.

"It always makes us feel better," agreed Maggie.

They had worked it all out in detail. Josef had volunteered his brothers - hypothetically. Clara had laughed and had felt a bit better at the thought.

*****

A few days later, Josef and Maggie had come to Clara to explain that all the brothers were on board and that they intended to proceed with the plan an hour before the bank's closing on the coming Friday.

"We just make these plans for fun!" Clara had whispered through her teeth. "If the bank finds out, I'm finished and there could be consequences for you, too."

"They'll never find out. None of us will go to your wicket. There are twelve wickets and eleven of us - Maggie will be with me."

"Don't you think it will be a bit obvious?" Clara objected.

"No, all my brothers look different. Unless you've seen photos of our grandparents, you'd never guess we're related," Josef explained.

"That's true enough," Clara agreed hesitantly.

"Relax! Everything will be fine," Josef assured.

Clara remained skeptical.

*****

On the appointed day, Josef had spaced out the entry of each brother so that there were one or two other customers between the siblings. Short, dark-haired Josef had signalled tall, blond Milo to go through the doors to join the line. Two minutes later, Josef and Maggie, the last of the family members, had joined the line. They restrained smiles as they watched Yanni - tall, stocky and chestnut-haired - now first in the queue, step on and off the electronic mat in order to confuse the machine. When the next wicket opened, Yanni strode up confidently, unapologetically giving the teller a list of complex tasks. The remaining brothers proceeded until the customer space at each wicket - except Clara's - was occupied by a Forrester brother. Clara could not look. She kept her gaze focused on her own wicket or on the customer in front of her. Even when the branch administration officer left his desk to lock the door, Clara, unlike the other tellers, did not scan the long line of customers remaining on the mats.

The waiting clients became restive. The brothers stood their ground with additional business or changes of mind. Only Clara's customers were served and politely dispatched.

"This line is hardly moving!" shouted an angry man. "What's the hold-up?"

Clara's stomach, and indeed all the tellers' guts gave a little lurch at the word "hold-up". The BAO charged out to the line to tell the client that such were words never to be uttered in a bank as this terrified the staff.

The plan went off without a hitch. While the brothers opened or closed accounts, started registered retirement plans, arranged term deposits, bought money orders and foreign currency, set up safe deposit boxes, checked on personal loan and mortgage rates, made deposits or withdrawals, and requested anything else that they could think of, Clara served the thirty or more people who had waited impatiently in the queue.

No money was stolen or misappropriated except for a $5.50 bank draft fee which Alex, the most charming of the brothers, had managed to persuade the teller to waive. It was a hold-up but not a robbery.

By the time Clara, the last teller, was ready to be "locked up" it was almost eight o'clock. Her cash had shown an approximate balance when the BAO had checked it. However, just as he had roughly pulled out the drop drawer, a dull thud sounded in the time-lockable space below. A look into the mini-vault had revealed a grease-covered half bundle of five-dollar notes. Adding this to Clara's blotter resulted in an overage of roughly two hundred and fifty dollars. The BAO had no choice but to admit that the two-hundred-and-fifty-dollar shortage of the week before could only be due, not to any error or carelessness on Clara's part, but to a malfunction of the drop drawer.

"I guess we'll have to keep you," the manager had told Clara the following Monday. "Your numbers were better than any other teller's last Friday."

He also congratulated her on the strange recovery of the half bundle of fives. Clara was careful not to allow triumph to cross her face.

"Do you have any idea what happened with the service statistics on Friday?" the manager almost demanded.

"No idea at all. I just serve whomever turns up at my wicket to the best of my ability. I didn't do anything different on Friday. Some people just need more time than others," Clara replied.

"It was as if all the other wickets were shanghaied," he pondered, watching her carefully.

"Have you read O. Henry, sir?" Clara asked.

"Like the chocolate bar?"

"No. 'O' as an initial and 'Henry' as a surname," Clara corrected gently. The manager shook his head.

"He was an author who wrote around the turn of the century, 1900 to 1910-ish. It was a pen name. He always had a little twist - usually humourous - in his stories. There's one I was just thinking of ... I 'm not sure of the title as it's been a long time since I read it. It's a funny little story about the spontaneous breaking of the law of averages. Maybe we had something like that on Friday. Life imitating art, I mean," she speculated, knowing that there had been artful manipulation of that law.

"Clara, I think you're wasted here. You should be studying literature or something."

"Well, most of the customers seem to like me and I like them ... most of them. But your fancy machine doesn't measure that," she responded humbly.

"You think too much!" the manager chuckled.

"That's what my last boyfriend said," she shot back with a nod and an enigmatic smile.

*****

Josef and Maggie had laughed when Clara recounted her conversation with the manager. They told her that the "hold-up gang" would be happy to hear that Clara would not be losing her job.

"They want to know if we can use them on our next caper," Maggie giggled.

"No, no ... the planning is just for fun!" insisted Clara.

"Doing *that* was fun!" Josef corrected.

"It was fun, wasn't it? But no! We can't ..." Clara had stated, a bit reluctantly.

*****

Clara's thoughts returned to the COVID-restricted present. She could still recall the grin Josef had worn all those years ago.

"A peaceful journey into the hereafter," she wished him silently as the tears gathered at the corners of her eyes. "Surely God has a place of honour for a man who was such a good friend that he'd involve himself in a bank hold-up."

Dinner Is Served?

The coagulating blood on the floor had been as thick as honey. The log farmhouse stood dark, silent and still. It should have been bright with the golden glow of oil lamps, aromatic with the almost-ready-to-serve meal and musical with the sound of Myrette's cheerful voice telling her sisters to set the table. Just the memory of the scene almost made Rosette upchuck. Five years had not erased the horror nor identified her sister's killer.

Rosette was cooking for company but not for her family, who seldom met for meals anymore. Knives had had no place on Rosette's table since that night. She planned dishes that did not require cutting, setting out a fork and a spoon at each of the two place settings. She was not naive enough to think that neither of these instruments could be turned into a weapon but she just could not imagine sitting down to eat with a reminder of that night's violence right there on the table. She wished that she could live entirely knife-free but realized that there was simply no way to cook her own food without at least a paring knife.

The scent filled the kitchen as the oven transformed a soft, doughy mass into her special lavender focaccia. Her mind flipped to the delicate perfume of the lilacs which had wafted around the sickly-sweet iron smell of blood that spring night. The younger sisters had all gone into town. Myrette had shooed them out in order to concentrate on cooking in peace. Perhaps she had wanted a few minutes alone with the new boyfriend who was to be introduced to the family that evening. It was strange how the half-heart locket Myrette had been wearing was the only thing taken that night - and strange, too, how the new boyfriend had never appeared.

Rosette folded fish and julienned vegetables into two heart-shaped pieces of parchment and tried to clear her mind for her guest. An unreasonable - so her friends said - razor-sharp fear had kept Rosette from dating following her sister's death. They had encouraged her when she described how Émile had charmed her in the supermarket and again at the ice-cream counter. After a few such meetings, she had plucked up the courage to invite him to dinner. He had seemed so ... polite.

Now the fish sat burning in its parchment while the bread, without a hand to lift it to the wire rack, adhered to the baking sheet. Émile had come in the front door. Rosette had seen him as he respectfully bent down to remove his shoes; she had gone straight out the back door.

Dialing 911 in her neighbour's kitchen, Rosette heard a voice telling her not to be ridiculous, that she was sabotaging a chance for a great relationship after all these years and that she had to have been mistaken in that quick glance when Émile had reached for his shoelaces.

Rosette paid no attention. She knew. There was no question. It was Myrette's locket that had dangled from Émile's neck.

Flowers in a Storm

Aunt Rose was not like my mother. She was barely older than I – the youngest of her generation – while, as Mother's youthful mistake, I was the oldest of mine. Rose and I had played together as children.

Mother's sisters, all named for flowers, said that Rose had "the gift" and that she was a little "fey" because of it. Although I did not fully understand what they meant, I noticed that the word was trotted out at every evidence of eccentricity.

"What is the matter with her?" asked Roger as he looked out the back window at the rain pelting down and the electricity cutting through the clouds like strobe-light sabers.

Mother, the oldest and unluckiest – or so she told everyone, because she had been named Daffodil – looked, then waved her hand to suggest that Roger should not worry about it. Aunt Jasmine and Aunt Lily – the filling in the daughterly sandwich between Mother's conservative white bread and Aunt Rose's hippy-dippy whole wheat – looked around to see if there might be another volunteer to go after Rose.

I knew exactly what Aunt Rose was doing; I just did not relish getting soaked to the skin. However, there seemed to be no way around it as she was waving at me to come out. She was sitting on the fence – astraddle, really. Tied to a fence post, she had an old skipping rope. With the ends, she was slapping the fence post and rocking forward as if to urge a steed to a faster gait.

"You're not going out there," insisted Roger. "That would be insane!"

Roger was afraid of insanity. His brother Kevin was institutionalized and it was a big secret - a secret at Roger's work and among his friends. I had been introduced as part of Roger's vetting process in preparation for "formalizing" our relationship. I liked Kevin. He smiled at me with his whole face - something I had never seen Roger do - and spoke to me from his heart.

Mother liked Roger. He was serious (read officious), dependable (obsessed with promptness), properly employed (a banker), thrifty (stingy) and tall. My previous boyfriend, a bit of a wild man who had died in a motorcycle accident, had been five foot five, just an inch taller than I am. Mother had no use for "little men".

I buttoned my slicker, stopped by the kitchen for an apple, slipped on my boots and braved the storm.

"Whoa!" called Rose, patting the fence post. She put her hand out for the apple, "feeding" it to her (imaginary) horse when I surrendered the rosy treat.

"Mount up behind me, dear," she instructed.

I placed one foot on the middle slat, stuck the other leg out behind, swung it over the top rung of the fence and put my arms around Aunt Rose's waist. Water ran down inside my collar as thunder rattled my ribs.

"Hah! Git up!" she shouted at the "horse" before addressing me. "I wasn't born yesterday, dear. I've just got to get you away from that dreadful man."

Details

"It's on the next block," Stephan insisted, scanning the stone features of the civic buildings.

"There!" he shouted, pointing to the stone carving of a beaver and the year 1896. It matched the image on the contest form.

While Jaynie parked, Stephan noted the street name and number. They leapt from the car. Stephan took the requisite selfie of the two of them in front of the building. They were off again in seconds.

It was called an architectural scavenger hunt, designed to call attention to the town's rich "built heritage" but it was really a contest of memory and attention to detail. The first prize was two $100 gift cards donated by an architectural antiques shop. This pleased Jaynie and Stephan. Though they were long-time friends, contrary to rumour, they were not a couple.

A wooden door with a distinctive owl-shaped brass door knocker was next. Stephan was confident this was on the ground floor in the downtown. Jaynie thought it looked residential and must be in the Annex area.

Jaynie would have preferred walking but she knew that their closest competitors, Martin and Sam, would be driving. With anyone else, Jaynie and Stephan would have walked, enjoyed the exercise and not cared about winning.

Just over two years before, Jaynie had noticed that Sam no longer responded to the little touches that she arranged when she expected his return from a business trip. Scented soap, extravagant pastries, formal table settings and other thoughtful gestures had evoked neither comment nor appreciative nuzzles and kisses. She had wondered whether, if she hid her pain, Sam's fling would run its course.

Stephan watched doors while Jaynie cruised up and then down Main Street. None was right. Still, she did not press Stephan to give up. Finally, he conceded that his memory was faulty. In the Annex, they found the door immediately.

Stephan and Martin had been a couple before same-sex marriage had been a legal possibility. Believing that they had an enduring relationship, they had never headed to the altar when the law changed.

The last illustration on the contest form was an eye-shaped window with leaded edgings suggestive of eyelashes. Stephan registered no familiarity. Jaynie wondered how he could forget this.

Stephan had appeared at her door one night during an electrical storm, his tears mingling with the rain. Over alternating gluttonous binges on ice cream and scented tea, she had learned that Martin had given Stephan a month to vacate the house. Jaynie had made up the guest room. There Stephan had stayed until Sam returned with divorce papers and his scandalous but invented accusations against the two friends.

Jaynie almost had to drag Stephan from the car for the photo at the three-storey brick Victorian that had once been his home with Martin. She wrote the address on the form. He could not. He wept. She did not stop to comfort him but, after checking the image, packed him back into the passenger seat and sped off.

They reached the contest office, sprinting in just ahead of recently married Sam and Martin. A handful of tissues and the gift card in his pocket stopped Stephan's tears.

Measure by Measure

The creamy marble Corinthian pillars, rendered in relief, were richly gilded at crown and base. The Arcadian Court evoked the feeling of warm afternoon sun on ancient classical edifices - a pleasant, welcoming formality. Its days as a palm court had ended before Sylvia's time. However, she did remember the separate children's menu presented the first time she had dined here (one did not simply *eat* in this room) with her mother on one of their seasonal shopping trips to "the city". Inside the formal cover, the offerings had nursery-rhyme names such as "Mary, Mary's Garden-Fresh Salad" and "Mrs. Jack Spratt's Fish and Chips". Dessert selections were printed in colourful balloons to the right of the main courses. In the late 1950's, the elevator operators sported smart uniforms and called out the merchandise and services available on each floor of the grand department store before reaching the eleventh-floor dining room. There may have been music then but Sylvia did not recall.

Twenty years later, Sylvia sought refuge in this beautiful comforting place by pushing "eleven" on the automated elevator panel with her own fingers. The architecture inspired the same confidence as before but the tables were "improved" with wipeable glass squares over the white tablecloths. None of the lightning-precision linen changes she remembered could happen now. There was, however, a piano tinkling with palm court melodies while she awaited seating.

The formally dressed pianist caught Sylvia's gaze as she came to the front of the line. She properly averted her eyes but allowed a pleasant smile to spread fleetingly across her features. Using a few transitional chords, he shifted to an arrangement of "The Arrival of the Queen of Sheba". Sylvia sincerely tried to withhold any sign of recognition of the music but her eyes drifted to his and she lost the struggle to restrain a smile. He beamed back.

The hostess relieved Sylvia of her dripping umbrella and soggy raincoat before seating her.

"The special is Rock Cornish game hen on wild rice," the server tempted.

Sylvia ordered the room's signature chicken pot pie. She understood the change to glass tops when the waitress returned with scalding tea in one of those dribbly stainless-steel pots which had replaced the traditional silver service.

"The pianist takes requests," said the waitress.

"Does he know 'Der Vögelfanger' from Mozart's *Magic Flute*?"

He did. He smiled meaningfully where both he and Sylvia knew that the lyrics would describe the bird-catcher's selection of a wife. The next week, the pianist greeted Sylvia by playing "The Girl with the Flaxen Hair". Sylvia requested Coates' "By a Sleepy Lagoon". Next, she matched his selection of "The Girl from Ipanema" with "Por Una Cabeza". "When I'm Sixty-four" by the Beatles welcomed her the fourth week. Her request, "She Didn't Say Yes, She Didn't Say No", elicited a smile. Finally, they traded "Could I Have This Dance" and "Beautiful Sunday".

When he found her at the tea dance that Sunday at the historic house in High Park, it mattered not at all that they had never been formally introduced. Each had measured the other by music.

Luggage and Baggage

When Charles awoke, Elinor was still packing the last suitcase, the small carry-on, which had to fit everything they would need should the checked bags go astray in transit. Of course, he renewed the argument started the night before.

"I don't understand why it is such a production that it takes you all night - and if it really is, why you can't start sooner. You never sleep on the plane and you're going to be beastly when we get there. You always are!"

"You could pack your own bags if you're that concerned!" she snapped back, leaving a colourful modifier for *bags* unsaid.

"You know it works better to have like things packed together. It's just more efficient for you to pack everything at once," he replied, stopping short of his usual smarmy comments about her being "the master packer". That might have sounded like praise - however faint.

She knew exactly why their things had to be co-mingled. Except for their wedding trip, when he had forgotten to take any socks or underwear, they had packed separately only once. Arriving, in that instance, at Gatwick airport, they had argued as they claimed their luggage. He had rejected her unsubtle hint that a proper breakfast would be appreciated. Charles preferred to get the long train ride into London over with first. Elinor knew that this would bring them to the hotel hours before check-in time. She could not understand why an hour to fortify her nutritionally was too much to sacrifice. When he had turned to arrange train tickets, she had picked up her suitcase and, concealed by the masses, hurried off to the airport hotel where she had checked in, enjoyed a room-service breakfast, showered, changed, napped and considered leaving him altogether while he frantically consulted security and police about his missing wife. They noted that he acted as if she were a camera or a briefcase rather than a woman capable of making her own choices.

The corridors in Shanghai's airport were patrolled by uniformed men armed with machine guns. In a crush of people who bore her and Charles across a crowded room to the customs and immigration desk without, it seemed, their feet ever touching the floor, Elinor felt tired and cross. Everything smelled damp and mouldy, triggering her allergies. The two travellers emerged into a day so overcast that Elinor wondered about a solar eclipse. People pushed and jostled her as she struggled with her bags and with tissues for her dripping nose. In an episode of rare restraint, Charles observed her cold, determined smile and said … nothing. Neither did he offer help.

Crap! It's going to rain, she thought as they boarded the bus.

Later, the clouds burst as the bus roared and beeped into a crowded city street. Suddenly she was charmed by a rainbow of plastic rain ponchos perched over a river of speeding, bell-tinging bicycles. She fell instantly in love again - but with the city, not the man.

A Matter of Currency

It was on the train between Bari and Matera. When he was on a job, he always tried to be unobtrusive - to keep a low profile, as the Americans termed it. His common-man looks and his plain brown suit and tie let him blend into the background. It did not do to be noticeable in his type of work. He would have done nothing to call attention to himself had it not been for that smile.

She seemed to be holding court, but informally and without ostentation. The art student in the corner was intently sketching the foreign lady who wore "that smile" while a few local people who spoke English were asking the lady questions and translating her answers for the others. There was a little joke about jet lag after which someone promised to wake the lady if she should fall asleep before her destination.

As if this friendly crowd would allow her to drop off to sleep! he thought. Then that smile appeared again. Her eyes swept the car, catching him as he looked at her. He should have averted his eyes guiltily but he could not have broken the shared gaze if he had wanted to do so. Though brief, it was intense.

What, he wondered, *could a man do but smile back?* He thought that it was equally as if you discovered that something you owned, and had thought little about, turned out to be worth a million Euros - no, a billion dollars, for inflation - or as if you discovered a shiny penny in the change handed to you by a sour-faced cashier.

By popular standards, the lady at the centre of all this was not pretty and certainly not beautiful. She was not young, either - maybe his age, about sixty then - but youthful. Her clothing itself was ordinary. All the pieces were out of fashion - some more, some less. However, she had combined them in a way that revealed she had a sense of style all her own. Her face was unremarkable until it lit up with that smile. It was the element of surprise that seized his attention.

An "It Girl" maybe? he considered but quickly rejected the idea. *No, that's just a ten-dollar concept. Her smile has both the simple joy of the lucky penny and the almost limitless possibilities of the billion dollars.*

She had come for the history and the architecture but could not wait to repeat the pleasure of hot *cioccolata in tazza,* she told them. Even though it was what passed for winter in southern Italy, she asked about gelato shops. This would be her first time in Matera but clearly not in Italy. When someone told her that Bari was beautiful, she replied that she would need to save Bari for a future trip.

Mmm, he thought, *willing to return to Europe.*

The business he had at the stop after Matera could not wait. Still, he knew he could find her again easily. He had chased more elusive quarry to ground. It would not be a problem. He knew just how to make it seem like a chance meeting. It would be different to hunt someone without intending to shatter the person's peace of mind. If his business could be tidied up quickly, he could take a bit of time to find out more about her. Maybe he could spend the rest of his life eliciting smiles instead of provoking anxiety. She had had that much influence on him and he did not even know her name. At least she had been prudent enough to withhold that. He intended to tell her to be more careful in the future.

She had answered all the eager questions from her fellow passengers without hesitation. Everyone knew that she would be spending ten days in the little city of caves, before returning home to Canada, and that her previous trip to Italy had been to Ferrara. She also liked shopping, museums, historic sites, chocolate, and gelato - even in comparatively cold weather. With all these clues, finding her would offer no challenges at all.

When the train arrived in Matera Centro, he jumped up to help her with her bags. Everyone called *"Buona sera!"* to her as she hopped lightly down the stairs. He handed down to her the rose-coloured suitcase and its matching flight bag. In that moment, he saw the colour of her eyes: green with speckles of gold. These were distributed randomly as had been the little disks of paper which were once tossed into banknote pulp as a method for verifying genuineness. (He did not like the new plastic banknotes. Still, once the counterfeiters had learned to bleach the lower value notes and reprint them as hundreds and thousands, something new had to be developed.) The genuine smile that followed his small kindness reached and enveloped the sea-green windows to her soul.

How could she not know the power of that smile? he pondered.

Still, she did not seem aware at all. She did not invite anything with it. It was simply a spontaneous and sincere thank-you. He felt an almost overpowering relief in the certainty that she would not be trying to pick anyone else up before he found her again.

After the doors closed, he approached the young female artist. The pencil sketch was quite a good likeness of the foreign lady with that lovely smile. One hundred and fifty Euros the pencil-wielder extracted from the plain-looking man. Did this young woman have an inflated view of her talent or did she just recognize a captive - or captivated - audience when she saw one?

"You had better sign it for that price ... in case you're well known someday," he needled as he counted off the notes. "Oh, and be good enough not to tear it out of the sketchbook!"

"I have others in -" she began to object.

"You may take them. I need the book to protect my investment," he insisted in a way that suggested that resistance would be pointless.

The artist tore half a dozen used sheets from the front of the book and an equal number of blank ones from the back. She placed them into the small black portfolio at her feet before surrendering the wire-bound album to the stranger. He noticed that she was making a faint attempt not to look too satisfied as she put the money into a small bag hanging inside her shirt. As if she felt she needed to offer something else for the shocking price, she told him that she rarely felt the limitations of a static art form but that she wished that she could have captured that smile in animation.

"I understand completely!" agreed the buyer.

Three days later, the plain man stood in a square on the upper level, a somewhat newer part, of the city of Matera. Old Matera, a warren of stairs and passages within a bowl-shaped habitation of caves, was bisected by a river. The old part of the city had a depth of history which had been suddenly cut off by an official order forcing evacuation sometime in the last century. In more recent times, there had been a revival with refurbishment and resettlement of many of the caves and stone caverns. He had observed the foreign lady over the previous two days, noting her movements, her choices of eating places, her longing gaze at the chocolate shop and the extended time she had spent in the knit shop. He had even noted the times she had left and returned to the Locando di San Martino - the very nice but not extravagantly expensive cave hotel where she was staying. He had easily ensured that she did not see him for, though she was cautious after dark - keeping to the busy main tourist areas and looking around herself - she seemed to feel safe in taking no noticeable precautions in daylight. This contrasted pleasantly with the often-obsequious subjects who consumed much of his usual attention.

He thought of the telephone conversation and brief interview he had had three days before. He had been standing across the street from the villa when his phone call was answered. The young cretin had some nice "toys" in the lane: a new Porsche and a vintage Bugatti. Signor Claudio Benedetti, the grandson of the original borrower and the one responsible for clearing the debts of the estate, had rented the villa in his wife's maiden name in a useless effort to evade discovery.

"Yes, yes, it would be fine to meet at the villa tomorrow," agreed the young Signor Benedetti. Twenty-five minutes later the door had given forth a couple who had hastily packed. The plain man allowed them just enough time to begin stowing the luggage in the boots - or "trunks", as the Americans said - of the two exquisite automobiles before approaching. He always found it insulting when debtors tried to run ... again. He had found these people once. Could they really imagine that he would not find them any number of times if necessary?

"I am just the skip-tracer," the plain man had explained to the couple. "Tomorrow the collections man will visit and I must insist that you be present. The process becomes a great deal less cordial if you are not."

The sound of the door chimes returned his thoughts to the present. After the foreign lady with "that smile" had entered the hosiery shop, the plain man counted to ten before starting for the door himself. He carried an overcoat on one arm and held an attaché case in his hand. Inside the shop, he found and stopped at a carousel labelled *Uomo* and began to check its offerings while surreptitiously keeping track of her. He could tell by her body language that she was not just browsing. This was to be a buying trip. He relaxed and, looking more carefully at the colours in the array of men's socks, had an inspiration. The next time she moved near the carousel, he engineered a close call. It was not quite a collision but was enough to make her look up. He began to apologize but stopped as she recognized him.

"From the train?" he half asked and half stated.

"Yes, yes ... I remember," she confirmed, smiling with innocent surprise.

He thought but did not say, *Didn't your mother teach you not to talk to strangers?*

He substituted, "A pleasure to see you again! Perhaps you could give me some advice?"

"About ...?" she asked, startled.

"Socks!" he replied, indicating the carousel.

"Oh! Yes ... of course," she agreed in a hesitant but kindly manner and waited for him to explain.

He indicated his conservative dark brown suit and, pinching the fabric at one knee, raised the cuff just enough to reveal a sock perfectly matched to the shade of the suit. He adjusted his serious brown tie so that she noticed it resting against the faintly ecru shirt - less jarring to the eyes than a crisp white would have been against the dark suit.

"As you see, everything is correct but there is nothing at all lively. I want to do something a little different. Nothing wild, mind you. Just a ... a..."

"Gesture?" she suggested.

"Yes! The very thing ... a subtle change," he agreed.

"Do you wear brown exclusively?" she inquired.

"Either brown or charcoal in winter. With charcoal, I wear pale grey shirts, charcoal socks and black shoes," he detailed.

She turned the rack, asked his size and pulled out a pair in a dark shade of teal.

"For the charcoal - though they would go with either," she declared confidently. "And these for the brown," she added presenting him with a pair of argyle socks in brown, taupe, black and buff.

When he looked uncertain, she wondered aloud, "Not too much, I hope?"

He stared at them, trying to imagine the effect.

"They're part cashmere and the teal ones have some silk. They should feel very pleasant on your feet," she encouraged. (She wondered briefly if it had been a mistake to mention a sensation and a body part to a strange man but cast off the concern, likening it to the Victorian fashion of covering table legs for fear that bare legs, even on a table, might be indecently suggestive.)

"Why not?" he said, convincing himself and interrupting her mental wanderings.

The saleswoman came over, saying, *"Signora,* you buy five, number six - our gift to you - *speziale* today. Ladies only," she explained, with a glance at the two pairs in the gentleman's hand.

"I need two more, then," the foreign lady responded, adding, *"Grazia, signora,* they're all so lovely. It's difficult to decide." She smiled at the saleswoman, who moved toward the wall-sized display of ladies' socks and stockings.

"Perhaps I can help you … since you have been so kind to help me?" the gentleman in brown offered.

"Because you have so much experience selecting ladies' stockings?" the foreign lady-with-that-smile joked lightly.

"And what about your qualifications for choosing men's socks?" he volleyed playfully.

"I used to buy my father's socks and he was *very* particular," she tossed back with another one of those smiles. "I chose his ties, as well. I suggest a nice brown tie with teal accents or, even better, a teal tie with dark brown -"

"Let's get your other two pairs of stockings before we think about ties!" he asserted - and just like that he had turned "you" and "I" into the much more pleasant, and somewhat more obligated "we".

"Let's see what you have there ... one brown, two black and one grey. Someone else needs a little more excitement in her choice of socks," he noted, laughing. He checked the size of those she had and pulled down a plaid pair in black, charcoal and dove grey. His hand hovered over a pair of dark violet but she shook her head.

"I wanted teal but they seem not to have any for women," she lamented.

"Then rose, perhaps?" he tempted, remembering the colour of her luggage. When she did not object, he passed her a pair.

He spoke in Italian to the saleswoman, who collected all the socks and stockings, took them to the cash register, and began ringing them into the machine.

"I'm sorry to ask but what did you say to her?" the foreign lady enquired gently but with some concern.

"I asked her to wrap them separately but to charge them all to me. I hope that I haven't overstepped. It's just that I'd like to impose upon you once again in the search for the ties you recommended," he said apologetically.

"My grandmother said that it was not proper for a lady to let a gentleman buy clothes for her," she replied. When a little dimple of concern appeared on her forehead, he was quick to respond with damage control.

"Please, *signora,* I do not want you to be even a little uncomfortable," he began respectfully, but continued conspiratorially, "but I really do not believe that your grandmother will know … and socks are surely a harmless little gift."

"If and only if you allow me to treat you to lunch. I'm afraid we might need some sustenance before we take on this quest for ties," the lady with "that smile" replied.

"Except for family, I have never been treated to lunch by a lady - and even then, not since I was a boy," the man in brown noted.

"New socks, new ties … why not throw caution to the wind and have a new experience at lunch, too?" she asked lightly.

"Why not?" he agreed with a nod and a smile - and great satisfaction that they were again back to "we".

They took lunch at a bright little restaurant on the Via Ridola. It was a name she remembered because the choice of the French word, *bistro,* combined with the English word, *Italian,* and the name of a famous American author, had struck her as intended to attract tourists. However, she knew the kitchen was good as she had picked up dinner there and had taken it to her room the evening before.

She had become disoriented twice in trying to guide him there. It was not quite as near to the archaeological museum as she had remembered. He could easily have corrected her but to do so might have required an explanation. He dared not say anything which might suggest that he had been following her for two days. (The drawing had been useful but he would have located her in any case.)

They had found it necessary to move to a table outdoors because the tobacco smoke inside was too much for her. The sunshine made it just possible to dine *al fresco.* That it was a little too cool to linger suited her.

"They have a foot or two of snow at home in Canada and here I am sitting out in the sunshine," she remarked before saying, "I don't even know your name."

"*Signora*," he had replied, "a little mystery adds so much to a small adventure, don't you think?"

She had laughed and agreed.

The *prima piatta* was *orecchiette con fungi* - mushrooms with pasta in the shape of little ears, a local specialty. That and the following plate - lamb with perfectly roasted potatoes, carrots and zucchini - were selected because she had told him that she could eat neither cheese nor tomato. He had observed that Italy was a curious choice of destination for someone with those dietary restrictions.

"I can always say *fromagio é pomodoro non mangera*!" she explained.

"Your Italian is terrible," he declared with a chuckle.

"It's true," she agreed, "but I always get food that I can eat. I have never had to refuse a dish in two trips to Italy. I can do it in Korean - *cheejuh to tomato moglesu oppsumnida* - and in Japan I just say I hate them. *Cheezeh to tomahto kirai desuh*."

"What about other countries, *signora*?" he asked with a smile. Travel was a safe topic.

"English works in many places - not just England, the U.S. and Bermuda. I managed without Gaelic and Welsh in Scotland and Wales - the Scots are fine with that as long as you can figure out their brand of English but, in many cases, the Welsh resent the use of English. My French and German are better than my Korean and Japanese, so France, Germany, Austria and Switzerland were no problem, at least for dining. In China, Malaysia and Singapore, the risk of finding cheese or tomato in the cuisine is low … and in the Czech Republic, you can always find someone who speaks at least one of French, German or English - Russian, too, but they hate it and I don't speak it, though I wanted to learn it when I was in high school. Beyond that I have not travelled much."

"Oh, no … not much at all," he responded in a genial form of sarcasm.

The portions of both courses had been generous as well as delicious. The result was that neither he nor she could be tempted by the rich array of cakes and pastries offered on the menu. Instead, they enjoyed steaming cups of *cioccolata in tazza*. She thought of it as halfway between North American hot chocolate and a creamy homemade chocolate pudding, just off the burner. It was rich, warming and especially welcome because the chill of the air had taken hold of her. She suppressed a shiver as she had no intention of accepting the overcoat which he would almost certainly have offered.

Finally, he excused himself for a trip to the facilities, not quite trusting himself to refrain from engaging in a struggle over paying the bill. He knew that she would be offended should he renege on their agreement.

When he returned, he had lost his volubility. She noticed that he seemed chastened and appeared to be making a great effort to conceal something - fear, perhaps. He reflected silently upon the fact that, with his experience, he could almost certainly have prevented her from perceiving the change. In that case, he would have learned nothing about how she would behave in a crisis. A little bit of shared stress or fear tended to strengthen a new relationship, he knew. He also felt that abandoning her without any foreshadowing would be cruel and dangerous. If he judged her character correctly, and he rarely misjudged, she would try to find him - perhaps even to the point of consulting the police.

The difference in his manner troubled her. She began shooting questions at him, allowing him barely enough time to ward them off.

"For your safety, I cannot - must not - answer your questions," he repeated to every attempt.

"We don't need to look for ties today if you don't feel up to it, *signore*," she assured him.

"Dear lady, there will be no other day," he asserted with finality. "Let us just go and try to find a teal one. I can put it on and then you can remember me always that way ... just as I will certainly remember your priceless smile, which has given me joy since I first saw you."

He finished with a bit of his former sparkle and a smile burst across her face. He struggled with emotion and sighed something that the little she remembered of her high school Latin allowed her to translate as "Thank you, God, for this beautiful day."

On the way to the tie shop they should have passed the chocolate shop with the beautiful wood grain storefront and the sign proclaiming a history spanning over a century of selling fine chocolate. Rejecting all of her protestations, he strode inside, picked up a basket and began filling it with everything she fancied, which he judged with amazing accuracy by watching her eyes.

"Just allow me the pleasure of doing this for you. Please, *signora*!" he whispered with a pained intensity. "I am sure that even your very proper grandmother would not proscribe accepting gifts of chocolate from a gentleman."

Milk, dark and white chocolate bars, plain and in exotic fruit and tea flavours; brightly coloured confetti (sugar-coated chocolate and nuts) flavoured with bergamot, lavender or fruit; artistically boxed chocolate-dipped almonds and hazelnuts; fancy ribbon-wrapped boxes of delicacies with edible gold decorations - and more - disappeared into the basket. With abandon, the man tossed in envelopes and envelopes of instant *cioccolata in tazza* in a variety of flavours, some with crushed meringue bits.

She had an idea of the store's prices because she had browsed there on her first full day in Matera. She felt she ought to decline this incredible generosity but he seemed to be having so much fun that she held back too long. It would have been ill-mannered to expect the staff to re-shelve so much. She thought of the little currency conversion chart she had written out and she tried to remember what that many Euros would amount to in Canadian dollars. She realized, at that point, that knowing the amount could serve no purpose. She must surrender to the occasion.

When they left the store with heavy, bulging shopping bags, he cautioned with mischief in his eyes, "Promise me that you will not consume all of it at once! I don't want you to upset your stomach. That's all I ask in return - that and one of your smiles."

His joy made refusal impossible. She agreed, her entire face erupting into one of those sparkling smiles. However, as they walked on, care creased his brows. She noticed and whispered, "I'm afraid."

"Please don't be. After we enjoy this lovely afternoon, I will tell you how to keep yourself safe," the man assured her.

"I am afraid for *you*," she persisted.

"Ah well, there I cannot make any assurances," he replied gravely. "I do not know what will greet me when I return to my office. Everything might be fine or ... perhaps not."

"We could run?" she asked and offered in one phrase.

"Then you most certainly would need to be afraid. There is nowhere on this earth where we would not be discovered. Believe me, my job is finding people who do not want to be found," he argued.

"Why is this happening? I don't understand," she said worriedly.

"If I tell you a little, you must promise not to repeat it and, whatever happens, you must swear that you will not look for me. You must say that you met a man you had seen on the train and that you had lunch and a pleasant afternoon of shopping - that you know nothing else. Remember, to no one. Not to your friends, not to your embassy, not to the police."

It seemed a poor exchange but her curiosity spurred her to agree.

"All right, I promise," she replied, trying to hide the reluctance she felt.

"Put simply," he began, "after I saw your smile, I asked to retire from my job. My boss viewed this with extreme prejudice. He declined my request and made it clear that I would not care for the consequences."

"But –" she began to object.

"No, *signora*! I have been promised that you will not be harmed provided I finish the afternoon with you without any alarms being raised. Please, *signora*, let's have a lovely time. Smile for me while we find that tie," he protested.

"Do you trust him to keep his word?" she asked skeptically. The potential for danger was expanding in her imagination.

"My business is about honouring obligations. If we both keep our promises, there should be nothing for you to fear," he replied confidently but his mind tripped over the "should". *How dependable, really, were two possibly senile nonagenarians?* he wondered but did not say.

She did her best. For spaces of time, she managed to forget her concerns while, together, he and she examined ties, rejecting many outright and holding aside others for further consideration. In the end they could not decide between two so he bought the one she preferred and she asked the shopkeeper to wrap the one that the man in brown liked best – as her treat. The former had a bright teal ground with a black, taupe, cream and chocolate-brown paisley pattern. The latter's main shade was taupe. It had slender teal, black and grey diagonal stripes.

He used a mirror to tie the teal one in a full Windsor knot. Though it was perfectly centred, she came over, straightened the tie and adjusted his collar. He closed his hand loosely and ran the backs of his fingers lightly across her cheek. She smiled - that smile - but did not look up. She did not step away either.

Is it possible for joy and agony to exist in the same moment? he pondered silently.

He broke the mood by asking the shopkeeper to wrap his old, nondescript brown tie so that he could wear the new one. They each paid for their purchases before leaving the shop with yet another bag. She suggested that the tie bag would fit into the hosiery bag, lessening the risk that they would lose track of any of their treasures. He adored this bit of practicality.

"One more stop before ..." he suggested, leaving the conclusion trailing. He found himself unable to say, "before we part never to see each other again."

He guided her down the spiral iron staircase at the famous historic cistern and through the passage with the fragment of ancient painting to the ragged stairs that seemed designed for goat feet. She accepted without reluctance the arm he offered and relied upon his strength when she lost her footing. They paused until she felt confident in continuing. She had climbed these stairs with little trouble. It was the descent which was dangerous. In the few days that she had spent in Matera, she had learned safer but longer, slower routes to the floor of the "bowl" where her hotel was located.

They passed the large cave restaurant where she had taken two meals alone and proceeded to the knit shop. There was a spacious cobblestone terrace leading to the twin wooden doors which opened to the narrow-fronted but deep, white-washed cave. The pleasant old gentleman had already begun taking in the mannequins in preparation for closing for the evening meal. The foreign lady hesitated.

"I've been here. It's a bit out of my league but we can browse if you like," she cautioned.

"*Signora*, please trust me when I tell you that it is not, as you say, out of *my* league and even if it were, I would gladly mortgage myself for life to see your delight," he insisted.

"My grandmother –" she began.

"No, gentle lady, you will not tell me of your grandmother's objections. I am sure that she is at her final rest and I promise to do none of the evil things she feared would be the result of accepting such gifts … well, except … *if* you permit me … I will kiss you goodbye – gently and respectfully," he declared with a shy smile.

The elderly couple who owned the shop – she, the designer and needlewoman, and he, the business and marketing man – smiled at whatever the man-in-brown-and-teal said to them in Italian. The *signora* helped the foreign lady remove her outdoor clothing, looked the customer over and went to a cupboard to pull out mylar-encased ensembles in the correct size. Each hand-knitted or -crocheted set included a dress and two or three matching accessory pieces: a cape or wrap, a hat, a purse or tote and, in one case, long stockings. While many were crafted in traditional white or ecru, there were sets in lavender, aqua, pink and baby blue. Some were expertly worked in cotton or silk while a few were of soft Merino wool.

"I have a brief telephone call to make. I will leave you in the capable hands of the *signora* and her husband. I will return very soon," he excused himself in English to the foreign lady. He explained briefly in Italian to the elderly proprietors.

The petite elderly *signora* held one square white package in front of the shoulders of the lady-with-that-smile. With clucking and head shaking the elder lady had her husband return all the white sets to the cupboard. This evaluation was repeated with each succeeding hue until there remained a few packages each of lavender and aqua and one Merino wool set in a deeper rosy pink, a set in a paler pink also having been judged uncomplimentary.

The man-in-brown returned in time to see the modelling of the first and all subsequent outfits. Finally, the choices had been narrowed to three: the rosy pink set with a frilled, hooded cape and a tote; a lavender cotton outfit with a long scarf, full-brimmed hat and small beaded clutch; and, finally, an aqua silk boucle dress trimmed in silver at the neck and cuffs, accompanied by a silver shoulder bag and ecru stockings embroidered with silver vines and aqua flowers. The designer had not surrendered the stockings for fitting but had promised that the correct size could be furnished before the customer left Matera.

All being beautiful, the choice had been shifted to the man-in-brown-and-teal. He had eliminated the lavender cotton then turned to the designer who shrugged and sent the decision back to the lady-with-that-smile who also shrugged and returned her gaze to the two gentlemen. They conferred. The older gentleman smiled adoringly at his wife and told her something in their first language.

"Change back to your street clothes, *proszę pani,*" said the man-in-brown to the foreign lady. "I'll take care of the business and be waiting at the door. Tomorrow the *artiste* will measure you for your stockings."

"So, you have decided upon the aqua?" she asked, wondering at his use of the Polish honorific, recognized from her years of living in flats in the west end of Toronto.

"You ask too many questions, my dear," he replied jovially but firmly.

The shopping bag they draped over her arm seemed a little heavier than she expected but the older couple held her hands as they escorted her to the door. There was no way to look into the bag either gracefully or furtively.

"Tomorrow, you come," said the husband in English.

"*Domani*!" echoed his wife in Italian.

It was sprinkling rain outside when the two customers left the shop. From his case, the man-in-the-teal-tie pulled an umbrella. The lady collected the bags she carried and pulled them closer to keep them from filling with droplets.

"Now," he said gravely, "we have come to the end of our lovely afternoon … and even the sky knows it. It is weeping on us. You have promised me that you will smile so please hold the sunshine in your heart. We will walk past your hotel to the restaurant with the bird on the sign - Tico, I think it is called. I will make a reservation. When you return to your room, you will rest a bit and then take your time dressing in the pink ensemble. The wool will keep you warm."

She smiled, realizing that he had purchased both outfits. Sufficiently distracted by the thought that they might dine together, she missed entirely the fact that he knew exactly where she was staying. She was about to protest his extravagance when he continued.

"You will go to the trattoria for dinner at eight thirty. You may carry your overcoat but please do not wear it. When I have not appeared by nine o' clock, you will order and have them pack your meal to take to your room. Except for the time between 8:25 and 9:30, you will stay in your room tonight. This is how you will stay safe, my dear. Going, you must have a smile on your face for the joy of seeing the lights of the city and for the anticipation of dining together. You will not see me again but I will be watching. Returning, you may show your disappointment and you may wear the overcoat if you need it," he instructed before leaning over to place a very light and chaste kiss on her lips. She did not step back. Each smiled shyly.

*****

After *Ispettore capo* Alfredo di Palma of the *Polizia di Stato Questura di Matera* had set down the phone, he cursed aloud. This was so uncharacteristic that his colleague at the next desk had looked up. A Canadian tourist was being threatened and di Palma did not want an international incident in his patch. Before an hour had passed, di Palma had contacted Simon Lock of Interpol, Carlo Vaccarelli in the *Carabinieri* and the Swiss authorities in the person of Fritz Jaeger-Elsenbach. They had worked together in the past and each had his part to play in finding a contract killer. They had the phone number, the date and the approximate time of the call which had ordered the hit. Vaccarelli admitted that they continued to monitor the telephones, both land lines and cell, of the few surviving old "family" heads because they occasionally learned snippets about cold cases. It was unexpected that one of these dinosaurs should be implicated in something current.

The commotion might have been barely noticeable anywhere else. Old Matera may always seem busy but it is a quiet place where the crowds stroll, shop, take meals and stand in awe of the history and architecture. Police did their best to be discreet but the arrest of the tough octogenarian could not be disguised. The removal of a case meant to take a contrabass but actually containing a sniper's rifle caused a great deal of interest and discussion. The people from the front desk of the Locando di San Martino and several guests came out into the courtyard hoping to satisfy their curiosity. The police were careful to conceal from the public the photo, which had been discovered inside the case with the weapon, of a man and a woman enjoying a meal at a local restaurant.

A man with a new teal tie watched with satisfaction from an observation point above the old city. However, the foreign lady who was staying in Room 24 heard and saw nothing. Perhaps she had been in the shower or was admiring her new outfit in front of the mirror.

Later, when she returned to her room with dinner, the message light on the telephone was blinking. The aromatic meal that she delayed unwrapping was chicken supreme. (Was that *pollo alla crema*? She did not know because the waiter had given her an English-only menu. She had resented this just a little as she, generally, liked to try to figure out the Italian using her high school Latin and French to guess at unfamiliar terms and asking waitstaff only when she was truly stumped.) She called the hotel's front desk to satisfy the blinking light. Flowers had been delivered for her while she was out, the night clerk with the softly accented English told her.

"Yes, yes, of course you may bring them to my door … but I know your face and I will open the door to no one else," she had said cautiously. The events of the day had made her alert to possible danger.

The only door to her room - a small, white-washed cave with brightly painted furnishings - gave onto the open courtyard. The tiny stone stairs were clearly visible through a turquoise framed window across from the elegant marble-and-stone shower room and water closet. She watched as the clerk came out of the reception area's glass door, walked across the cobblestones and climbed the stairs. No one could be hidden on the little landing. The lady would have seen. The clerk set the basket in front of the door before rapping firmly and stepping down two stairs. When she unlocked the door and pulled it open, he reported, "They arrived at 8:35. The card is attached and we have checked that there is enough water, *signora.* If there is anything at all … no? Then sleep well, *signora.*"

When she handed him, in gratitude, what she hoped was an appropriate amount, he replied, "*Gra-az-ie, signora,*" without checking.

She closed the door, set the dead bolt and put the shutter and bar on the window before opening the waxed tissue which concealed the bouquet. "Orchids!" she exclaimed, her hands trembling as she struggled to extract the note from the envelope.

"Matera is beautiful. Take pleasure in your holiday. Just think of me sometimes and smile. Signor Teal Tie," the note read.

The writer had watched unseen from a promontory until the lady had taken the basket inside and closed the door. He hurried to the train station. He had had another of his inspirations. There was work to do and there would be hours of travel before he could begin. He would thank di Palma when all was done.

Staring at the pink and purple orchids, she felt at once pampered and devastated. She watched the BBC news late into the night, unable to settle or to withhold the intermittent floods of tears. She awoke with just enough time to throw on some clothes to catch the end of the breakfast period. As always, there was no shortage of fruit, preserves, cereals and baking - sweet and savoury. She passed on the cheese platters, of course, but was able to secure a generous portion of scrambled eggs and ham before the hot serving dishes were cleared away.

*****

At the lavish Swiss apartment of his boss, the man-in-the-teal-tie set his cell phone to record and hid it in his jacket before striding through the door for his meeting with Signor Albanoni.

"You return to me, Tino. What is all this about retiring? Why would you want to upset an old man?" he demanded. "I have been grooming you to succeed me. Do you bite the hand that feeds you?"

Signor Albanoni, who sat in a wheelchair with a cashmere lap rug tucked around him, wore a perfectly tailored brown suit not unlike that worn by the man he addressed, though certainly more expensive. The older man was somewhere in his late nineties. He resented the betrayal of his ancient body and had not noticed the decline of his mind.

"I felt joy when I looked at her face, *patron*. I am not unhappy but I had forgotten what it was like to feel joy. I remembered that my name is not Tino - not Vitorio - I am Viktor and I am Polish not Italian. I have served you well for many years. I have been loyal. I have worked hard and that has both earned you and saved you a great deal of money. I am almost sixty-one years old. Surely, I deserve to retire," he answered.

"I have not retired!" shouted the older man petulantly. "You know too much to leave us, Tino. The kind of retirement I can offer you, you would not like. If you are lonely ..."

"No, thank you, Signor Albanoni. Your daughters hold no interest for me nor do I for them, as lovely and charming as they may be," the younger man responded. He thought of how beaten down and bitter the daughters were after a life with this unbending father. A forced marriage with either of them would be as unappealing to the groom as to the bride. He believed that no amount of wealth could compensate for the lack of harmony and affection in the home.

"They would do as I tell them, Tino," the old man growled.

"I prefer not to marry at all than to take a wife who is forced to accept me, *patron*," the younger man replied.

"They learn to love after a time. Mine did, though she cried at first," said Signor Albanoni, referring to his first wife who had died in childbirth at the age of twenty-two. The second marriage had been a love match, however.

"Yes, sir," Viktor replied quietly but without enthusiasm.

"There will be no more trouble about this retirement business, Tino," ordered the older man, shaking with rage.

"I would not want to find it necessary to arrange an accident for an innocent lady."

"No more trouble, Signor Albanoni," agreed the younger-but-not-young man.

"Then go now and take care of that mess that Antonio has left. I want it settled by the close of business today," Signor Albanoni instructed.

"Certainly, *patron*," the younger man answered, knowing that Antonio Albanoni, had died of influenza over fifty years earlier and Ezio, the overindulged son from the second marriage, had been killed two decades ago in an accident fuelled by alcohol and velocity. Viktor felt a twinge of conscience for was he was about to do. The old man had been good to him but the risks could no longer be ignored.

"And Tino, get rid of that garish tie. No banker should wear such a thing."

"Yes, *patron*," he had said with a level of respect he did not feel. His recording of this meeting would certainly be sufficient for the competency hearing even if neither Simon Lock nor Carlo Vaccarelli could supply tapes or digital copies of the conversation between Signor Albanoni and his childhood friend. Fritz Jaeger-Elsenbach had agreed to describe in detail the joint police operation for the hearing, should it be necessary.

*****

As she brushed her teeth after breakfast the next day, the telephone rang in the foreign lady's room. The caller identified himself as Chief Inspector Alfredo di Palma of the state police. The conversation that transpired was simple: Did she know anything about the arrest the previous night near the Locando di San Martino? ***Nothing at all***. Was she acquainted with a Signor Contadini? ***Not that she knew of***. Had she eaten lunch with someone on the tenth of

December? ***Yes***. What was his name? ***She did not know.*** Was she in the habit of dining with men whose names she did not know? ***Certainly not***. Then why? ***She had seen him in a shop and had recognized him from the train***. She had not seen nor spoken with him since that day? ***No***. Did she know his address or phone number? ***No***. Did she know anything else about him? ***Other than the fact that he was a pleasant conversationalist, no.***

"I think that you may safely enjoy the remainder of your holiday in Matera, *signora*." the inspector had said in closing. (She wondered if she had imagined that he had subtly emphasized the word "safely".)

"Thank you, Chief Inspector di Palma. It is reassuring to know that the local police are working to protect a lady travelling alone."

"*Buona giornata, signora*."

*****

Alfredo di Palma did not wait for Signor Contadini to telephone. He was on the phone again at the start of his lunch break. After a brief overview, he told Contadini that, though she was very pleasant, she had told the police official nothing about the gentleman stranger except that he had made good conversation.

"I'd like to pick her up as a material witness just to get a look at her. I am sure that the photo could not have done her justice and …" di Palma needled, "you seem surprisingly worried about her."

"No one wants an innocent tourist to suffer for his mistakes," said Signor Contadini as casually as he could manage.

"You can tell yourself that if it works for you," replied di Palma with sarcasm but no malice.

*****

Her days were spent walking around both the old city and the near parts of the new. Checking off the historic sites and museums as she visited them allowed her some sort of purpose, if not organization, to her wanderings. She bought a few gifts for friends, found a gelato shop and developed a real sense of where everything was located in relation to her hotel. Two days before her scheduled departure, she bought her train ticket to Bari and arranged with the front desk for a taxi to take her to the station. Although it was easily walkable unencumbered, the terrain was impossible with luggage - even in her improved state of fitness from hiking and climbing around old Matera each day. She also picked up her new stockings from the knit shop and expressed warmest thanks to the delightful couple for their kindness and speedy service.

When she arrived at Bari Airport, she checked in as usual. The flight to Frankfurt was delayed. It was a small plane. Passengers had to walk, in the rain and driving wind, from the bus at the edge of the tarmac to the open-air wheeled staircase in order to board the aircraft. That she was cold, and more than a little damp, put her in a bit of a sour mood. She reflected on the fact that she had had to abandon the pretty basket in which the orchids had come. It was simply too large for either her carry-on or her suitcase. She had, however, kept the beautiful frothy teal bow as a memento.

At Frankfurt, the disorderly crush of people trying to get through passport control was maddening. Eventually, she emerged and found her gate for the trans-Atlantic flight. The ground crew warbled last call as she approached. She was able to present her passport and boarding pass immediately as no line remained. The ground attendant was about to wish her a pleasant flight and send her through when it became clear that there was a message on the computer.

"Oh, *genadige Frau*, you are changed to business class. Just a moment. I re-ticket you," said the smiling young attendant.

"How odd! That hasn't happened to me in years," the lady said.

"Today is *glucklich* - your lucky day," said the attendant as the machine chugged out the crisp new documents. "Here is your ticket and this is your boarding pass. Enjoy your flight - and last call. Board quickly, *bitte*."

"I will, *danke sehr*," the lady called as she hurried through the warm, dry retractable boarding tunnel.

Having checked the lady's boarding pass, the flight attendant closed and secured the aircraft door immediately. Another flight attendant guided the passenger to her seat and spirited away her hat, overcoat and rose-coloured carry-on. The lady stowed her purse in the cubby provided, fastened her seatbelt, and did a quick review of the laminated card showing the aircraft's safety features before she examined the contents of the business class amenities pack.

"Gentle lady, is this seat taken?" came a familiar voice. A smile overtook the lady's face just as the flight attendant interceded.

"Herr Contadini, we're not full today. We could certainly provide you with a seat to yourself," the attendant offered apologetically.

"No, no. Thank you. This is where I prefer to be. Who knows? If I present myself properly, this lady may become the future Mrs. Contadini," he replied lightly.

"Herr Contadini, that hardly seems fair when all of the crew have been hoping that you would choose one of us," joked the flight attendant in a manner that suggested sufficient acquaintance to know that the gentleman would not take the remark as unacceptably familiar.

"How sad that they did not speak up before I met this charming lady," he jested in return before the attendant melted away to prepare for take-off.

"How? … What? … I don't even know your name," the lady-with-that-smile stammered.

"Viktor Contadini at your service, *signora*. Originally it was not Contadini but something in Polish that would be impossible for you to pronounce. I am happy with Contadini if you are."

"Very happy," she replied, smiling, and he knew it was not just about the name that she was happy.

"There has been a change in the management of the business in which I work. Unfortunately, the result is that I will be needed and will be unable to retire immediately to devote all my attentions to you," he explained mysteriously, concluding with a sparkle of humour in his dark aquamarine eyes. When the dimple of concern appeared between her brows, he asked apologetically, "Perhaps I presume too much?"

"Well, I think I ought to know what kind of business it is that you –" she started.

"*Proszę pani,* last week you were prepared to run away with me!" he jested with a grin.

"That was when I thought your life was threatened. I think that I ought to be a bit more practical now," she countered.

"And so you should, dear lady … so you should. Briefly, I work for a small, family-owned – no, not *that* kind of family, it is all eminently respectable – Swiss bank. I call myself a skip-tracer but I am an investigator and some-time director of operations. I like the administrative part less than the fieldwork," he confided then continued, "I assemble the information that others use to accept or decline borrowers and I find borrowers who … shall we say … go missing. I also consult occasionally for Interpol and several national and local police forces. I am not being immodest when I tell you that I am very good at what I do."

"If I had not been upgraded to business class, I might never have seen you again," she remarked, wide-eyed.

"I must confess to having a little influence with the airlines. Please remember that I find people who do not wish to be found. It is much, much easier to find someone who is not trying to hide, my dear," he admitted.

"But you don't even know my name," she objected.

"That is adorable, gentle lady. I do not know what you wish to be called. I have known your name, Signora Graham, since before we met in the hosiery shop," he explained in a tone halfway between a declaration and a confession.

"You followed me? Where I come from that is called stalking," she retorted, almost indignant.

"No, dear lady, that is called surveillance. However, if you ask me to stop - assuming that I have no legitimate business in doing so - and I do not stop, *that* could be stalking. You have not asked me to stop," he explained, ending in a tone that was hopeful but not quite confident enough to be a question.

"I feel that I ought to be frightened by this. It is … unsettling … but, somehow, I'm not," she said, smiling tentatively. "I like to be called Pearl. It's my middle name. Regina seems far too glamorous for me … and I don't care for Reggie at all."

"Nor Gina? … No?" he asked at the slight shake of her head. "It would sound so very pleasant with Contadini. Signora Gina Contadini!" he pronounced, rolling it musically over his tongue.

"People would expect me to do better than *'fromagio é pomodoro non mangera'*. No, just plain Pearl – nothing fancy, just plain and reliable," she replied with a self-effacing aversion of her eyes.

"My dear, pearls may not be as sparkly nor quite as showy as faceted jewels but their modest lustre appeals to me far more ... and when they are well treated and kept close to the heart," - he touched his jacket just over the place where his heart would be - "they increase in warmth and beauty," he explained.

She smiled, knowing what he said of pearls to be true though not usually so poetically expressed. She hesitated before asking, "I still do not understand what happened that day. Can you ...?"

"My dear Pearl, had not your precious life been threatened, and perhaps mine as well, it would have been laughable. As a crime comedy film, it would almost write itself. It starts with two boys born in Italy between the wars. Those were tough times. One boy rescues the other in some way and a bond is formed for life. The former is destined to become a respected Swiss banker but the latter also reaches the heights of his chosen path - in the mob. In the present they are two old men suffering from the beginnings of dementia or some sort of mental decline. The banker no longer has the discernment not to call in the favour when he feels his authority is threatened. Add an aging hit man who requires one more success to retire with a round number for his bragging rights. The order is given that he should follow through only if the two subjects meet again. However, with his professional pride, he does not want to be paid for a job without completing it ... and there is the issue of the count. In the movie, instead of the efficient and co-operative police work which saved your life, there would be turf wars and a Clouseau-like character. I'm certain that it would make a fortune and be no more unbelievable than the reality," he explained, pausing to wait for the tension in her face to fade.

"The banker's daughters will spend the next two weeks announcing their father's retirement and their succession to his position. I will return then to keep my hand on the rudder until we establish the continuity that investors and depositors require and, of course, until I can find my replacement - a more difficult task. Unfortunately, it will be a few years - perhaps three or four - before I can retire and devote all my attention to you," he explained.

"But you know nothing about me … or my faults," she objected.

"You underestimate how much an observant person can learn from watching another for a few days and, of course, I have access to all the resources available to a bank in assessing a candidate for a loan."

She ignored or did not notice the suggestion that she had been thoroughly investigated.

"I have been told that I am 'fierce' and I know that I have a bad temper."

"I am sure that both will disappear when you are well treated. If I fail to listen to you or to attend to your needs, I shall deserve the sting of your rebuke! May it happen rarely if ever," he responded solemnly.

"No one except my parents and a doting aunt has ever showered me with gifts as you have. It feels strange … even a little uncomfortable."

"Gentle lady, this is more of an indictment on the quality of the men you have met than the degree to which you deserve to be honoured. If my resources were fewer, my gifts would need to be more modest but they would be no less frequent nor less carefully curated to delight you," he insisted. He paused, checking his pockets for something.

"In fact, I have a little something for you now. Here it is," he announced joyfully, as if he had recovered something that had been lost. He presented a small flat box to her with a gesture of studied casualness.

"Mr. Contadini ..." she began to object.

"It's Viktor and, if you open it, you will see that it is the one piece of jewellery that a lady can always accept from a gentleman who is neither her fiancé nor her husband. Your grandmother would most certainly agree."

She gently pried open the spring-loaded box and inhaled sharply as she set eyes on its contents.

"A 'regards' brooch? How ever did you find one? I love it ... but it is much too extravagant."

Nestled in the midnight blue velvet lining was a small silver-coloured bar pin with a ruby, an emerald, a garnet, an amethyst, another ruby, a diamond and a sapphire. By the fire in the stones, she guessed that they were genuine and of high quality - not that she would have known for sure as she had never been the recipient of genuine faceted stones. The mother of a former sweetheart had given her a string of pink pearls and a jade pendant. These had constituted her entire wardrobe of 'good' jewellery, until that moment.

"I had it made for you, my dear. It is just silver - so really not extravagant at all."

"And can you look me in the eyes and tell me that the stones are -"

"Paste? No, dear lady, I cannot lie to you."

"Then whatever will I do at customs? With all your lovely gifts I am already pushing the limit," she worried aloud.

"Ah, sweet Pearl, is that what concerns you? I will hold it for you until you clear customs - if you will just give me the pleasure of knowing that you will accept my small token."

"On condition that you promise that there will be no gifts over five dollars for the next week," she insisted.

"You and your adorable conditions! Make it ten dollars and I will promise," he assented.

"Ten it is ... but no cheating!"

"Certainly not! Not when you have just agreed not to send me away for at least a week, provided I restrain myself," he affirmed.

"Am I being manipulated, Signor Contadini?" she returned a bit playfully but with serious intent.

"Well, I hope so," he laughed, "but you are always free to make it stop. And now that the manipulation is not a secret, how dangerous can it be?"

She was silent for a while before launching her next concern.

"Mr. Contadini, what do you expect in return for all of your attentions and generosity?" she asked warily.

Before he could respond, the plane bounced in an air pocket. Instinctively, she reached out her hand for his. He took it, stroking it soothingly, while she recovered her composure.

"Ah, my Pearl, while you take the time you need to decide whether I am … what is it that the ladies say? … yes, 'husband material', you must call me Viktor. It will be sweet, after so many years of being known as Vitorio, to hear the name my mother gave to me … and perhaps you might treat me to lunch from time to time so that I may enjoy the memory of our first meal together … and …" he continued solemnly, "I most fervently hope that you will smile for me. You have that billion-dollar smile, my dear, and I must admit that it is, as you say, just a little out of my league … so perhaps I could rely on your being generous with that smile."

"That's all, Viktor?" she asked, using his name but still suspicious.

"Most certainly, dear lady. Unless you tell me differently, I intend to behave as a perfect gentleman. Your grandmother would insist upon nothing less," he pledged. "Well … except for the gifts. That prohibition is a little too restrictive for me."

"No one wants a hesitant suitor but you seem unusually confident," she observed.

"I am relentless. The victor is always the one who puts on his best face and competes with his whole heart and all his endurance regardless of any lack of confidence inside. My mother gave me this name to remind me," he explained.

"There is no other man in my life. You can hardly call that a competition," she challenged.

"My dear Pearl, I am competing with your satisfaction with the life you have now. I can see that you are undaunted by travelling alone. I suspect you have preferred it. This is rather more difficult than competing with another man. I have no doubt that I have the determination to best any other suitor. However, I have no way to measure how life with me would compare, in your estimation, to what you now enjoy."

Then, again, there was that smile!

Garbage Out - Garbage In

Mrs. Patrick O'Halloran - she still preferred to be "Mrs. Patrick" rather than "Mrs. Eileen" because the latter reminded her with the force of a slap that she was a widow - stood shivering in her driveway. She had dimly heard the front door open and shut behind her as she placed her small plastic sack of garbage at the curb. The scraping and clicking sounds of the dead bolt lock being fastened claimed her full attention. She looked back but there was nothing to see except the closed door, exactly as she had left it save for the fact that it was now, she knew, securely locked.

Minutes before, she had pulled on an old pair of Patrick's corduroy trousers over her flannelette nightgown and topped it all off with one of his hooded sweatshirts. This ensemble was her usual choice for the weekly early morning chore, especially in winter. She always felt cozy, as if wrapped in one of his loving hugs, when she wore Patrick's clothes for this less-than-pleasant task. She had been glad of the warm thoughts because the radio announcer had reminded listeners that the temperature was minus twenty degrees Celsius. (She remembered that they had called it "centigrade" when she was in school.) She really should have put on a coat but it was such a short trot out to the street that she had never found the need before, even in more extreme temperatures.

"These pants have been putting out garbage for more than ten years," she said to herself, "but I have been in them for only the last two of those."

Patrick had been very clear that taking out the garbage at any time - and especially on dark and icy winter mornings - was not women's work. Eileen had been amused by his firm views on division of labour. Anything with heavy lifting was excluded, in his mind, from women's work and he had cheerfully taken on such tasks. He clearly had found no understanding of how strenuous floor scrubbing was or he would not have expected her to be responsible for that chore.

The evidence of the cloud of condensation from her breath brought her thoughts back to the present and the sub-zero temperature. She was beginning to feel the chill. She regretted her haste and her resultant failure to put on a coat and grab her house key. Having accidentally locked herself out of the house twice - with the attendant, and very expensive, visits from the locksmith - she had invested in "idiot-proof" locks which required either the use of a key on the outside or the careful turning of the dead-bolt toggle from inside. She focussed on the fact that, since she was now locked out, there had to be someone inside who had turned the lock.

She looked around. Almost everyone else on the street habitually put their trash out the night before collection; there was almost never anyone else in sight at 6:00 a.m. when Eileen toddled out. In fact, she always looked through the little window in the door, sweeping the view to ensure that she would not be seen, before slipping out of the door.

My, how fast the cold penetrates when you're without a coat! she thought as her teeth began to chatter.

She knew none of the neighbours well. The people she and Patrick had known had all died or had been moved into care by adult children annoyed about being summoned repeatedly to deal with crises, both health and practical.

There was no one left in Eileen's family - at least no one who maintained caring contact - who might have tried to urge her into an old people's institution. She and Patrick had cared for every one of their kin in turn - her parents, his mother, sisters, brothers, in-laws and even a favourite niece - until Patrick became ill.

When the boxes of dishes, photos and keepsakes from each lifetime had arrived in sequence at their house, Eileen had had no time to unpack them and no strength left to carry them up to the attic nor down to the already crowded shelving in the basement. Boxes clogged the living room, dining room and kitchen. Eileen had tried to keep the upstairs neat and tidy so that Patrick, by then unable to navigate stairs, did not see what had become of their once-welcoming living spaces. When he had reached the stage where he had had to be hospitalized, there had been too much commotion for him to take in the condition of the downstairs as the paramedics bore him out on the stretcher. Running back and forth daily to the hospital so that she could hold Patrick's hand and try to keep his spirits up as he endured the treatments left Eileen with no energy to maintain even the upstairs. It was becoming almost as cluttered as the downstairs when the hospital visits ended and Eileen found herself numbly walking through the required decisions and, later at the funeral parlour, the visitation hours and service.

The grief at Patrick's passing had been debilitating. Just getting meals, keeping up with laundry and dishes, and doing the shopping took almost everything she had left after keeping her person reasonably clean. However, she did walk and did go to a functional fitness class twice a week because she knew that these were needed if she meant to maintain physical health and to hope for a return to mental health.

Oh, dear God, what am I going to do? It is so very cold, she thought. It seemed to her that The Almighty must have been listening as a voice called from across the street.

"Hey, lady, are you okay?" the young man - one of several students who lived in the house facing Eileen's - asked. He was out at that hour because he was still clinging to his New Year's resolve to work out at the gym and hit the library twice a week before class time.

"I'm locked out," she began as a great shiver passed through her body, "and I'm nearly frozen."

"I can see that. You'd better come in here!" the young man replied to what he noticed was the oddly dressed old lady shivering in the sub-zero darkness. He waved his arm to indicate the door to what Eileen knew was a student house where five - or was it six? - students were living. She reflected on the fact that there always seemed to be so many different people coming and going from the ragged brick Victorian. It had once been the carefully kept home of the Hennessy family, whose many children had grown, married and moved away long before the older generation had been taken off to a distant nursing home. The house had then been sold and turned into its present use.

The young man had ushered Eileen into the living room before reminding her that his name was Latham and asking her to recount what had happened.

The young have such odd names now, thought Eileen as she noted the splayed pizza boxes which harboured bits of cold crust. Her gaze lingered on the assortment of open but most likely empty pop and beer cans on every flat surface in the room. She dismissed the eclectic collection of threadbare furniture but lamented the old and badly abused Aubusson carpet which to her eyes had come from a place of quality. She was sure that professional cleaning and some small repairs could still reclaim much of its once considerable value.

Though Latham listened carefully to what Eileen was trying to say, he could not grasp the content for she dithered about, adding and retracting bits parenthetically here and there. A girl (young woman, really, Eileen corrected her thoughts) wearing pajamas and a chenille housecoat came into the room.

"I think she's trying to say that someone went into her house and locked the door while she was putting out the garbage, Latham. We should call the police!" the young woman instructed before turning to Eileen with the introduction, "I'm Rain, by the way."

"It's a pleasure to meet you, Rain. I'm Eileen O'Halloran," Eileen responded, thinking that here was another peculiar name.

"Cool!" said Rain before instructing Latham to watch out the window of the front door in case the intruder left while he called "the cops" on his cutting-edge new phone.

They speculated on why anyone would do such a thing to an old lady. They decided, however, that nothing they could think of made any sense.

"You could have fallen or frozen or caught your death of cold," fumed Rain as she placed a fuzzy (and, Eileen noted, not entirely clean) throw over Eileen's shivering shoulders.

"I think you need something hot to drink. I'll make some tea, how's that?"

It came in a mug with the bag still in it and was somewhat past the "in-and-out" stage which was Eileen's preferred way of taking her tea. Eileen hesitantly asked for a spoon and something on which to place the bag. As Rain disappeared once again into the kitchen, Eileen thought of how her own mother would have been scandalized by such a presentation to a guest - no teapot, no spoon, no saucer, nor milk, sugar, serviette or tablecloth. Still, decided Eileen, it was thoughtful of Rain to offer. The warmth of the drink, and the welcome as well, went a long way toward helping Eileen cope with the calamity.

"He's out!" called Latham. "I'm getting him on video but his hoodie is hiding his face. Do you think I should try to stop him and hold him for the cops?"

"No, Latham," Eileen objected. "Suppose he has a knife or worse? I'd never forgive myself if you were hurt."

"But he's getting away!" Latham countered.

"Is he taking anything?" Rain asked.

"Just a camera - do you have a small digital camera, Eileen?"

"No, just a big old clunky Pentax that takes film," Eileen answered in response to Latham's question.

"Then, no, he doesn't seem to be taking anything unless it's something small in his pockets," speculated Latham as he was joined at the door by another presence who was hurriedly putting on his winter wear.

"Go together and follow the guy at a distance," commanded Rain. "Try to get a licence plate number, if you can do it without getting hurt."

"That was DeLorean. He has an early class and he's always late for it," Rain explained to Eileen as the front door closed behind the two young men.

"DeLorean - like the car?" Eileen wondered aloud.

"It's a car? I thought it was a sci-fi reference. I'll google it later," Rain replied.

Rain helped Eileen to her feet and led her to the window. Rain and Eileen watched as Latham and DeLorean kept the intruder in sight. The students appeared intently involved in a discussion. The intruder looked back but clearly dismissed them as inconsequential. Following the intruder, Latham and DeLorean turned the corner. Eileen and Rain lost sight of them at that point.

With excitement, Latham returned about fifteen minutes later with a somewhat fuzzy but still readable image of a licence plate. DeLorean had gone on to catch the bus.

"Give me a minute to get dressed and I'll go with you to check out your place and get you a coat," Rain offered.

"Should we disturb anything before the police arrive?" Eileen asked tentatively.

"Maybe you're right. We should wait but I'm still going to get dressed anyway," agreed Rain. "Latham, could you stay with Eileen for a sec?"

"I wanted to go to the gym and then get some research done in the library … but since I called the cops, I guess I've got to be here when they come. Sit yourself down, Eileen. I'll watch your front door until the Holstein car gets here," Latham promised.

Eileen laughed. It had been years since she had heard that expression.

"Grandpa always called the cop cars that because they were black and white like Holstein cows," Latham explained. "Like the cows on his farm … He was a dairy farmer and I used to love to go and spend time on the farm when I was a kid … but it just got too hard for too little return so he had to give it up. Broke his heart and his health … Selling the farm is what killed him. I wish we still had the farm. I think I liked farming better than anything I can learn at the uni."

Eileen looked puzzled so Latham explained that students hardly ever say "university" anymore.

"It's difficult to be a farmer these days," Eileen commiserated.

*****

Later that day, after the police had done a thorough walk-through of the house, Rain went over with Eileen to support her while the police officers asked their questions. Eileen told the story for the third time and affirmed that, as far as she could tell, nothing had been taken. Her purse was undisturbed in the bedroom where she had left it. The gold Waltham pocket watch which had been her father's remained suspended on the little wooden stand that he had whittled for it. The sparkling garnet necklace, given to her by an old beau before Eileen had met Patrick, was still in the jewellery box. The pairs of Japanese wood block prints continued to decorate the living and dining room walls and all her fine china resided untouched in her grandmother's mahogany china cabinet. Even the collectable coins - some of them Patrick's, some inherited from Eileen's uncle and others that she herself had culled and treasured over time - were all in their proper places. The old Pentax SLR sat on the desk, its case a bit dusty, Eileen noticed as they walked through. Perhaps a vintage camera enthusiast might be interested but otherwise few people would look twice at that heavy old thing now that digital cameras were smaller, lighter and more convenient … cheaper, too, when you took into account the price of film.

The officer, with a young police cadet in tow, promised to follow up on the licence plate but, since nothing had been damaged or stolen, he indicated that the event would not likely generate a lot of activity.

"What about reckless endangerment?" demanded Rain. "Somebody left an old lady outside without a coat. She could have frozen."

"Well, it's not like they broke a window or picked the lock," interrupted the cadet, who was barely older than Rain.

"Do you mean that we all have to lock the door behind us when we take out the garbage?" Rain chipped back.

"It might be wise," said the officer levelly in an effort to defuse the contest.

"Thank you, officer," Eileen acknowledged in a calming voice.

*****

Following the strange event, Rain, Latham and DeLorean came over regularly to shovel snow, to check that Eileen had groceries in and to do tasks, such as changing the furnace filters and swatting down cobwebs from the ceilings. These chores were easy for the students to do but overwhelming to Eileen. They continued to speculate about the mystery. They also asked Eileen if they could help her sort through the boxes of papers and household goods that had come to her as her family members dwindled.

Rain was with Eileen when the notice of the competency hearing arrived. The older lady crumpled into a chair and began to cry. Rain put her hand out to signal a request to see the document. Eileen surrendered it meekly. After a quick examination, Rain first soothed Eileen's jagged feelings.

"Now we need a plan," announced Rain confidently. "I have a friend in pre-law who can help us find legal advice and another in the MSW program who'll give us some guidance on what constitutes evidence of competence. You're certainly not insane or suffering from dementia - just grief … and loneliness sometimes. The house is a bit of a disaster but Reading Break is coming up so we should be able to make a real dent in that - if you want our help?"

"Mostly, I don't want to throw things out. They mean something to me. There are memories attached to almost everything," Eileen explained, sniffling just a little.

"No worries, Eileen. I think we can make a difference without chucking out anything that's important to you," Rain replied. "The first thing we have to do is hang up all those pictures you've inherited. That would give you a lot of space to work with. So, what d'ya say? Do you want our help?"

"Yes, please," Eileen accepted.

"I'll go to the hearing with you and Latham and DeLorean, too, to show that you're not alone in the world … to show that you have support. I'm sure Crystal and Barry - his real name is Baryshnikov; his mother was wild about ballet - will help, too. Napoleon goes home for Reading Break so we can't count on him but Barry's girlfriend, Magda, might be persuaded."

*****

By the time the hearing arrived, the lawyer had discovered the source of the complaint and had gained access to the evidence: photos which must have been taken the day of the intruder. Organized by Rain, the six students had helped get Eileen's house, if not in shipshape, at least in reasonable condition. Magda, Barry's girlfriend and the daughter of a builder, knew how to wield a hammer and how to hang pictures on plaster walls without inflicting damage. This she accomplished with Barry's assistance. Piles of papers had been collected by the crew to be sorted, and then filed or shredded as judged appropriate by Eileen. Furniture and carpets had been moved by DeLorean and Latham to allow a thorough cleaning of the floors. Crystal and Magda dusted, polished or vacuumed the furnishings. Walls were all scrubbed and, those that needed it, painted. With Rain's help, boxes of carefully wrapped knick-knacks were unpacked, sorted and either displayed, repacked or given away as Eileen chose. Cupboards were emptied, scrubbed and reorganized. Old spices and outdated cans and boxes of food were discarded. Latham had taken charge of the refrigerator. It sparkled and contained only fresh food when he finished with it. As the women corralled, sorted and inventoried the overflowing bags and boxes of yarn, Eileen insisted that each of her six helpers choose yarn and a pattern that, by way of thanks, could be turned into a hand-knitted wearable.

Crystal, a better-than-average photographer, produced proof of the improvements which she processed into letter-sized, evidence-quality prints. These were submitted to the lawyer who surrendered two sets to the relevant authorities.

As the date for the hearing approached, the lawyer advised Eileen on what to wear - something serious and correct but not dowdy. He coached her on how to present herself and even bullied her a little so that she could practise remaining calm and holding her temper under pressure.

"No tears!" he had warned her at their last meeting before the hearing. "You want to show them that you are strong and capable."

*****

On the day of the hearing, an astute police officer noticed a plate number that seemed familiar for some reason on a car in the parking lot at the courthouse. Calling it in, she discovered that it was the licence number from "that weird event with the old lady where nothing was taken".

Eileen entered the hearing room with her lawyer and six student supporters. Each of her neighbour-saviours sported an example of Eileen's hand-knitting in a complex Fair Isle design. This provided additional evidence of a mind capable of following and executing intricate instructions. Rain, Magda and Crystal each wore an elegant sweater jacket while "the boys" - Latham, DeLorean and Barry - were resplendent in vests. (An added advantage was that the projects had consumed over forty skeins of yarn and had freed up the space these had occupied.)

There were hugs between Eileen, her student friends and even the lawyer when the officiant declared Eileen competent - or rather, when the charge of incompetence was discharged. Unknown to them all, as the officer of the court - a senior citizen himself - spoke strong words to the distant cousin and her photographer friend who had started all of this, their car was being fitted with a wheel lock.

"You have been of no comfort or assistance to this lady. You have not called to check on her well-being. There is no evidence that you attended her husband's funeral or did anything to comfort her in her grief. Yet you sent someone to lie in wait to find evidence that you could use to have her ruled incompetent so that you, as her surviving next of kin, could gain control of her assets. You put her at considerable risk to achieve your wicked purpose. I would be pleased to grant any application from her for a restraining order against you so that you cannot now or in the future impede Mrs. O'Halloran's right to enjoy her remaining days in her own home or such place as she may see fit. If you had cared at all for this lady, you would have been aware of her efforts to keep herself fit. Her walks, her attendance at functional fitness classes and her ability to form friendships such as these with her kindly young neighbours, who have demonstrated that they have her best interests at heart, show that Mrs. O'Halloran remains competent to manage her own affairs.

"Ms. Howard, as a family member, however distant, you should be ashamed of your treatment of this lady … and Mr. Totton, did you even stop to consider the distress and potential for harm that your actions created? You are fortunate that you may leave my presence without becoming guests of Her Majesty's correctional system.

"Mrs. O' Halloran, I cannot recommend strongly enough that you put your legal affairs in order so that this woman is expressly prohibited from claiming power of attorney over your affairs during your lifetime and from benefiting in any way from your death. I further recommend that you make a living will so that people you trust can be appointed to care for you, should the need ever arise.

"However, these are simply my recommendations. You are fully competent and entitled to make your own choices."

Eileen and her friends left the court building in a celebratory mood. Ms. Howard and Mr. Totton left to discover that not only could they not move their car, but also that an interview with the police awaited them.

Legacies

The young woman behind the thrift store counter examined his selections curiously. The man had made lengthy examinations of all the plates and bowls on the shelves, even to the point of checking the maker on the bottom of each. She had expected, after the care he had taken, that the fairly large pile would contain the best pieces with the most famous names. Instead, he had assembled orphaned pieces of the lowest grade, and among those, the examples in the worst condition. It puzzled her. His care in handling the dishes and his apparently knowledgeable scrutiny contrasted with the array before her and with his tidy appearance. She might have asked him to explain his choices but, though his smile was not unpleasant, there was something about his body language that discouraged conversation. She added up the amounts stamped on the pale blue adhesive tags and told him the total. He paid with a handful coins and accepted, with a nod, the offered newspaper and box for wrapping and transporting his purchases. As he left the store, he allowed his expression to drift from the benign mask he had used in the store to the rage he actually felt.

*****

Amy Hannah Sterling entered the last reading test mark into the correct column, clicked *Save* and put the computer to bed. It took its sweet time powering down but she did not mind. She was in no hurry to return to the house. She took a piece of scrap paper from the pile and began listing the items she would pack for her trip. She paused after she wrote *black-and-white sweater coat.* It would be chilly this time of year - both the weather in France and the mood at home.

The memory of how they had met on that blistering day in Winnipeg tugged at the corners of her lips. She had gone to the Manitoba capital to evaluate her crumbling and, according to Madeleine, the friend whom Amy was visiting, abusive marriage. Amy's father had bought the ticket in consultation with Madeleine and had informed Amy's husband that it was non-refundable. Her dad had made it clear that he would pick Amy up and drive her to the airport and that there would be no argument about it. Amy feared Sam Sterling's reaction but, in the end, Sam had decided that a showdown with Amy's father, a man Sam had done everything possible to alienate, would be a mistake. Sam figured that it would be easier and more effective to punish Amy when she returned home.

*****

Walking with her head dropped forward, she watched her toes emerge from and disappear into the pink-and-baby-blue flounce on her ankle-length peasant dress. As she considered that there was little point in continuing a hopeless life, Amy was barely aware of the world around her. A car accelerating down the street toward the pedestrian crossing had been about to grant that wish. She realized too late that her suicidal thoughts did not mean that she was ready for death at someone else's hand - or rather, vehicle. Two long arms shot out, snatching her out of the trajectory of the car. Without stopping or even slowing down, the car sped off while she remained, stunned and clasped in the embrace of the man who belonged to the arms. It was a few moments before she had the presence of mind to feel indignant that the man had not let go. As she inhaled - to what? shout or scream, she was never sure - he pivoted and set her neatly on the sidewalk. The scent of his expensive masculine soap lingered around her for a moment after he let go. She knew little of the perfumer's art. She could not identify the earthy foundation of the scent but she recognized the spicy notes as nutmeg and bergamot. She knew the fragrance was expensive as the cheaper versions invariably irritated her allergies; this scent was all pleasure and no allergic punishment. It surprised her since nothing else about him suggested wealth or refined tastes. Freed from his grip, she knew that the appropriate thing to do was to thank him - so she did, in a voice that quavered from the full realization that she had almost "bought the farm".

"That surely was close. I think I'm as shaken up as you!" he had said. "Let me get you a coffee or somethin' while we settle ourselves."

He was tall, though not lanky. What then? Not svelte ... that was too chichi for his homespun type. *Wiry,* she decided, was the word. His eyes, the light amber of first-run maple syrup, had followed her gaze to the wedding set on her left hand.

"It's been a little while since I've been so close to a near-fatal experience and I know that's not somethin' you just brush off. You're goin' to need to sit down, ma'am. You suit yourself but there's a coffee shop on this block - don't even need to cross a street," he assured with a grin and a raise of dark chestnut eyebrows. The craggy face testified to a life spent mostly outdoors.

As he was making sense and she was starting to tremble, she let him guide her into the shop to a table by the window. (It was public, so probably safe, she hoped). He fed her herbal tea and cookies while she told him what she was doing in Winnipeg. When she seemed talked-out, he had given her a capsule summary of his life.

"I don't even know your name. Mine's Amy ... Amy Hannah Sterling," she offered when he paused in his recitation.

She was short, slender and pale. A wide-brimmed hat protected her face from the sun. Her hair was not quite as light as corn silk but was just as luminous.

"If you was anyone else, I'd give you one of the many generic names my mother used to keep us anonymous and safe ... Fred Smith, Bobby Jones ... Mike Davies ... but I want to do some better for you. The earliest name I remember is from a song she used to sing to me, maybe you've heard it? 'Angus McFergus McTavish Dundee'?"

She nodded, a black-and-white image of *Captain Kangaroo* taking shape in her mind, while the stranger took a breath to go on.

"I don't know my real name - I don't even know if a person whose birth was never registered has a real name - but the first one I remember is Angus McTavish."

She was unable to suppress a short, rising-pitch, staccato burst of laughter.

"What's tickled your funny bone, darlin'?" he asked with one raised brow.

"I just cannot imagine you as a Fred or a Mike - and certainly not as a Bobby!" she declared.

"Most people I consider friends just call me Mac. What do you think would suit me?" he asked with a playful lift of his chin.

"You don't use Angus?"

"Not since my mother stopped callin' me that."

"Mac works fine ... or Gus, even better," she considered.

"What makes you say that?"

"Well ... there must be millions of guys who answer to Mac but Gus is more rare these days ... and you seem exceptional ... unusual ... rare, I guess," she replied, working hard to find words that would both express what she meant and not cause him to take offence.

He chuckled, a warm baritone sound.

"'Nothin' rare or special 'bout me," he insisted.

"Of course! Regular guys just go around plucking people out of the path of speeding cars!" she intoned in mock solemnity.

"That was just instinct, ma'am. Any decent person would do the same," he argued, waving the idea away as if it were smoke in the air.

"Assuming he was astute enough to act in the first place, an ordinary person would just have gone about his business afterward," she contested.

"That's real simple, darlin', I've got no pressin' business to go on about," he replied, punctuating the end with a laugh.

"That would almost make you unique in this madly busy world," she observed, "but I'm sure that you were going somewhere."

"An old pal is stationed at the air base. I told him I'd be in town but I didn't give him any firm time I'd be by," he explained.

"Instead, you're sitting here trying to settle my shattered nerves with tea and cookies."

"Tryin'!" he echoed, but with indignation. "I'd like to think I'm succeedin'."

She fixed him with her gaze as though she were making an effort to frame him in a viewfinder for an official portrait before saying, "I'm not doing a very good job of thanking you."

"None required," he volleyed back. "Just promise you'll be more aware of what's goin' on around you. I wouldn't like to think I'm spendin' my last dollar on someone who..." he trailed off, reluctant to speak the words.

"Are things that bad … financially?" she asked, reaching for her purse.

"No, darlin', put your money away. I just …" he began but hesitated.

"Wanted me to stay in the land of the living?" she finished for him.

"That's right!" he agreed.

"I had a great-uncle who refused to wear a safety harness when flying. He was thrown clear and survived more than one plane crash - in the early days of aviation, of course. Low altitudes and open-air seating." She spun the yarn that she had heard repeated at family gatherings.

"I get the picture," he encouraged.

"He concluded that he would have been killed if he'd been restrained. It made him a fatalist. He believed that when your number is up, you go and not before," she finished.

The stranger looked at her appraisingly, considering carefully what to say next but ending up with, "Does that mean you think I interfered today?"

"No, I think you were there because it wasn't my time to go today," she answered readily.

He looked perplexed. With a subtle shake of his head, he told her, "I wouldn't want you to be walkin' around countin' on that kind of outlook! Some reasonable caution is surely called for!" He argued a bit more loudly and forcefully than he had intended. All eyes in the coffee shop turned to see what the fuss was about. Did she pull back from him in her chair in response? He made soft apologetic noises until she relaxed again.

"I promise I'll be much more alert from now on," she vowed.

"Be a lert. Lerts have more fun?" he joked.

"I'm not promising to have fun … just to exercise, as you say, reasonable caution," she insisted.

"Somethin' wrong with havin' fun?" he questioned in a voice just above a whisper.

"Not of itself," she responded. "It's afterward. Anytime I've forgotten myself enough … I mean, relaxed my vigilance enough … to have fun there's been something terrible happen right on the heels of it. I work very hard at not having fun. That's not to say that there aren't pleasant moments … like this." She waved her hands to include the table and him before averting her eyes and covering her mouth as though she had tempted fate in being so frank.

When she raised her eyes again, she could see that his were focused on her rings. Her question was in her face; no sound emerged.

"Well, ma'am, I know marriage is no walk in the park … takes work on both sides … but I don't figure I'd marry or less I thought there'd be some fun in it," he started and, then to remove some of the sting of implied criticism, continued, "just my thoughts, you understand."

She scanned the room seeming to verify that she recognized no one there. In the firm belief that she would never see him or anyone else in the café again, she decided what she would say next.

"Well, I wouldn't be here … in Winnipeg … if there was any fun or even any peace in mine," she whispered. "In fact, if he knew I was sitting here with you, then you might have wasted your effort at that corner."

"He wouldn't be harmin' you while I'm here. I figure I can handle myself," Gus replied with quiet confidence.

"I'm sure that you can but he doesn't pick on anyone who could give him a real contest … and the operative words would be 'while you're here'. It would be worse for me when you're not … but he never hits me anywhere that it would show when I'm wearing street clothes. Not since my arm got broken … but that was my fault."

"Hold on just a minute, Amy Hannah! I want to be clear on this. Did you accidentally break your arm or did he help that along some?" Gus asked evenly, but it was clear that he was working hard to retain his temper. He was thinking about his mother and of all the sudden changes of venue that had punctuated his early life.

"I wouldn't get out of the car when he told me. I don't know what comes over me. Sometimes I just refuse to do what I'm told. It's my fault. I bring it on myself."

"No, you don't, ma'am," he objected as he poured more tea into her cup.

"You don't understand," she interrupted.

"More than you know, darlin'," he confided.

He told her about his life with his mother on the run from his old man, noting that he would not dignify the guy with the title "father".

"Where is your mother now?" she asked.

"I'm sorry, Amy Hannah, I can't talk about that just now," he declined.

*****

In the end, he had urged her to phone Madeleine for a ride as he could see that Amy was still unsteady. When Madeleine arrived, Amy realized that the volume of tea consumed would make the ride home agony. She excused herself.

"Ma'am, you keep in close touch with your friend?" Gus probed when Amy was out of earshot.

"Every week or two. I worry about her. Why?" Madeleine asked.

"I'd kinda like to check on how she's doin' from time to time. It was a close thing, this brush with death, maybe closer than she knows, an' somehow, I feel some responsibility for her well-bein' ... some need to follow up."

"Why don't you give her your number or ask her for hers?" Madeleine challenged, knowing that Amy, for fear of Sam, could never carry home such evidence nor accept calls from anyone but her parents and one or two of her oldest and closest friends.

"I move around a lot. I c'n call you when I'm back this way ... and I know she's a married lady an' I don't want to give her no trouble."

"I'm a 'married lady', as you put it, too."

"It's not like I'd be askin' after you so it shouldn't give you trouble with *your* husband. I'd just like to know that she's still livin' in the world ... an' livin' well, I hope."

"And if, God forbid, she isn't ... living?"

"I'd hope you wouldn't be uncomfortable tellin' me where to find her grave so I could take flowers an' say a proper good-bye – but I'm hopin' after today that she's got a better appreciation for stayin' among the livin'."

In the end, Madeleine had surrendered her phone number, agreeing that Gus could call a couple of times a year. Mindful of what the man had said about not wanting to cause trouble, Madeleine also decided not to mention the agreement to Amy.

*****

On one call a couple of years later, after reporting that Amy's husband had died of heart failure following one of his violent rages, Madeleine had asked Gus if he wanted help getting in touch with Amy.

"No, ma'am. You remember somethin' called *Desiderata*? If the universe is unfolding as it should and has plans for us, I figure that we'll run acrosst each other somehow."

Five years later, still struggling with guilt for having formed the wish in her mind that her husband would not survive his heart attack, Amy had visited Madeleine again.

Because the dishwasher had failed the previous week, Madeleine was washing the breakfast dishes while Amy dried them and put them away. When the phone rang, Madeleine waved her wet hands to signal that Amy should get it.

"Hunter residence! Good morning, how may I help you?" Amy chirped into the phone. There was a longer than normal silence before the response.

"Good mornin'," a man's voice began tentatively.

"Madeleine is just drying her hands if you –"

"I'll speak to Madeleine if you don't want to talk to me, Amy Hannah. It's –" began the voice.

"Gus … Gus McTavish!" Amy finished for him.

Madeleine smiled. "I wondered if he'd call while you were here. It was getting around to the time I was expecting –" she began.

"You're not stepping out on John?" Amy asked, shocked.

"He's calling for *you*, silly," Madeleine admonished. "You'd better talk to him. I'm tired of giving reports on how you're doing … and you should sit down before you fall down."

"I'm in Winnipeg, Amy Hannah. How about herbal tea an' cookies at the same coffee shop. It's still there. I checked. I check ev'ry time I come through. I kept hopin' I'd see you through the window."

*****

Amy had returned to Winnipeg in the summer of each of the next three years. When, in the third summer, it had become too painful for them to say good-bye, Gus had accompanied her home to Ontario. He was a bit overwhelmed by the house – a small two-storey Victorian labourer's cottage which Amy had decorated in feminine shades of rose, pink, sage and lilac and had stuffed with furniture embellished with traditional needlework doilies topped with knick-knacks. Upholstered love seats (a full-sized chesterfield could not be shoehorned into the tiny living room) were decked with antimacassars embroidered by her grandmother and great-aunt. Perhaps the most intimidating of all for Gus was the stairwell. Its walls were crowded with photographic portraits of five generations of Amy's family, collected from closets and blanket boxes of cousins who no longer wanted to give them houseroom, and from her father who was happy to have copies in his albums rather than the originals. The only real picture Gus had of his mother was in his mind's eye - and he worked very hard to keep it from fading. The police reconstruction of her face, which he had saved from the newspaper and had laminated in a coin-operated machine, was not a good likeness. Even so, he kept it in his wallet.

Gus and Amy Hannah had had one year of deliriously happy days before the novelty of being settled in her house had worn off for him. He had been accustomed to moving frequently - and, too often, suddenly - throughout his more than forty years on earth. In the midst of his second summer with Amy Hannah and feeling himself weighed down by her possessions and commitments, he became frustrated that there was little work for him, and that most of that was intermittent cash-only security and night watch temp jobs. These put money in his pocket but offered him no satisfaction. It further stung him that she laboured long hours to keep a roof over their heads and tasty food on the table. She had warned him that teaching was more than a full-time job but, never having gone to school himself, he had been unable to imagine what she meant.

In the worst days there was little communication between them. They had had a small argument over why he was unable to do the dishes while she spent all day at work. The chill started after that and had become colder as he avoided talking - not wanting to appear threatening - as his anger simmered. She was able to hide in her work but he simply withdrew into himself. The depression which settled on him, like a black sweater caught over his head, held him in a localized but unending night of anger and frustration. He knew how to be contented alone but he had no idea how to deal with being lonely with someone who slept beside him but might as well have been miles away. His single concession was that, though they now slept turned away from each other, he always ensured that one of his feet touched her on the foot or leg. If not for that, she might have recommended that he sleep in the spare room - or she might have crept off to do so herself.

Once, she was sure that she had been awakened by the sound of his sobbing in the darkness. She had turned toward him and placed a hand lightly on his shoulder. When he neither spoke nor turned to face her, she had abandoned the overture. In the morning, she dithered over whether to remain stubbornly silent or to try to offer comfort.

"I could have sworn that I heard crying in the night," she began tentatively.

"Mustuh bin a dream," he replied, deadpan.

"Yours or mine?" she probed.

"Makes no difference," he responded icily as he walked away. He paused at the bedroom door to add, "A man worthy of his supper don't cry in the night."

She had wanted to run after him, leap at him and scream, "I love you and I can't live with this coldness between us!" However, she held herself back because she resisted being the one who precipitated the final break.

From what he knew of his mother's marriage, he understood too well that violence or the threat of it was abuse but he failed to understand that silence could also be abusive. She, fearing that his silence meant that he had one foot out the door, booked a trip to France for herself without discussing it with him. She had felt that she needed something to look forward to in order to propel herself through the term should she one day come home from work to a house empty of him.

Gus could not have come along in any case as he had no passport and no existence in documents, his mother never having registered him. She had been on the run from her abusive husband by the time of Gus's birth. She had moved the child around from rented room to rented room and from job to job - often on ranches or at stables because she had a way with horses - homeschooling the boy as much as she could while staying nowhere long enough to put down roots.

With this as his history, it would not have surprised Amy if he had just wandered off. She was certain that he still loved her but he clearly did not love the life he had with her. For his part, he kept hoping that she would ask him to stay - would assure him that he meant more to her than her anger over a sinkful of dirty dishes. Still, he would never admit to the tears and it would take him some time to realize, with a large share of guilt, that his not doing the dishes might have demonstrated to her that he did not value her more than the argument over this domestic task.

With her suitcase sitting at the door and the airport limousine waiting in the driveway, she had had a moment of inspiration. She placed the phone book open on the table at his place and circled, with her red test-marking pen, the number of a gardening service owned by one of her former students. The fact that it was within walking distance of the school where she worked was, in her mind, a bonus. It was a gesture but not one she held much hope of working.

He had been more than angry when he had first seen the copies of her flight and hotel reservations, which she had left in plain view so that he could be notified without an actual exchange of words. It upset - no, enraged - him that she had done this without talking it over with him.

Though he knew that he never wanted to turn into the monster his father had been, he had struggled with the urge to break things. He had visualized dashing to bits her treasured fine china, passed down to her through multiple generations, about which she had carefully educated him. When the visualization had not satisfied him, he had gone to the thrift store to purchase orphaned crockery that he could destroy while Amy was out of the house. He knew that he needed to release his rage without frightening her. Somewhere inside he was still able to recognize that taking away her connection with her female ancestors would be unforgivable - a step too far.

First, he threw the thrift store dishes piece by piece against the outside wall. Then he took a hammer to the shards. The goggles, left over from a summer field school in archaeology that she had taken years before, protected his eyes and told him that, as much rage as he felt, he had not entirely been deserted by rational thought.

As he cleaned up the evidence, he was able to recognize that, after her hard work, she deserved the rest and escape that the holiday would give her. Knowing that without a passport or the documentation required to get one, he could not have gone with her, he concluded that he wanted good things for her - such as this trip - despite the rift that had developed between them.

*****

He had hugged her wordlessly before she left for the airport. Avoiding eye contact, he had pressed his forehead gently against hers. He was afraid that tears might betray him.

After she had gone, he put the energy from any residual anger into painting every room in the house while he awaited her return. He retained all of her colour choices except in their bedroom. He chose a neutral which the paint chip folder titled *French Vanilla Ice Cream.* In the thrift store, he found a set of toile curtains with a matching duvet which had the same creamy colour as the paint. The fabric had figures of vintage country life printed in sepia tones on the warm background. The woodwork, he painted in one of the sepia shades poetically dubbed *Afternoon Tea* by the paint company. The desire to give himself presence in this most private of spaces by replacing her *Cottage Rose* with a soft blue called *Old Denim* had given way to what he hoped was the more inclusive neutral selection. He had laughed at himself for devoting so much time and thought to paint colours when, for most of his life, he had never stayed anywhere long enough to notice anything about a room beyond whether it was warm and reasonably clean, and, if he was lucky, had a sturdy lock. He hoped that she would not be offended but he realized with a crooked grin that a woman who booked a trip to France without consultation could hardly complain about his initiative in decorating.

He also found satisfaction in taking her suggestion. He got a paid-under-the-table part-time job in the greenhouse at the gardening service. Helping things grow proved to be unexpectedly therapeutic for him.

*****

In Belfort, France, she climbed up each day to view the huge stone relief of a lion created by Bartholdi, the same man who had designed the famous Statue of Liberty. The first day she had been so exhausted by the climb that she had fallen asleep afterwards while sitting inside the landmark's accompanying museum. She had paid the small amount extra for a seasonal ticket which allowed unlimited visits. Soon she could make the climb with energy to spare for shopping and for seeking out the best, but still affordable, places to eat. She bought a set of French milled soap cakes with a manly scent that she knew Gus would like and a large box of tiny dark, milk and white chocolate replicas of the *Lyon de Belfort* to show him that she had been thinking of him - though she worried that he might be gone.

Well, she thought, *if he isn't there, I can always eat the lions myself and give the soap to Dad.*

*****

The day she was due back, Gus ensured that there was not a single dirty dish in the kitchen. Chuckling at the temptation to just break the dishes and throw them out instead of washing them, Gus wondered how he could have let a small thing like putting a bit of soap on some plates and cups get in the way of Amy Hannah's happiness - and his own. He decided to meet her at the airport.

As they sat on the edge of the bed the next morning, he enclosed her in his long arms, found the nape of her neck through her long hair and kissed her there gently. He had learned a long time before that allowing himself to fall asleep after intimacy - no matter how much his body craved the rest - left her feeling lonely, rejected and betrayed. When he had proven that he could and would keep himself awake for her, she, feeling confident in his care, had sometimes whispered, "Sleep, my sweet Gus. Really, I'm okay."

This day, overjoyed to have her back and to be speaking again, he declined her offer to let him rest and, instead, paid close and tender attention to her.

"I've missed your love and affection - not just while I was away but since summer, really," she whispered as he sighed into her ear.

"You always have my love, Amy Hannah, but I guess I've been a bit light on the affection," he admitted.

"A *bit* light?" she demanded with a smile. She was wary of discouraging his efforts to share.

"That's in the past, darlin'."

"Please don't shut me out again. I need you to know something. When I was a child and my mother was angry with me, she shouted. When she was very angry, she shouted and spanked me in rhythm to her shouts. When she was furious, she would stop speaking to me for three or four days."

"How did you deal with the not speakin', darlin'?" he asked, knowing instinctively that she had opened an important window.

"I never asked for anything that she could refuse and I kept busy so that I wasn't underfoot," she confessed.

"An' I hardly spoke for four - or was it five? - months. I'm sorry, darlin'," he whispered, caressing her cheek. "I was afraid that you wanted me to leave since you never asked me to stay."

"I thought that asking would just give you the chance to say no," she responded, matching his volume - or, rather, the lack of it.

"There'll be no more of that, Amy Hannah, I promise. I 've learned how to deal with the anger that I inherited from my old man. I've bin afraid of turning into him. The solution's a bit hard on crockery but it works," he told her with a mysterious grin.

"I was afraid that you wouldn't be here when I came home," Amy confessed.

"I was a little afraid that you wouldn't come home," he admitted.

There was a long pause while he hugged her more closely and while they both contemplated how near they had come to losing each other.

"Now that you told me about your mother, I guess I better speak plain about mine," he began, checking to see that he had her full attention.

"It's a strange and terrifying thing to see a man in a car with an older version of your own face and to have to stand by - not able to do anything but watch - as this older version of yourself runs down and kills your mother on purpose," he told her holding his head in his hands. "I was too far away to save her. I was nineteen and we'd had words because I wanted more independence. I told her that I was a man - not a child to be led around by the hand by his mother."

Amy hugged him in silence. What words could be sufficient, or even useful, in such a situation?

"I need you to know that every moment that you are away from me I am afraid that something will happen to you because I wasn't there when my mother needed me," he added.

"You never told me. I'm sorry that I worried you so much," she responded softly.

"Amy Hannah, I share this nest with the most beautiful, magical bird imaginable. I could never clip her wings like a common hen that's got to be kept in the barnyard. I never want my fears … or my anger, either … to frighten you or limit you."

"I never guessed."

"I couldn't tell you that he caught up with us … with my mother and me … and that he killed her. He ran her over with a car - stolen car, I found out later. I saw him but they never caught him. I couldn't save her. I couldn't stay for the police. I never knew his name - my mother never told me. I had no name, no identification myself. She was my mother but she was a Jane Doe in the newspaper. Until I came here with you, I used to call every couple of years to ask if the case was solved. That stopped when I came here. I won't bring the law down on you so I don't call from here. If I hadn't argued with her, she might not have died. I might have been able to do something."

"You can't know that, Gus! You might even have died, too," Amy argued.

"Would that have been so bad - if it was my time?" he shot back.

"No! You don't get to use that argument. You wouldn't have taken it from me the day we met and you can't use it now!" she cried in desperation.

"Hush, Amy Hannah. Hush, now. I never meant to upset you. I just want you to know the whole ugly truth. I just want you to understand why I didn't talk to you. I thought you'd be as afraid of me as my mother was of him, if you knew. I get so angry - I'm afraid that I'll turn into him," he not-quite sobbed.

"You have never been - could never be - like him in that way, Gus."

"The rage is so huge that I want to break things," he countered.

"Welcome to the human race! Most of us feel that angry from time to time. I want to throw furniture when I'm furious. It's not how angry you feel, it's what you do about it that matters. My grandmother said that an angry woman should scrub the living daylights out of the kitchen floor and an angry man should chop wood for the wood pile. I see how scrubbing the floor helps dissipate the anger in a constructive way. Still, I've always been more than a little skeptical that an angry man with an axe or a hatchet could be a healthy combination. My ex liked to break things - sometimes me. I had to store all my family china at Dad's place. There would have been nothing left. Only one cup and two saucers survived from my wedding set. You are not, and could never be, like that," she insisted.

"Well, darlin', I've been breakin' things," he admitted.

"What things? This house looks great. You've painted and cleaned - I love what you've done with this room, by the way - and I haven't noticed anything missing."

"And you won't. Nothin' o' yours nor mine either," he guaranteed before telling her the story, even revealing that he had imagined destroying her treasured dinnerware before settling on the second-hand store plan. As he finished, he stood, lifting her and clasping her firmly but gently from behind in the way that he had done that first day but this time he rested his cheek against hers. She inhaled the scent of his expensive soap - his one extravagance - and felt that they were home at last.

The Pneumonia Love Song

The lady wearing the purple angora coat arrived in mid-morning on a frosty day at the Basel-Mulhouse airport, where depending upon which exit was used, a person could come out into one of three countries. Her old joints resisted efforts to limber up after the hours in transit. The ghost of her breath hovered in the air as she caught a tram into the central part of the city, having come through to the Swiss side and taken the rail shuttle to the station with the surety of one who had done this many times before. She had thought about stopping for a snack but, remembering that The Krafft had tea stations on every floor, opted to proceed, without delay, to the hotel for check-in.

*****

The call had come in just as the men had made the first stroke at pulling down the thin strip of crown moulding to begin the kitchen renovation. It had not been the first time that an unexpected event had stalled the work on this room but it was the first time that the work had actually begun. She had needed to hush those assembled as she scrambled to find the phone under the box protecting it from the detritus of the teardown.

"Yes, this is she," she had confirmed to Karel's nephew, whose telephone voice she just vaguely remembered. Clearly, he had not recognized hers.

The assembled company watched as her lips pursed and her forehead wrinkled in distress at what the voice was saying.

"I'm sorry to hear that, Oleks," she replied, remembering the nephew's name just in time. "Where is Suzette, then?"

Squeezing the telephone receiver more tightly, the elderly lady had asked this with a great effort to keep the contempt she felt out of her voice. She listened at length before cautioning the man at the other end of the line, "I don't know when I can get a flight out."

All eyes that had not already been upon her turned to look in case the sight of her would somehow fill in the missing parts of the conversation.

"Of course, Oleks. I do care for him and I'll come as soon as I can. I'm so sorry. I'll get back to you as soon as I have flight information."

When she cradled the handset, she was clearly shaken. She blinked back a tear and worked to steady a little tick at one corner of her lips.

"It's Karel. He has pneumonia and it's very serious. Oleks, his nephew, says that Karel is asking for me. I can't refuse to go," she explained.

Two men averted their eyes to hide the resentment they felt. One, the elderly lady's present husband, remained silent but the other, Suzette's former partner, recovered first.

"Where is he and why do they need *you*? Where is Suzette?" Georges almost spat.

"Karel's in Basel. Now that she's really needed, Suzette has made herself scarce," the lady replied.

"It serves Karel right," Suzette's ex declared with a cynical but not quite bitter edge to his voice.

"*Granpère*, is that the same Suzette who was your ..." Yvette began to ask.

"Yes!" snapped Georges. "I will talk no more about her."

*****

The tiny reception desk at The Krafft was just as the lady remembered it - staffed with people both gracious and helpful. As was usual for her, she had slept little on the flight and was running purely on nerve. The renowned polite efficiency of the Swiss was calming and reassuring. She herded her rolling suitcase into the miniscule elevator and pressed the number for her floor. A quick glance at the seductively beautiful sweeping staircases reminded her that these were meant for dramatic entrances, not for dragging luggage. Except to transport luggage, no one able to climb stairs would choose the confining elevator in the time between check-in and check-out.

Compact and cozy, the hotel room had cool white walls and pale blond furniture with clean lines. What might otherwise have been a chilly effect was enlivened with bright, folk-inspired textiles: curtains, carpet, cushions and coverlet. She placed her suitcase in the closet before taking the tea tray out into the common area. There, the tea-making station offered a variety of special tea blends in clear jars with sparkling chrome lids. A bowl of red and green apples - so artistically arranged that she hesitated a moment before she disturbed it by taking one - sat beside a flat dish containing individually wrapped fancy cookies and Swiss chocolates. She chose a floral-scented green tea and, when the kettle had come to a boil and settled back to the correct temperature for the more delicate needs of the tender green leaves, she added water to the two-cup iron pot. She arranged the green apple, three cookies and one chocolate on the tray and bore it back to her room. After a few heavenly sips and one slowly savoured cookie, she telephoned Oleks to let him know that she had arrived and to get the name of the hospital. She respectfully declined his attempts to give her directions, assuring him that the efficiency of the front desk staff would ensure that she had a map and precise instructions for the required trams, with which Oleks, possessing a car, would be less familiar.

After ringing off, she finished her tea, enjoyed the two remaining cookies and tucked the chocolate and the apple into her purse. She brushed and re-pinned her silvery hair, passed a hot wet washcloth over her face and changed to the fresh blouse she always slipped into her carry-on bag for fear that her checked luggage might fail to arrive at her destination. This was no longer a worry but she preferred not to open the suitcase just then. When the shoulder pouch where she kept her passport, bank cards and most of her cash was settled into place, she topped her outfit with her jacket and covered all with the deep purple angora coat.

The memory of a Japanese friend nicknaming her Murasaki because of her love of purple brought a gentle smile to her lips. Today, in order to navigate the difficult path between her commitment to her present husband - the love of her life - and her lingering sense of … what? - not quite obligation - to Karel - her ex-husband, she needed to think of herself as someone else, perhaps someone mythical. She would be Murasaki. She put her shoulders back and straightened her posture. "Bra up," her singing teacher had repeatedly told her.

"You cannot face the song - let alone life itself - without giving your lungs the space they deserve!" the Welsh woman had insisted.

With bra up, Murasaki arranged her hat, plucked up her purse and, locking the door behind her, set off for the hospital.

The clear, concise directions from the reception desk ensured effortless tram connections to her destination. At the hospital, more Swiss efficiency brought her to Karel's room and assisted with correct enrobing in infection control gear before her entry into the patient's room. Asked if there was anything else she required, the silver-haired lady replied, "He will want me to hold his hand and not through gloves."

"Be sure to wash your hands thoroughly, use sanitizer and be careful not to touch your face or hair before touching the patient," she was told. It was clear that the medical staff understood the therapeutic value of touch.

Karel called her name as she entered the room.

"I'm here, Karel," she responded gently but, as he continued to call for her, she grasped that he was unaware of the sound or movement around him. Despite this, she continued to respond with, "I'm here, Karel," after every outcry.

He looked pale and weak, an effect that the plastic "moustache" attached above his upper lip for oxygen delivery did nothing to soften. One of Karel's hands had been tapped with intravenous tubes, reminding her of the systems some maple bushes used for sap collection at sugaring time. The tubing piercing Karel's hand, she reflected, unlike those for maple trees, was intended to put nutrients in, not bear them away.

Ensuring proper hand hygiene, she sat down in a chair on the side opposite the hand with the tubes. She took the free hand in hers and began to stroke it softly. It was some time later that he erupted with an extended coughing episode. The sound split the air with kettle drum resonance. When it eased off, he opened his eyes and spoke her name with surprise, setting off another round of coughs.

"I'm here, Karel," she assured the now-aware patient as she continued to stroke his hand. He smiled, and seeming satisfied, slipped back into a state of sleep. His body was restless but the expression on his face declared that his mind was at peace. She sat with him all afternoon, stroking his hand and re-assuring him of her presence whenever he seemed to awaken. At some point, one of the staff brought her a plastic-encased magazine with the explanation that it should be safe and the recommendation that she should still be vigilant about potential pathogen transfer to the patient. While he slept, she was careful to turn the pages with the hand that she did not use to stroke Karel's. Though she had spoken to them in German, the staff had somehow known that a magazine in English would be appreciated. She wondered whether it was her appearance or her accent which gave her away.

At supper time, Oleks' wife Katya arrived.

"You must eat now while I stay with Oncle Karel," Katya insisted in the sing-songy French which Murasaki recognized as a match for that of a friend who had left Canada to take her last year of high school in Switzerland.

The food hall at the train and transit station provided tasty meals at the best prices to be found in the downtown of Basel. The city, a government town where too many dined on expense accounts, was notorious for astronomical restaurant prices. Murasaki purchased a meal of *Rahm Schnitzel mit Spätzle,* purple cabbage and peas as vegetable sides and an *Apfelstrudel* for dessert. All was efficiently heated and carefully wrapped by a server with a smile. Not a morsel remained when Murasaki returned to the patient's side.

Karel slept into the evening, punctuating the time with brief eruptions of coughing. He no longer called her name, however, seeming satisfied to know that she had arrived. She held his hand or stroked it gently and she smoothed his dishevelled hair away from his face from time to time. At 9:00 p.m., Frau Knecht, the *leitende Krankenschwester* – the equivalent of the charge nurse for the ward – came in to check on the patient and to explain to the visitor that a special duty nurse would come in soon for the night shift.

"Please give her my number at the hotel and tell her that she can call me at any time of the night if Karel awakens asking for me," the visitor insisted.

"It is unlikely that he will but I will tell her, *aber genädige Frau*, you must go and take some rest or you will have no strength to come back tomorrow."

*****

Karel was calling for her when she arrived the next morning. His complexion was less waxy and his breathing the faintest bit stronger than the day before.

"I'm here, Karel," she assured him. "Don't try to talk. I'll just sit here and tell you about my flight and the lovely room at The Krafft, which Oleks so kindly arranged for me."

He seemed to be struggling to say something but she could not make it out. She looked around but found no water except a bit in a tube attached to a pink sponge. How she hated the thought of using that on him but clearly nothing else was authorized. She gave his mouth a quick swipe with the instrument, being careful not to cause any dribbles which might provoke choking. It seemed to do some good as he was able to thank her for coming. He tried to say something more … something that she assumed was an apology … but his effort was obstructed by another coughing fit.

She reminded him that the small allowance that he had reluctantly agreed to during the divorce negotiations now allowed her the financial freedom to work only occasionally and, still, to afford to pay for air tickets. It was this that allowed her to be present when he needed her, she explained.

She talked about the weather and anything else she could think of to fill the air so that he would not be tempted to talk.

"I'm dying," he whispered sadly when she paused for a breath.

"Nonsense!" she insisted. "I have come all this way to look after you. Don't you dare die. I'll be terribly offended."

He tried to laugh a bit but was overwhelmed with another spate of coughing.

"Don't talk. Save your strength for getting better ... and no more about dying. I forbid it!" she needled.

He smiled and she smiled back but it showed only in her eyes as the lower part of her face was masked to keep him safe. Soon after, he slipped off to sleep again, clutching her hand.

*****

"Pneumonia is very tricky in the elderly," the young blond doctor explained to Katya and Murasaki in a consultation later that morning.

He is too attractive for his own good, thought Murasaki. She observed that Katya sparkled just a little in response to this doctor's gaze.

"Some patients who should recover, succumb and some who seem too weak show the heart of a lion and find somehow the will, against all medical indications, to defeat the disease," he further explained.

From Katya came the fact that Karel seemed to have given up after he discovered that Suzette was not coming back. He had been found half dead in his apartment by a neighbour who had called Oleks and an ambulance. Suzette had not even bothered to lock the door when she left.

"He has not been fighting and he cannot survive if he does not," Herr Doktor Kranz insisted in almost native-speaker English.

"I came as soon as I could. I got the first flight available," Murasaki told Katya and the doctor.

"What is your relationship with Mr. Stohryn?" the doctor asked quickly.

"I'm Karel's … ex-wife. When he is able to talk, he will tell you that I am the love of his life. I care enough about him to be sad that he is not the love of my life … though, despite what happened with Suzette, I still love him enough, as one loves a family member, to want to see him well. I promise to stay here as long as I am needed."

"He looks better today than when I saw him yesterday. His condition has been very serious. I have twice been tempted to order assisted respiration and now we have a *nicht wiederleben* designation - what you Americans would call a DNR order."

The elderly lady ignored the doctor's erroneous identification of her as an American to jump upon the issue of the "do not resuscitate order".

"Who ordered that?" she demanded sharply. Katya looked away and tried to make herself unnoticeable.

"Oleks Stohryn," replied the doctor, reading from the chart in his hand.

"I am fairly sure that I am the power-of-attorney for medical matters," Murasaki insisted.

"Fairly sure, fifty or sixty per cent?" the doctor challenged.

"Fairly sure, eighty to ninety per cent," she shot back. "Karel would have told me if he no longer wanted me to do this. He might not inform me if he were changing his will for his material possessions but I know he would never have given Suzette this power over his life and health. I am confident that if he wanted Marina, his niece, or either or both of his nephews, Oleks and Rudy, to take over this responsibility, he would have told me."

"I will need up-to-date documentation. In the interim I will remove the DNR," the doctor affirmed.

"I think we found something like a power-of-attorney in his apartment," Katya said hesitantly.

Murasaki wondered if Katya and Oleks had been going through Karel's papers while they stayed at his apartment and whether they had called her in Canada because Oleks had found something telling him that he had no authority to make life-and-death decisions for Karel. She controlled the urge to question or comment.

"I can bring the paper tomorrow," Katya offered.

"And I know the lawyer. I will call to find out if there is anything more recent," declared the elderly lady, continuing with, "Assuming Karel recovers enough to return home, my husband - my current husband - will come to help me take care of Karel at home."

"The world just becomes stranger and stranger. Every time I think I have heard everything, I am once again surprised," the doctor pondered. "You say your current husband is willing to help you to do convalescent care for your ex-husband?"

"Yes, to simplify, my current husband believes that, as the victor, he can afford to be generous," the grandmotherly lady explained.

"Perhaps if you are here for a while, you will have time to help me make sense of this," he suggested with a grin. She smiled and gave him a subtle nod.

"Our parents are needing more and more help and that is the same for Rudy and his wife," Katya told them by way of apology. "We can not afford to take away any more time from work to care for Oncle Karel, so we are very relieved that you are here."

"It would be a shame if you have come all this way and he does not respond to treatment," the doctor added. He had decided that he quite liked this spirited *Großmutter*-type.

"I have cared for Karel in sickness before and he is not an easy patient. I will need clear instructions and justifications for any treatment you might need me to help with but I assure you that if it is medically possible for him to survive, he will find the will," the silver-haired lady stated in a tone that no longer surprised the doctor. She continued, "The difficult part is that he is going to ask me to come back to him and I can never do that. He made his bed with Suzette and he lied about it. Even if I were not happy in my current marriage, I could never trust him in intimacy again. We will just have to make sure that he does not see that as a cause for despair and that he doesn't use it as a reason to malinger to keep me here."

"One thing at a time. If we can get him to fight enough to clear his lungs and breathe without oxygen tubes, it will be a great victory," replied the doctor. He did not actually wink but there was, in his face, the suggestion that he wanted to do so.

"Has he taken any nourishment at all on his own?" the ex-wife asked.

"As he cannot control his coughing, there is risk of choking. Feeding by mouth is better for the whole body than feeding into the vein but he is not yet ready for this," the doctor told them before asking, "Is there anything else you can think of that would make Herr Stohryn more comfortable?"

"He'll do better in his own pajamas … and he'll want me to sing to him. I know that that won't meet infection control standards so we could do it remotely. If someone could call me and hold the phone to his ear, I could sing into the phone and there wouldn't be any risk in that - if the phone on his end is properly sanitized," Murasaki explained.

"I can arrange that," agreed Herr Doktor Kranz, "and I will check on him tomorrow."

This closed the consultation. The doctor hurried off. The two women returned to Karel's room. Because Karel appeared to be sleeping, Katya prepared to leave. When he knew that his niece had gone, Karel opened his eyes and, smiling, demanded with one word that Murasaki talk to him.

"You old fox!" the silver-haired lady accused. "You pretended that you were asleep. Don't you want to talk with Katya?"

"You - only to you ..." he managed before his speech was arrested by a coughing fit. Describing her dinner of the night before, she continued to hold his hand until sleep overtook him again.

Throughout the afternoon, she talked to him during the brief intervals when he was awake. She also swabbed his mouth with the sponge apparatus that sat on the side table. This combatted - barely - the dryness caused by his being fed only intravenously. She knew this from caring for her parents during their last days. She reflected upon the fact that she was now older than the age reached by the first of her grandparents to pass on. She shook off this melancholy thought and felt even more determined to nurse, cajole or encourage Karel to choose life.

When the private duty night nurse arrived, Murasaki insisted that she could be called at any time of the night should Karel ask for her.

In her hotel room, she prepared a pot of tea before taking a quick shower and putting on her nightgown. Just as she was raising the teacup to her lips, the telephone rang.

"Monsieur Stohryn is asking for you," said the night nurse's voice.

"Of course, I will speak with him," Murasaki replied.

"I am here in Basel, Karel. I will be there to see you in the morning," she re-assured adding, "I was just getting into bed. I'm glad you called."

"Sing!" he begged.

"Certainly ... but I must sing quietly. Maybe something like a lullaby?"

"Maybe 'Hanzel und Gretel'?" he croaked in request.

She stood, corrected her posture, drew a few slow breaths through her mouth, releasing each one carefully through the nose. When properly prepared, she began Humperdinck's "Abendsegen" in German, describing the seven pairs of angels who guarded sleepers. After singing about the final two who stood by to guide into heaven those not surviving the night, she admonished, in her English speaking voice, "Don't even think about going anywhere with those two. There's to be no trotting off to heaven now that I am here, Karel. Just have a good sleep and I will be there in the morning."

The nurse's voice came back on the line saying that the patient had tears in his eyes and that, perhaps, a cheerier song might help.

Murasaki offered to sing "How Do You Like Your Eggs in the Morning?", the up-beat Vic Damone and Jane Powell treasure. The patient agreed. The lyrics described the importance of affectionate hugs and smiles regardless of how the eggs and toast might be prepared. Murasaki put all the swing into the song that she could muster after a long day.

"Now get some sleep so that you can get better. I'll see you in the morning," the singer told him.

"Yes, *chou-chou*," he promised.

"He seems better now," the nurse reported before ringing off.

It was 4:00 a.m. before the phone rang again.

"Help me! I'm sick," Karel's voice pleaded.

"Yes, that is why you're in the hospital. I promise I will be there in the morning," she soothed.

"Sing?" he asked.

"Of course, Karel," she agreed, offering several familiar titles for his consideration. They settled upon "We'll Gather Lilacs in the Spring Again". She sang with warmth and tenderness ... and the promise of something that she knew she could not honour beyond the measures of the song.

"Mmmm," he responded appreciatively. Once again, she urged him to sleep and to expect her in the morning.

After ringing off and having little hope of sleep herself, she picked up the paperback novel she had been reading. Minutes later, the book landed - for the third time - with a bounce on the floor awakening her with a start. She retrieved it, placed it on the nightstand and curled up under the covers.

The clock read 7:30 when she next opened her eyes. Leaping out of bed, she immediately regretted her rashness. She sat back on the edge of the bed until the wave of vertigo - some kind of syncope, her doctor had told her - passed.

"Silly old girl!" she said to herself. "You're not young enough for that anymore!"

An hour and a half later, showered, dressed and breakfasted, she sat gently stroking Karel's hand and talking in her smoothest, most soothing voice about the weather, the tea and cookies she had enjoyed at The Krafft and anything else she could think of that was not related to her beloved current husband. Karel needed encouragement to return to health - not a reminder that she would never come back to him. She would not deceive him but she was not averse to avoiding the subject. She paused to reflect upon her long-ago description of the wonderful trip on which she would have taken her mother. Murasaki had woven aloud this fantasy into words even though it was clear that life was slipping away. Murasaki had wanted the last images in her mother's mind to be beautiful. She contrasted this with her confidence that Karel's body, more than twenty years younger than her mother's had been, stood a good chance of recovering.

"Help me!" Karel called out to her.

"I'm here, Karel," she told him.

"Sing?" he begged.

"Not here," she cautioned but offered, "I could hum?"

"Please?" he wheedled.

"It has to do with infection control, Karel. Humming is less dangerous."

"Mmmm," he assented reluctantly.

"How about the melody from the humming chorus of *Madame Butterfly*?" she suggested.

"'One Alone'?" he croaked, requesting the love solo from Sigmund Romberg's musical *The Desert Song*. She recalled its being performed by the local musical society during her time as an elementary school pupil. Mr. Reginald, her teacher at the time, had had the leading male role. Her mother had agreed to allow her to stay up late one night in order to attend.

"I think not. That song deserves full voice and it really is not appropriate," she disagreed, remembering his dalliance with Suzette during the time when he had promised complete commitment to his wife. "Take what I can give, Karel."

"Mm-hmm," he accepted but burst into a coughing fit. She held the kidney-shaped pan to catch the product of his efforts. The night nurse had detailed the positive change from dry to productive cough. Murasaki had celebrated by wielding the equipment at the appropriate moment to catch the small yellow masses that he expelled from his mouth.

She congratulated Karel on this evidence of improvement and waited until he was able to breath calmly again before she began to hum softly. Though it lost a lot in the translation to a single voice, he smiled his approval. Before she reached the closing crescendo, his mouth had dropped open from his relaxation into slumber. She slowly withdrew her hand from his, watching to ensure that he did not awaken. She used the opportunity for a quick washroom visit and a check-in with Frau Knecht, who bestowed upon

Murasaki a wrapped sterile replacement for the pan. The nurse promised a timely removal of the used one.

At noon Oleks and Katya arrived with the document that confirmed that Karel's ex-wife remained his agent and effective next-of-kin for his care. This matched what the lawyer had told Murasaki on the telephone. The couple stayed to cover Murasaki's lunch break. She returned well fed and carrying a bag of purchases from a nearby yarn shop. (These, she was told, would have to be held at the nursing station until she left for the day as they could not be taken into the patient's room.) When Oleks and Katya heard her approach, they met her in the hall.

"We're very sorry that we thought you were a gold-digger when you married Oncle Karel. Now that we have met Suzette, we know what one really looks like. You were so very good for Oncle Karel. It is unfortunate that it could not last," Olek apologized. "There was a box with your name on it in the apartment. It seems to be some clothes and shoes - though we did not look carefully. We sent it to The Krafft and we asked Oncle Karel's accountant to cover your room until you no longer need it."

Murasaki noted that Oleks did not say "until Oncle Karel is well". She wondered if they still expected that Karel would not survive. She was a bit offended that they clearly did not want her to stay at the apartment that had been one of her homes during her life with Karel. Still, she liked The Krafft. It was also convenient - cleaning was the staff's responsibility, not hers.

Oleks was recounting the demands of parents and jobs when Murasaki's attention returned to his words. She assured him that she would be there for Karel for the duration of his hospitalization and that her current husband would come to help with caregiving from the point of discharge.

"We are just in Freiburg if you need us – not so far but we must get back to work tomorrow. Do you really think he is any better?" asked Oleks uncertainly.

"Oh, yes. He's spoken to me and he is starting to cough up some of the phlegm that has been giving him trouble ... and you must have noticed that his colouring is better. He still seems to have some fight left in him," she noted. "I really do care for him, Oleks. I can never go back to him after all that has happened but I assure you that I will take good care of him."

"We all know that you will but we cannot imagine why. Thanks, good luck and keep in touch. Marina and Rudy and their families asked to be remembered to you," Oleks closed.

"Send my warmest regards to them, please, and take care of yourselves," she said by way of launching them. They had said that they were in a hurry to go but they seemed to be dragging their feet about leaving. She wondered if there might be something more that they wanted to ask but were unsure how to broach. The only thing that she could imagine would be related to inheritance and she had no intention of smoothing the way for such questions.

After gowning and masking, she returned to Karel's bedside. He opened his eyes.

"They said you slept through their visit. Are you pretending again?" she needled.

"I love you, *chou-chou*," he declared, avoiding the question but setting off a violent round of coughing.

"That's right! Cough it all up. I want you to get better as soon as you can," she cheered him on.

"I want you to come back to me," he insisted as soon as the coughing had subsided and she had caught a rainbow of mucus in the vessel.

"One of us could get her wish! If you want my caring attention, you will not try to extort more than I can give. You must get better because you can and because it will give me joy," she pontificated.

"Will it?" he demanded with not a little skepticism.

"Of course. Just because I can't come back to your bed does not mean I have entirely stopped loving you, Karel … so, of course, I will rejoice in your restored health," she replied, responding just as certainly to his gaze as to his question.

"Does your husband know?" he joked.

Her response was swift and serious.

"Certainly, he does. He will be coming to help me care for you as soon as they let you go home."

"And to remind me that you are *his* wife!"

"That, too."

"He loves you," Karel gasped in a tone that was a statement but was also suggestive of a question – perhaps a hope that there was still a chance that she might leave that man.

"Yes, I am the love of his life and he is the love of mine. I am sorry that I didn't know he was still living when I met you, Karel. We might all have been saved a lot of pain …" she apologized. "But then I wouldn't be here now to care for you. I have never hidden any of this from you."

"You are the love of *my* life," Karel whispered.

"Things don't always work out the way we hope but we must still embrace life and find our best possible path forward. It will also be the best revenge on your heirs – for you to live long while you enjoy spending your money," she cajoled.

"You are my heir," he revealed, as a magician pulling a rabbit from what had been an empty top hat.

Astonishment registered on her face and snatched away any words she might have uttered.

"You don't think I would have made Suzette my heir?" he rasped before beginning another extended coughing fit.

"What about Marina, Oleks and Rudy?" she asked when he settled again.

"There is something for them but most goes to you," he barely got this out before he began to cough again. He expelled a green-and-yellow lump into the pan she held.

"You must rest, Karel. We can talk more about this when you are feeling better."

He was not quite sleeping when the doctor arrived. After checking the chart and vitals, the doctor fixed the lady in his gaze.

"You seem to have the magic touch, *madame*. He's much improved today," the doctor congratulated her before turning to the patient.

"How is the cough?"

"Not so bad if I don't talk too much," Karel replied, crackling into a light cough at the end of the sentence.

"I want to try you on some soft food, Mr. Stohryn, if you promise to take it slowly and not try to talk during your meal. I want you to try even if the food is not your favourite. The menus have been finished for today. Tomorrow, if this goes well, you can have some choice but today you take what comes, *richtig*!" the doctor commanded.

"Ja!" agreed Karel adding, "This angel will insist." He waved toward his ex-wife and flashed a sparkling smile her way.

"Sehr gut!" laughed the handsome doctor. "Even your oxygen levels are better. What did she do to cause such a change?"

Karel cleared his throat and hacked up another globule of phlegm before answering.

"She held my hand … and sang to me in the night when I was afraid and … she told me to get better so that my heirs would have to wait for my money!" Karel explained with a smirk before succumbing to another coughing episode.

"Ah, this is the miracle cure!" Herr Doktor Kranz joked. "I may need to retrain the hospital staff and make presentations at conferences."

He became serious as he looked back from the door, saying, "The plan is soft food moving slowly to full diet. When you are successful at getting enough nourishment by mouth, we remove the IV and the catheter. Then, with regular elimination and some physiotherapy to get you ambulatory, we can look forward to sending you home. I want to prescribe a mild expectorate for tomorrow. I want you to cough up the mucus that is on your chest. You did not seem strong enough before. I will check again tomorrow."

Frau Knecht came in with a tray soon after the doctor left. She explained that she would be feeding the patient and that Karel's visitor should take a well-deserved break. Murasaki squeezed Karel's hand gently, and making way for Frau Knecht, promised to be back within the hour.

"Heiße oder kalt?" Frau Knecht asked the patient.

"Hot first," he replied in English.

The egg custard was smooth and light, as well as warming. It was savoury rather than sweet but he still had to restrain himself from gulping it down. He chewed to activate the necessary saliva - though the consistency was just fractionally more firm than a cream soup or a milkshake.

Karel's ex-wife, after shedding the infection control garb, left the hospital for a nearby coffee shop where she ordered, Grießnockerlsuppe, the clear vegetable-and-dumpling soup that she had so enjoyed on holidays in Austria. This she would follow with a slice of beautiful, layered cream cake, perhaps Black Forest or hazelnut torte, and a pot of tisane. She hoped that Karel would find as much pleasure in his first hospital meal as she would in this light repast. A wave of guilt passed over her before she chased it off with the thought that he would soon be able to indulge his sweet tooth if he continued to improve at the same rate.

When she had telephoned her husband in Canada the night before, he had asked after the patient and had reported finding an affordable flight, leaving two weeks later, which he hoped would suit.

"That should be just right," she assured him. "I miss you so very much and I can't wait to see you, my treasure."

As he rang off, he made a little kissing sound into the telephone which she had prized all the more because, although he was a warm and caring husband, he would normally have thought such sound effects embarrassing. She always visualized their bond as tiny bridges connecting heart to heart, mind to mind, soul to soul and body to body such that they could not be disengaged from each other without damaging both. She knew that their love augmented both and diminished neither. It had been that way before he had been lost and thought dead. It was that way again now.

In the years between, she had finally given up hope that he would ever be restored to her and had applied for a declaration of presumptive death. Eventually, she had met Karel. She had loved Karel but, as she knew that she could not survive so great a hurt again, she had not given herself as completely as to the lost one. Karel's betrayal with her oldest friend, Suzette, had angered much more than it had wounded. Anger management was easier for Murasaki to achieve than restoration of a broken heart. This accounted for her ability now - while he was hospitalized - to care for Karel so tenderly with neither debilitating guilt nor any hint of temptation around his requests for her to return to him.

On Murasaki's return from the coffee shop, Frau Knecht reported that the patient had taken the entire meal almost without incident - just a little cough which caused him to expel one mouthful of the orange sorbet. Karel was triumphant. His ex-wife patted his hand and congratulated him. After such an eventful day, sleep tugged at him and claimed him despite his desire to resist.

"We will talk more tomorrow. You need to rest now," she soothed.

The night calls had been reduced to two - one at midnight and one at 2:00 a.m. The first time, she sang the lullaby from a film popular in her childhood where the sleepers-to-be were urged, with reverse psychology, to remain wakeful. The second call opened with a weepy Karel lamenting his poor luck with relationships.

"Dry your tears, Karel. You can't be crying - it's bad for your breathing. I will sing you the pneumonia love song," she bargained.

"Do I know it?" he choked out.

"I don't know. It was huge in North America years ago but I'm not sure that it got to you in Europe. It cautions against rushing into love again after being hurt," she detailed. "It seems like the right song for the moment but you must promise me that you will see the humour in the words."

"I'll try," he conceded.

She put on comic voice and responded, "Try? There is no try, sir! There is do or do not."

His chuckle, she felt, put him in the right frame of mind for the song. He gave a bit of a wry laugh when she finished singing and affirmed that he could see the humour in it. He had laughed lightly but, still, it had evoked a fit of coughing. As she waited for this to subside, she thought about how he had spent his life trying to balance pursuing excellence in his profession with caring for family members who were ill or in declining health. His last aunt had died just before he had taken the vacation on which he had met the love his life. This was at an age when most people were thinking of retirement. Murasaki rang off, assuring him that she would be there in the morning.

*****

He was wearing his own pajamas and sitting in a chair when she arrived a few days later. The remains of breakfast sat on the clip-on tray which both kept him from slipping out of the chair and provided a reservoir for the meal tray and a kidney pan. He was still attached to all the same tubes as on the previous day but he looked more positive.

"Hold my hand?" he had begged as soon as she arrived.

"Of course," she agreed, sanitizing her hands carefully after she pulled a chair over close to his.

"It looks as though you've done well with your breakfast this morning. What did you have? A soft-boiled egg, some kind of hot cereal and - what's this? Did they try you on a bit of toast?" she enumerated as she examined the evidence.

"That was not so successful. Crumbs make me cough," he lamented before being ambushed by a spate of coughing. She caught the phlegm in the kidney pan and rubbed his back to soothe him as he bent forward.

"I would have given up. You would have inherited -" he rasped.

"I'm not trying to get your money, Karel. I want you to be healthy so you can enjoy it yourself," she contested soothingly.

"That is why you are my main heir," he replied.

"That's a kind thought but I didn't know that and I would have come to help you in any case," she insisted, "but I don't really want to talk about anything to do with death right now. I want to talk about preparing the apartment. I don't think you'll be staying here much longer."

"The cleaners will have been there by now. Oleks would have arranged it."

"True ... but I will need to stock the kitchen and make sure that the guest bedroom is ready."

"For you and *that man*!" he almost spat.

"If by *'that man'* you mean my husband, yes."

"When I met him the first time, he told me his name was only for his family and friends and that I was neither."

"Then call him Cash," she suggested.

"It's a ridiculous soubriquet," he sniffed. "How did it start, *chou-chou*?"

"When he found his way back to me, he was legally dead so he couldn't get any ID. Until we could get a reversal of the presumptive death ruling, any cheques he got for odd jobs had to be made out to cash. It became a joke at the bank and then around town. When he gets here, you can't just call him *'that man'* or *'hey you'*! Everyone who met him after he returned calls him Cash."

"But you don't," Karel challenged.

"Of course not!" she retorted, pausing to consider how to avoid discussing the affectionate terms she was now in the habit of using. She continued, "When you and I were together, I rarely called you Karel. It was *caro mio* or *Liebchen* or *chéri*."

"So it was. Whenever you called me Karel, I knew you were angry - very angry!" He looked at his feet and sighed.

"Back to getting the apartment ready, please," she urged, changing the subject to safer ground.

"Fritz will give you a key," he assured her, referring to the maintenance manager.

"You should telephone him ... and Oleks and Rudy, too, to let them know that you are on the mend," she suggested.

"Would you do that, *chou-chou*?" Karel wheedled.

"I could. I just thought that they might like to hear your voice," she recommended.

"You are the only one who really cares if I live or die," he sniffled.

"I don't believe that, Karel, but I may be the only one who would sing to you at four in the morning," she told him solemnly.

"Is that what time I asked the night nurse to call?"

"Midnight, two, four, five … but I said anytime and I meant it," she told him.

"You are too good to me … but you won't consider coming back to me?"

"No, Karel, I care deeply for you and I'll help you and take care of you but I am where I should be now … with the one who truly loves me. So much so that he's coming to help me to take care of you."

"I need to stop asking you?"

"Please! Content yourself with what you *can* have."

"I love you, *chou-chou*," he declared.

"Perhaps … but not enough to keep me safe by resisting Suzette."

"You are still angry," he observed.

"Yes, I am!" she barked before continuing more mildly, "Karel, she left you to die. I don't think of myself as any kind of saint but, in similar circumstances, I would have called an ambulance for my worst enemy."

"But you are still angry for yourself, too," he observed.

She detailed her reasons, counting off on her fingers. He and Suzette, occupied in physical intimacy, had failed to meet her, as they had promised, at the train station on her arrival in Italy from Canada. It had been raining and she was wrangling several pieces of luggage. He had betrayed his commitment to his wife with her oldest friend and had tried to lie about it. He and Suzette had not used protection. Suzette and Georges "enjoyed" (Murasaki emphasized the word sardonically) an open relationship and had each had many lovers. Finally, Karel and Suzette had acted as though Murasaki had been the crazy one when she had insisted that this was grounds for ending the marriage.

"How would you know about protection?" he demanded with a heat in his voice that reddened his face and provoked a violent coughing jag.

"I went through the garbage!" she shot back before recognizing that this level of emotion was not therapeutic. "Karel, this is not good for your recovery. I don't want to upset you and I'm asking you to extend me the same courtesy."

When he settled again, a little smirk crossed his face.

"You hate anything sticky, messy or dirty. I can't believe you picked through the garbage."

"Every bit of it – extreme measures for extreme circumstanceses," she admitted.

"How did you know it wasn't flushed away?" he demanded.

She thought about the finicky plumbing in the small Italian "bolthole" that they had restored and decorated together. He had lost that place to her in the divorce, retaining at least half a dozen other properties around Europe that he had bought and rehabilitated before he knew her, against which she would have had no claim. There were three or four others bought after they married on which she might have had a claim if she had asked – though she never would have.

"There would have been a visit from the plumber …" she began.

"You have all the answers," he despaired. "My mother told me that lies were the gateway to the devil's pit."

"Your mother was a wise woman. I am so sorry that I never met her."

"I'm sorry about everything with Suzette and especially about how stingy I was with you in the divorce settlement. Can't you forgive and forget?" he asked. He flashed her the coy little-boy grin that she had found almost irresistible when they had first met.

"Forgive, maybe ... someday. But forget? Never," she replied, struggling for a measured tone.

"Maybe I should have died ..." he mused sadly.

"Stop that! Just because I haven't let go of the anger doesn't mean I don't care about you. I'm here, and where is Suzette?" she shot back.

"What do I have to live for? Suzette is gone and you will never come back to me," he moaned.

"You have exactly the same things to live for that you had before you met me - your work, your family, your friends and social life, and your pleasure in music. You are not exactly hurting for money ... and you have something else, too. You have me to sing to you and to encourage you to get well and 'that man,' as you call him, to come and help me care for you at home so that you can expect an early discharge from the hospital. You really are very fortunate, Karel," she insisted.

She rubbed his back and patted his hand. He tried not to give in to the smile that was fighting to take over his face but he was unequal to the task.

When she returned to her room at The Krafft that evening, a large box had been delivered for her. Pulling out clothes and footwear that she had all but forgotten offered a festive, Christmas-like diversion for her after the stressful discussions of the day.

She returned most of the clothing to the box but, in anticipation of the following day, she set out an outfit that had been an extravagant gift from Karel. It was one that he had especially liked on her. The red-and-blue tweed hooded cape matched a pair of flannelette-lined tweed slacks which revealed a flash of red lining at the cuffs. Even the hiking boots continued the theme with blue leather toecaps and twisted laces of red and blue. The set had included two thermal turtle-necked sweaters: a red one and the blue one which she selected for the morning. She imagined what her husband's amused response would be – "outdoorsy clothes for rich folks". In her life with him, they spent most of their days in jeans or cords – and not the designer type.

Karel had bought her a sapphire pendant with a stone the size of her thumbnail to complete the ensemble. Perhaps, she considered, Karel had given Suzette the piece and his other gifts of jewellery that she had left behind. It would not be polite to ask him, she decided.

Waking naturally after an uninterrupted and restorative sleep, Murasaki enjoyed a continental breakfast before catching a tram to the hospital. The door to Karel's room was open and all infection-control notices and garb had been removed. He was delighted by the sight of her and, especially, with her choice of outfit. It was with obvious pride that he told her that all the tubes, bags and monitors had been removed early that morning on the doctor's orders.

"I have even had a short walk – with lots of support – from the bed to the chair this morning and I ate everything on my plate," he almost crowed.

"That *is* good news, Karel!" she congratulated.

"You need the sapphire to complete the effect, *chou-chou*. I want you to know that I put all the nice pieces in the bank to *save* them for you – not to *keep* them from you. You do believe that?"

"I do, Karel, but if you preferred to sell them all, I could hardly fault you," she affirmed.

"Do you not want the things I gave you?" he asked, his eyes tearing up with hurt.

"I treasure the memory of the affection that inspired each gift, Karel. My life is quite different now. I can't imagine an occasion where I would need evening wear and most of the pieces are really not for everyday outfits. The pearls would go with a suit, though. I'd be pleased to have those."

"You could have the other pieces redesigned," he suggested.

"You know me. I wouldn't do that. You chose them for me to please me. I would never want to dishonour that impulse by changing them."

"Suzette wanted to get rid of everything that was yours. You can have them back as soon as I am well enough to go to the bank."

"That's very good of you, Karel, but could I suggest something?"

He nodded cautiously.

"I keep the pearls, the sapphire and one or two more pieces of your choice and you can divide the rest between Marina, Katya, and Rudy's wife," she said, unable to summon the name of Rudy's wife from her memory. These memory lapses seemed to be more common recently. However, she always remembered the elusive name or fact a few days later when it was no longer useful or important.

"I am ashamed to say that Suzette left with much more in the way of jewellery than I ever gave to you but then, unlike her, you never asked for anything."

"And that is why I was always delighted with your gifts ... they were always your own idea."

"But you are willing to give them up now?" he puzzled.

"If that would soothe relations with your nieces and nephews, I would be more than happy," she explained.

"*If* I do that, I will let them know that *you* wanted them to have these things."

"Whatever you prefer, I don't mind. One other thing, though. I would like you to go over the provisions of your will with your family - with Oleks, Rudy and Marina - sometime when I am not around," she recommended.

When he demanded to know why, she explained that she wanted his relatives to know what to expect and she did not want them to feel that she had unduly influenced his decisions concerning his bequests. There could be quite a lot of bitterness and even litigation when the terms of a will were unexpected. She knew this from experience.

"It's my money and my property and I should be free to do what I want with it."

"I'm not suggesting otherwise," she soothed.

"I want you to have most of it because you have always cared more for me than for my money ... and because you don't want it and you will never be waiting for me to die so you can get it."

"I'm just asking you to consider a bit of diplomacy. Come on ... you can be so good at that when you put you mind to it," she cajoled.

He laughed. She smiled and asked him to think about how he would like to be remembered - whether there was something he would like to set up now which would continue his life's work, such as an award for a young architect for best adaptive re-use of an historic building. She told him that she thought he might get some pleasure out of presenting such an award when he was restored to health.

"Would you help me with this when I'm better? You might have some other good ideas. There is rather a lot of money," he urged.

"Karel, I don't want to be indelicate but what kind of money are we talking about here? A few hundred thousand Euros ... a million ..."

He waved his hand to indicate that the amount was higher.

"Two million?" she guessed in disbelief.

"More. Closer to twenty million and that does not include the real estate or the business."

"Karel, I had no idea," she gasped.

"I inherited a bit from aunts and uncles. I worked hard, invested well and picked up underpriced properties in poor condition and restored or adapted them. Many, I sold at a significant profit and a few of the smaller gems I kept. I was careful with my spending ..."

"Yes, very! I always thought you were cash poor and property rich - and, though we had ... I mean, you have ... lovely properties, all of them are cozy and none of them is extravagant."

"Would it have made a difference if you had known?" he solicited.

"We would have been talking about scholarships and charities and legacies long ago ... and that other time when you were sick ... while we were married ... when you ran me ragged ... I would have insisted on your paying for help with meals and laundry."

"I didn't want any strangers around. I just wanted you to take care of me," he offered by way of explanation.

"You know that I was happy to care for you ... but I could have sent out the laundry and ordered in food! It would have saved my strength and my time so that I could have given you more attention."

"I am sorry, *mia amora*. Maybe I was a bit selfish but I liked and still like your cooking better. To be honest, I think I could taste the love you put into the preparation."

"One of my mother's friends - an excellent cook - told me that the punishment for being a good cook is rarely being taken out for dinner, though you were quite good about dining out when you were well. Good food is one of the great joys of my life."

"And mine. I am grateful that I can eat again - and not from a tube!"

*****

The next day, Karel was surprised to see that his ex-wife was connected to a tote bag by a filament of yarn when she entered his room. She held a crochet hook and a handcrafted rectangle of variegated colours. His gaze was hopeful and childlike.

"It's very pretty. Is it for me?" he coaxed.

"What would give you that idea?" she toyed with him, observing the beginnings of disappointment flit across his face. "Of course it's for you. I bought the yarn when I first got here but I couldn't work in this room because of the infection control. I have barely made a start on it but it should go faster now that I can work on it here without risk to your health. It's a lap rug to keep you warm when you're sitting."

"I like the colours but am I such an old man that I need a lap rug?"

"Or such a baby that you need a security blanket?" she joked, provoking a chuckle from him.

"The yarn is called *Basel in the Spring.* It's soft – a merino wool blended with cotton, angora and a bit of silk. There was a series of cities ... *Summer in Strasbourg, Freiburg in the Fall* and *Winter in Colmar.* Since we're in Basel, I thought this one best."

"And it is Basel – the rosy-red of the *Rathaus,* the yellowish green of the infant spring leaves, and the verdigris of the weathered patina on copper rooves and some creams and greys – the stone buildings in sunshine and shade. I like it!" he approved.

"I thought you might," she agreed.

"How long will it take?" the little boy in him asked.

"'I'm hungry' ... 'I have to go to the bathroom' ... 'Are we there yet?'" she mimicked, as if an impatient child.

"That, too!" he mocked himself.

"Now that I can work on it while we talk, two or three days. The yarn is chunky but I was never fast and my fingers aren't as nimble as they once were."

She shed her coat and hat, sat down beside him and let her fingers do a slow dance as they worked the hook and fed the yarn, creating an image of the city - part abstract and part impressionistic - in stitches. He watched quietly for a few moments.

"If I want you to finish quickly, you can't hold my hand," he reasoned.

"That's true, Karel, but I must rest my hands from time to time, so don't worry," she replied with amusement.

They talked happily of their memories of dinner parties, concerts, and other events - social and business - enjoyed in Basel. When he went suddenly quiet, she looked up in time to catch a wave of melancholy skitter over his features.

"I was a fool!" he declared before continuing. "Suzette was the centre of attention when we went anywhere together. It nourished my male ego but she was not as widely liked as you. You put everyone at ease."

"At one time, Suzette - and Georges, too - could work a room, making each person feel that he or she had been transformed, as if by magic, into the most fascinating person in the world. Georges with his golden curls and his limitless blue eyes and Suzette with her sleek black bobbed locks and her dazzling dark eyes - they were the 'Sun King' and the 'It Girl'. It was something stunning to watch. Long before they met, though, from high school days, I was always on the edge of Suzette's universe - until there was a new love or a break-up. Then I was needed in the way of a sounding board or a pan of comfort food."

He noticed that she had stopped working the crochet hook and wondered aloud, "What happened?"

"We got older and some of us - or rather, one of us - didn't take it very well," she explained, "and in the midst of this, Georges - I don't know whether it was intoxication, innocence or idiocy - decided to tell me, in front of Suzette, that while his wayward body and wicked soul were devoted to her, his pure heart belonged to me. A large part of that was a joke but Georges has been kind to me over the years at some of my lowest points so I know that at least some of it was a compliment. Suzette was not used to having less than the full portion of attention. She was also beginning to suffer from many of the small age-related changes that most of us noticed in ourselves over a decade ago. It seemed that everything was raining on her parade. I, who had been awkward and unlovable in high school, suddenly seemed to be the darling of or, at least, an object of interest or respect to several men - you included - whom Suzette desired. Georges could have had no idea of the consequences. Otherwise, he would never have said such a thing," she explained.

Before picking up the crochet hook and winding the yarn around the fingers of her left hand, she patted Karel's hands and squeezed his shoulder. He gloried in the warmth of even this small amount of affection from her.

*****

Three evenings later, Murasaki tucked the newly finished lap rug around Karel's hips, squeezed his hand and kissed him lightly on the cheek before leaving. She tried not to hurt Karel by too obviously beaming in anticipation of her husband's arrival. The forty-watt smile she was aiming for and the one hundred-watt smile that reflected her feelings settled out into a sixty-watt version.

"*That man* is arriving tonight," Karel complained. "I can see it in your face."

"I told you about that. He'll be at The Krafft when I get there. That's why I'm leaving a bit early but I'll be back in the morning."

"Thank you for everything, *chou-chou*. I love the lap rug - so soft and cozy and the colours are so beautiful. I know that I must not ask you while he is here but I can't help it now.

Just one more time … you wouldn't consider coming back to me?" Karel asked with resignation.

She grinned and shook her head.

"No," she said softly, "and no more of that after today."

Karel raised his hand as if taking an oath, saying, "I promise, and I want you both to dine at The Krafft this evening. I arranged it while you were away for lunch. The reservation is for eight o' clock … and don't worry, it will be charged to my account."

"That's very thoughtful of you - and generous," she accepted.

"You deserve it, *mia amora,* and so does he … but don't tell him I said so. I'm still - and always - envious of him," Karel whispered, placing his finger to his lips as though shushing someone.

*****

She swept gracefully up The Krafft's grand staircase to find her husband sitting in the common area by the tea station. He winked at her, smiled, stood and opened his arms to her. She scanned the open area, her eyes alighting on a sulky youngster with the word "Hate" inscribed in the remaining hair on an almost shaved skull. The girl was occupied with a graphic novel. Murasaki's husband stepped forward, embracing his wife warmly but briefly.

"Zo has had a few tense words with her family, haven't you, Zo?" he told his wife, offering an introduction and an explanation all at once.

Zo looked up and smiled with a warmth and sweetness that belied the stylist's inscription. She was dressed in black sweatpants and a black T-shirt with slashes in the sleeves. Her heavy mascara and black eyeshadow put Murasaki in mind of ancient Egyptian kohl. Chunky black boots of a brand popular with young people completed the look.

"I'm just gonna hang out here and drink tea and read 'til it blows over. If I go back too soon, they'll think they've won," Zo confided merrily.

Murasaki smiled, assured the young person that it was a pleasure to meet her and wished her a pleasant evening.

*****

"You are the most beautiful woman I have ever seen in my life and I've missed you beyond imaginin' since you've been away from me. The calendar says it's been just about three weeks but it feels like an eternity," he declared as he stood behind her at the long mirror on the closet door.

They made eye contact through the reflection. He could see that she was gathering facts to mount an argument. She looked at her own wrinkled hands and gazed in the mirror at the goiter which rose whenever she swallowed. She silently noted the slightly saggy jowls, the erosion of her lips and her greying hair. She would have found more faults but he spoke sharply.

"No profit in winnin' that argument, my beautiful wife - just prideful ... not worth it! I enjoy your beauty but I treasure your kindness, your warmth and your wisdom and I'm countin' on your kindness and wisdom to allow me to keep the delusion, if it is a delusion, and I don't believe it is - of your beauty. Tell me that you're not goin' to take that away from me," he urged with a sly smile.

"You always had a silver tongue!" she accused.

"Never did - 'til I met you," he bantered, turning her gently around to face him before embracing her heartily.

"Mmm," she purred, drinking in the familiar warmth and scent of him.

"I hate to spoil this sweet reunion by askin' but how is the patient?" he inquired before planting a chaste little kiss on her lips and, thereby, delaying her answer.

With a laugh and a smile, she recovered her composure, recounting Karel's progress and the preparations for the imminent move to the apartment.

"He's asked you to come back to him, I s'pose."

"Several times, yes," she replied matter-of-factly.

"I take it I got nothin' to worry about in the answers you give him?" he said smiling and giving her a little tickle behind her ear.

"Nothing at all," she confirmed. "I can't be sure that he'll stop asking but I've told him it would be an exercise in frustration because he isn't going to get an answer he likes any better, no matter how many times he asks."

"I just can't figure how Karl never learned what a stubborn woman you can be while he was married to you. For such a smart man, he seems awful thick on some subjects," said her current husband, who had the curious distinction of being both her second husband and her fourth, with Karel in between as number three.

"Whereas you figured it out right away?" she teased.

"I did - and most of the time I like it," he shot back.

"When do you not like my stubbornness?" she challenged.

"I'm jus' mesmerized by your beauty so I can't think of an example right now. It might come to me later," he laughed.

She smiled so broadly that the healing dry spots on her lips separated, releasing tiny specks of blood. She pulled a tissue from her pocket and dabbed gently.

Beauty, indeed! she thought as she checked with the tissue again to see if the bleeding had stopped.

"If I hadn't already done it, I'd cross the ocean for one look at that smile. Such natural beauty!" he thought aloud.

"Karel has arranged for us to have our evening meal in the hotel dining room. It's on his nickel," she said. "It's a bit fancy - white tablecloths and formal service. You'll need a dress shirt and a tie, at minimum."

"Good thing I come prepared," her dear one replied, pulling a white shirt, a grey and buttercup paisley silk tie and a deep plum sports jacket out of the tiny closet. The jacket, she reflected, had once belonged to her father. Still looking barely used, its classic cut never seemed to go out of fashion.

"What about trousers?" she asked.

"Now, darlin', you said shirt and tie. I upped the ante with the jacket. I heard nothin' 'bout pants," he contested cheekily.

She looked at him with her lips pursed and the little muscles at the base of her nose tensed. She tried to maintain the look of annoyance but failed. He caught her as she dissolved into silent laughter.

"I thought I'd wear my best jeans. Once I'm sittin' down no one will know!" he needled. She added sound to her laughter.

She remembered the day when he had bought the jeans. His hand had recognized the quality of the fabric as he moved through the offerings on the rack in the thrift store. The jeans had a designer's name that even he recognized. At ten dollars, much less than a tenth of the original price, he decided, they were worth a try-on. When he seemed to be taking an inordinately long time in the fitting room without re-appearing, she had called in to ask if he was all right.

"They're my size but a bit … um … snug," he had called back.

"Snug as in you can't get them done up or snug as in formfitting?" she had asked.

"The second, darlin'. They fit good … real good. Just not my usual style," he had explained.

"Don't be shy. Get yourself out here and let me have a look," she had cajoled.

A small but sudden intake of breath followed by a tiny sigh escaped her control when she had seen him. She chased away a fleeting look of longing covering it with a practical analytical expression as she evaluated the garment. Despite her efforts, he had caught the first response.

"Nothin' wrong with ... umm ..." He searched for a word that would be acceptable to her. "Desirin' ... yes ... desirin' your husband, darlin'."

"I'm sorry, sweetheart."

"What for?" he asked.

"I don't want to objectify you, my dearest," she replied, guilt and contrition each passing over her features.

"Hah!" he exploded with the beginning of a laugh followed by a strangled cough. "Darlin', you wouldn't even know how to begin."

"Maybe I also don't want other women to objectify you," she added.

"Not a thing you can do 'bout that. I figure that would be their problem. Only person you can control is yourself ... an' maybe me with that deadly stare you get sometimes," he chuckled.

"That sounds like it's from a psychology textbook!" she sniffed.

"More like a waitin' room magazine," he explained.

She examined the way the jeans hugged his muscular thighs and, as he turned in a playful mocking of runway models, how they smoothed over his *derrière*. There had to be a bit of some sort of stretch fibre - maybe two percent to ninety-eight percent cotton, she guessed.

"No, they won't do at all. I don't think they're roomy enough for you to work in them," she evaluated, "and what did you mean, I 'wouldn't know how to begin'?"

"I mean bein' objectified by you has never been a risk. When you told me on our first weddin' night that you had to have the light on because you needed to see my eyes ... well, let's just say I was a little skeptical. I thought you were bein' coy but you never were. You wanted to see that I was present ... with you ... and not havin' my mind elsewheres. You wanted - and always want - to see and know that we're two lovin' people bein' intimate - heart, mind and body - and never just two bodies havin' sex," he told her just above a whisper.

"How do you know that? More of your waiting room psych course?" she challenged.

"No, darlin'. I just know my beautiful wife - and the more I know about her the more I want to make sure that we never get lost or separated again. I even hope that we have peaceful and gentle deaths within minutes or hours of each other. I can't stand to think of you alone again and I never want to be without you, either," he detailed.

She had looked at the jeans again and dismissed them, suggesting that he find another pair that would be more in keeping with his usual style. He had bought them despite her protests and had insisted that she liked them regardless of what she had said.

When she thought of male physiques at all, she measured them in terms of the dancers from the golden age of the silver screen. Astaire was compact and elegant. His dancing was memorable for its precision and grace. Logic would dictate that there had to be an excellent musculature to make the moves possible but this was never obvious. It was more likely that his clothing would be noticed than his body. Karel's form (though not face) made her think of Fred Astaire. Georges, at average height, was aware that he had a beautiful body and, though *flaunt* was too strong a verb, she knew that he saw no sense in hiding this beauty. There was a power, exuberance and sensuality there so she thought of Gene Kelly when she paid any attention to Georges' form. Her husband was tall and lanky in the way of Dan Dailey. Both moved with a sort of latent strength and could play for laughs or shine as a romantic lead. Her husband could also appear quite menacing if the situation called for it. In cords or flannels and most of his jeans, his contours were all hidden but his new jeans showed him off to his best advantage.

*****

"If you wear those jeans into the dining room, all the women will be panting after you," she teased.

"That why they call 'em pants?" he joked as he produced his one and only pair of grey flannel trousers from the closet. "I'm goin' to be as well turned out as David Niven. I'm not sure you brought anything good enough to be seen with me!"

"I didn't but Oleks arranged for a box of my clothes to be sent over from the apartment. Have a look. See if there's anything suitable. When we shower, it will steam out any creases," she directed.

He pulled out a floor-length black silk dress, long-sleeved on one arm but sleeveless on the other. He set it aside with a firm, "No!"

The next was a powder blue cocktail-length dress with silver beading. It had a modest neckline in front but when he turned it around to discover a plunging back, he laughed as he said, "Never! I can't believe you ever wore this stuff."

"It was a different life with Karel! You know that it's important to fit into your environment," she explained.

"Like you don't wear jungle camo in the desert."

"Exactly!" she affirmed.

"What's this?" he asked hopefully as he pulled out a midi-length black velvet pencil skirt. There was a slit in the back which closed just above knee height allowing the wearer to walk without revealing too much leg.

"Keep looking. You should find a jacket and a satin blouse with a stand-up collar to go with that," she urged.

"That sounds more like my wife's taste," he observed as he extracted a velvet jacket that appeared black in the box but which, in the room's light, revealed small colourful patches of blues, purples and crimsons surrounded by black tracery. It reminded him of a stained-glass window at twilight. The boxy cut of the jacket contrasted with the form-fitting skirt. When he found it, the Prussian-blue blouse was a treat to the touch: a smooth silk satin with tapered fit and lace at the cuffs and collar.

"Mmm, yes! We'll look good together if you wear that," he declared, "but weren't you cold in that other stuff? I still can't imagine you in those things."

"I could put them on and let you see, if you like," she offered.

He set the three pieces of the approved outfit on the bed and came over to embrace her.

"Bad idea. I'm sure that neither one would look right with what I've got and then I'd just have to help you take 'em off. We might be late for dinner time an' I'm starved," he crooned to her, a bit suggestively, as he lightly circled a finger on the nape of her neck.

"Mm-hmm? And you're right that I would have been cold, but I crocheted a wrap to match each of those dresses. Somehow the wraps are missing from the box. Everything else is there. Someone must have pinched them," she complained.

"Take that as a compliment, darlin'. Let's jus' keep our tempers and think 'bout enjoyin' our dinner," he soothed, knowing that the thought of Suzette in those wraps could set off a major rage. He hoped that it was Katya or the cleaner who had "liberated" the garments. His wife, he was sure, could forgive either of them.

*****

After showering and towelling off excess water, she brushed her teeth while he stood to the side fixing his hair. They were at ease together in their nakedness. When she bent to rinse her mouth, the chill of the porcelain sink against her shower-warmed chest caused a yelp and a sudden pull back from the basin. From the rack overhead, he snapped a hand towel and ceremoniously placed it over the edge of the sink. She bent and rinsed comfortably before looking at him with adoration through the mirror reflection. He smiled back until he saw her glow crumple like cellophane in the presence of heat, a tear forming at the corner of one eye.

"Tell me," he whispered.

"You are so thoughtful. So kind. Another man ..." she paused.

"Another man would be a fool – was a fool!" he concluded, knowing that this memory was from her first marriage. It predated his first acquaintance with her and, thus, could have nothing to do with Karel. Wanting to embrace her and hold her but knowing that it was not the time, he went on, "Trust is the foundation of everything with you. When you know that you're safe and won't be molested for a moment's ... gratification – is that a good word? – there could be no one warmer and more ... I don't know what word to use ... My Heart, My Joy, My Wife ... you know what I mean. I'm sorry your past is still causin' you pain."

"There have been so many memories to ambush me while I've been here and away from you, My Love, My Treasure, My Husband," she said responding to his tripartite marital mantra with her own for him.

"I'm here now. If you think it'll be too difficult for you stayin' in that apartment and you want to go home, I'll stay and make sure that Karel is taken care of. I don't mean it that way ... I mean that he receives the care he needs. I'd give him the care he needs for your sake," he promised.

She was able to smile at his assurance.

"I'm sure that I'll be fine. Let's dress and enjoy our dinner," she suggested.

*****

Zo was still in her chair when they left their room. She turned and examined them carefully.

"You look real good for old people," she told them, clearly meaning it as praise.

"Thank you," they said in unison.

"Your style is quite distinctive, too," Murasaki said, returning the compliment.

"That's one of the sore points," Zo replied. "They went ballistic when they saw the word. I just thought it would be cool – you know, really 'bad girl' but they think … they said … they believe that I am trying to promote hate and that's not what it's about at all. I think that we gotta dialogue on tough issues – that's what I want to promote. The bad part is that I'm starting to think that there might be some truth in what they say … and now I don't know what to do about it."

"Your hair will grow back in quickly," he suggested.

"Not soon enough, mister," she told him, hanging her head.

"You can just call me Cash. Almost everybody does."

"I've got a ball of yarn left from a project. I could crochet a headband or hat for you, if you measure your head for me and tell me which you prefer," Murasaki offered.

"How long would that take?" Zo asked skeptically.

"About two to three hours. I could start after dinner and have it ready just after midnight, maybe."

"You'd really do that?" Zo wondered.

"Certainly. We have a reservation for dinner first, though, okay?" she replied.

"They took my sister out for dinner but they said that they don't want to be seen with me like this. I'm hungry … and hurt and embarrassed 'cause they might be … you know, right or sumpthing."

"I expect that I can get the kitchen to help with the first problem. I'll see that you get a little care package. Any restrictions? Vegan? Pork?" elicited the salt-and-pepper haired man.

"I eat everything … but not too much red meat, Cash," she responded.

"And I can help with the last problem. Just tell me, hat or headband," promised the lady.

"But only you can help yourself with the problem of feelin' hurt. Can we leave that with you?" Cash asked.

"I think so … thanks," Zo agreed with a sunny smile.

*****

Soon after the couple were seated in the formal dining room, a boxed meal - consisting of a container of dumpling-and-vegetable soup, a mound of hot German-style potato salad and a generous slice of cherry strudel - was delivered to a young woman in the common area on the hotel's third floor, with greetings from the chef.

Two hours later, the couple, fortified by an exquisite feast and glowing from the pleasure of the dining room's excellent service and ambiance strolled up the stairs hand in hand. They found Zo curled into an approximation of the fetal position, manga in her lap, sleeping peacefully in the chair she had occupied when they had passed through before. The empty food containers sat neatly gathered beside her.

"It seems a shame to wake her," Cash lamented.

"Yes, but I'm sure that there'll be tears tomorrow if I haven't kept my promise," Murasaki contested.

"You do the honours, then. I don't want anyone thinkin' I'm forcin' my attentions on a vuln'rable girl," he insisted.

"Zo ... Zo ... I want to get started on your headgear," Murasaki called softly while putting gentle pressure on the girl's shoulder.

By midnight, Zo, who had had to be wakened again, sported a chic headband in the mix of shades described as *Basel in the Spring*. The item hid entirely the sculpted inscription on her head and provided a softening effect on the severe eye makeup.

"I have rose and green eye shadow that would work with this!" declared a delighted Zo.

"I'm glad you like it!" the maker replied.

"Thank you, thank you! I think I better get to bed. My little sister will wonder where I am," Zo exploded with a mix of gratitude and worry.

"Do you have a key, Zo? We can go with you to the desk if you want to ring the room. Just let us know what you want to do," the silver-haired lady fussed.

"Can you?" she almost begged.

Their approach to the desk coincided with the arrival of Zo's family at the hotel's front door. Relief was evident on the parents' faces when they learned that Zo had eaten without leaving the safety of the hotel. They were careful to admire Zo's new fashion item without commenting upon the function that it was serving in disguising what had set off the argument in the first place.

*****

"This is not quite how I was expectin' to spend our evenin' on the night of our reunion," Cash whispered in his wife's ear as they snuggled into bed. "Still, do you ever wish that we had had a Zo or a Poindexter?"

"Not if those are names you might have given them!" she shot back.

He chuckled and she giggled.

"You don't like the name Zo?" he asked.

"It would be Zoë and remember how old we are. We were almost too old - or I was - when we first met. You men have an advantage. If you had wanted kids, you should have chosen a younger woman," she reminded him.

"Oh, my darlin', let's not think about what-ifs. Let's just think about how lucky we are now to have each other … and just for the record, you are the one and only one I've ever wanted for my wife."

"I *do* feel fortunate but I would feel even more so if I weren't so exhausted," she told him before kissing him lightly on the cheek marked with the old battle scar.

"I couldn't persuade you …?" he whispered suggestively and clearly not referring to her previous statement.

"Sleep! I need sleep! And I haven't told you that the night nurse has instructions to call if Karel wakes up asking for me."

"If you ask me nicely, I could get out of bed early, shave this face that you love despite it's deficiencies and come back to bed," he offered. "Mornin's are your preference anyway."

She loved him for many reasons, some of which could be articulated and others which could not. This sort of offer - generous and without pressure - was one of them.

"Mmm, we'll both have sweet dreams knowing what awaits us in the morning," she agreed in acceptance of his offer.

"Well, then, until the night nurse calls, darlin'. One of the many things about you that attracts me is your kind heart but sometimes I begin to wonder if you're tryin' to punish yourself," he whispered before kissing her goodnight.

"Mmm," she replied, already flowing through the membrane into slumber.

Three hours later, the phone jangled. She awoke, reaching for it. He sprang up prepared to repulse any attack. When there was none, he switched on a light and returned to snuggle her while she spoke.

"I cannot sleep. Sing to me, please," Karel moaned.

"What would you like to hear, Karel?"

"Anything you wish. I know *he's* there," Karel not-quite complained.

She opened with a spritely rendition of a British folk song she had learned in childhood which, in the rhythm of the refrain, suggested the gait of a horse. She was about to follow it with a lullaby called "All the Pretty Little Horses" when her husband told her that he had a song for Karel. The song was "When I Take My Sugar to Tea." It was sung with a bluesy swing to it in a bit of a gravelly baritone and was clearly meant to remind Karel of whose "sugar" she remained.

When she returned to the line, she asked if Karel wanted the lullaby or something else.

"Well, it will not be 'Tea for Two,' will it?" he asked with just a small measure of bitterness.

"No, it won't but I have another thought. How about 'Where E're You Walk'?"

"That would be lovely, *chou-chou*," Karel accepted.

She wanted to remind him not to call her that now but she thought that telling him might add to the stress that he was hoping her songs would reduce. She used the richness of her voice to paint a picture of all the beautiful, if fanciful, benefits that would accrue to the listener including temperature moderation and protection from a blazing sun.

"That was wonderful … and very soothing, my dear," Karel whispered.

"I hope it soothes you into a restorative sleep, Karel," she offered sincerely.

"Thank you and thank *him*, too. His song was suitable in many ways," Karel admitted.

After ringing off, she embraced her husband warmly.

"Was that really necessary?" she asked with skepticism.

"I think so. He expected it. Better we get it over right away," he answered.

"It wasn't exactly kind," she continued.

"My beautiful wife, you are more than kind enough for both of us," he declared, "and men can be territorial … and they can be bundles of testosterone, too. I'm defendin' my wife and myself. That was just a warnin' shot. If yer wantin' to shoot to kill, you never bother firin' a warnin' shot. You take 'im out with your first shot."

"I don't much like this metaphor, sweetheart," she chastised.

"I understand and I apologize, darlin'. Mus' be that testosterone-fuelled territorialism," he replied with a smirk. This provoked a thump of her fist on his upper arm. The action had yielded a sharp sound but was not strong enough to cause actual pain.

"Hormones must be gettin' to you, too!" he laughed. "You got any voice left to sing somethin' for me?"

"What would you like?" she asked. "Nothing too strenuous, darling, please."

"That song - Al Bowlly sang it - and Bing … and I think Nat, too. You know, the one … with 'hours' and 'flowers' … an' 'very'," he murmured as he struggled to recall the title. Much of his memory had returned but there were still things from their first marriage to each other, and especially from their long courtship, which eluded him or which were there only in shadowy form.

"You mean 'The Thought of You'?" she supplied confidently.

"You remember what I like even when I can't," he sighed.

"You used to sing it to me – it actually suits your voice better."

"You start and I'll join when I can," he promised.

They finished softly together. She sat back and regarded him carefully before embracing him again. She reminded herself that it would be a rare husband who would agree to help his wife care for her ex.

*****

Two days later, she prepared lunch while Cash went to fetch Karel home from the hospital. Karel had been annoyed that his ex-wife was not coming to accompany him home. She had explained to him, as if to a moody child, that she could be at the hospital and they could have a takeaway lunch or she could have his favourite soup and bread ready when he arrived but he could not have both. He had fussed a little with the result that Cash had offered to make chicken and dumplings for the noon meal to allow the lady to help Karel into the taxi. Since that was not what Karel wanted either, the matter was settled.

The aromas of potato-and-corn chowder, fresh Irish soda bread with tiny black currants, and double chocolate pudding cake greeted the men from outside the door. Karel had refused suggestions of a wheelchair or rollator and was most indignant when *that man* had picked the patient up and carried him up the two flights of stairs from the ground floor. Karel was set down in front of the apartment door at his own insistence, struggling to stay upright, with only his elegant walking stick for support. He knocked and was welcomed, with a congratulatory hug, by his ex-wife who, with great effort, assisted him the two steps to a chair facing into the living room.

"I've set the table but we could eat in here if you prefer," she had offered on seeing how exhausted Karel was from getting as far as the chair.

"No, *chou-chou*, I want to dine properly. I have had enough of trays in the hospital," he insisted.

"Well, I will ladle the soup while the gentlemen find their way to the table," she commanded.

She hurried to put the linen-wrapped bread, with the correct serrated knife, on the cutting board at the head of the table so that she could be absent when the men had what she knew would be a less than subtle contest of wills over how the transit would be accomplished. She had arranged a half bottle of wine beside the cork remover, an engineering marvel which Karel liked to use to dramatic effect. A pitcher of ice water and a chilled bottle of sparking apple juice were within reach of her place. Fine china bread-and-butter plates were bisected by butter knives, while chargers for the soup plates gleamed at each setting. These were bordered by sparkling sterling silver salad forks on one side and soup spoons on the other. A linen serviette in the bishop's mitre fold pontificated over each of the three chargers. Everything had been placed to precise measurements just as Karel liked it.

When she knew that the men were seated, she served water into the larger glasses. Karel opened the wine, filling to three quarters of the volume the smaller, second goblet at his place, while Murasaki asked her husband to open and serve the sparkling apple nectar into the remaining two empty glasses - one at her setting and one at his own. At last, she brought in the filled soup plates one at a time, serving Karel first, her husband second and herself last. In a final trip before seating herself across from her husband, she brought the butter curls atop a silver bowl of shaved ice. Tiny silver tongs sat ready near where she placed the bowl. Karel surveyed his domain with satisfaction. At his suggestion, they bowed their heads for a blessing (or, as she called it, "grace"). He managed to get through the Amen before being caught by a brief cough which he immediately suppressed with a sip of water. He cut the still-warm bread and passed it before taking some for himself while she circulated the butter curls. Karel nodded to her. She picked up her spoon and, filling it from the far side of the dish, raised it to her lips to signal that the meal could begin.

Soup and bread were followed by small crystal plates of endive, radicchio and roasted pear salad, delicately sprinkled with a maple vinaigrette. She had found it necessary to give her husband a sharp glance and a subtle shake of her head to discourage his intention to help her clear the first course and serve the second. Karel would not approve. He wanted Cash to feel like a guest instead of an intimate of the household, she knew.

She prepared tea after removing the salad service. She then spooned the still-hot pudding cake into footed crystal bowls nestled in crystal saucers at the verge of which balanced dessert cutlery. When the tea was almost ready, she placed a dollop of vanilla ice cream on each bowl and conveyed these to each place setting in two trips. She set the teapot on an engraved tray already arranged with a silver tea strainer in its reservoir, cups, saucers, teaspoons, a milk-and-sugar set and a small plate holding thinly sliced lemon circles. She wielded the teapot and tea strainer with grace, ensuring that each diner had his preference. For Karel, she placed lemon in the cup before pouring. Her husband took tea with a dash of milk and a spoonful of sugar - to cover the taste of the tea, she knew. She preferred hers clear so that she could appreciate the flavour and fragrance of the tea itself. They lingered over refills of tea after the last morsel of the rich cake and sauce had been consumed.

Karel was clearly fading at this point. The conversation which had been polite, if occasionally strained, turned testy.

The problem of moving Karel to his room and preparing him for a nap evoked posturing between the men.

"Gentlemen, I will be happy to clear the table and put away any remaining food. I am not averse to washing, drying and putting away the dishes as I begin the preparations for our evening meal. However, I am eager to avoid any tasks which involve refereeing conflicts between the two of you or which include heavy lifting - such as helping our patient move more than a few steps. Anything else you must figure out between you. I do not wish to hear any arguments from you nor between you," she pronounced.

"I'm sorry, *chou-chou*. That was a delicious luncheon elegantly served. Thank you for a wonderful welcome home," Karel agreed.

"Right, my darlin' wife! When I get Karel settled, I'll come and help out," promised her husband.

"What are you planning for dinner, *mia amora*?" Karel inquired, adding the affectionate Italian term as a velvet gauntlet for Cash.

Hoping to set an example, she decided to ignore this, though she felt it was an irritant. Replying without rancour she told him she thought something light would be pleasant, suggesting sole almandine on rose-saffron rice with steamed broccoli and some squash mashed with apple.

"Crème caramel for dessert?" he entreated.

"That's a bit involved. I was thinking something simple, maybe just ice cream. However, if I have time, I'll do that for you. If not today, then maybe tomorrow."

"Is there any more pudding cake?" he asked.

"There is a little. I thought we could have it for lunch tomorrow but ..."

"If it is less work, we could have it tonight," Karel suggested.

"We could," she affirmed with a grin, "if I don't have time for crème caramel."

She worked in the kitchen until she was sure that the men had left the dining room. She sliced the bread, wrapping it lightly so that it would have just enough dryness for French toast the next morning. The remaining soup went into one of the micro-wave safe bowls with a snap on plastic cover, as did the pudding cake. All the pots, serving dishes and utensils used in the preparation and presentation of the meal, she loaded into the dishwasher.

She made a final clearance of the table and checked that the tablecloth had not been too heavily soiled. After brushing away crumbs with the little silver brush and pan designed for the purpose, she determined that there were two small spots over which she placed "patches" of matching linen serviettes. The last crystal goblet emerged from the water just as she was joined by her husband. He took over washing while she dried, and then replaced on the table, the six goblets. Six crystal plates, followed by three crystal bowls, were washed, rinsed, dried and put away. He moved on to the bone china bread-and-butter plates, which also went back to the table and the soup bowls, which were returned to the cupboard. The cutlery was last. Since it was not breakable, he felt no guilt at all in distracting her with little kisses whenever she reached for another piece to dry.

"You look about done in, darlin'. Can't you rest a minute?" he urged.

"I'll sit down and write the critical path for dinner and then you'll be able to see what needs to be done so that you can help me, if you're willing," she told him as she pulled a lined yellow pad and a sharp pencil from a hidden drawer in the kitchen table.

"How complicated is this goin' to be?" he asked with concern.

"I think we can get away with just four courses," she murmured.

"Four courses! What does Karel think this is, The Ritz?" he objected.

"Sweetheart, four is the minimum. I usually did five or six unless we had formal dinner guests when I might be expected to produce as many as twelve. In such cases, I would buy some things - dessert, salad and maybe the cheese tray, ready-made," she explained.

"Thank heaven for small mercies!" he exclaimed with sarcasm.

"So … we'll need an appetizer, the main course, salad and dessert - that's not so bad," she assured him.

As she wrote, Cash described getting Karel ready for his nap.

"He's nappin' in his clothes. He didn't think much of that idea but he's not able to undress himself and he didn't want my help. I told him you were busy so he wouldn't be gettin' your help. I have to tell you, I'm not much in favour of you doin' that even if you're not busy, darlin'."

"Well, I don't think he would try anything inappropriate with me alone, sweetheart, and even if he would, he can't take more than a step or two without help so I'm not too worried. Still, it might be best not to give him the opportunity. Until he can do it himself, either he'll get used to you or we'll help him dress and undress together," she suggested. "Does that work for you?"

"I guess. Sure," he acquiesced with a hint of a frown.

"I was married to the man, darling. There's nothing there that I haven't seen before - nothing that would shock me, disgust me … or interest me, either," she argued.

"I s'pose," he responded as though not quite convinced, "but I'd like to spare you that if I could."

"He may be a little afraid of you," she observed.

"You jus' tell him that I respect *you* and you would be upset if I did anything to hurt him and I would *never* want to do something that would upset you. I think he might believe you before he'd believe me."

"I'll try that but, in the meantime, we need to get the dinner going," she replied.

After she had written the plan, she made a drawing of the table setting, explained where to find the dinner china and silver and sent him to set the table while she organized the kitchen.

She prepared the dessert while he washed and tore or cut, as appropriate, the salad fixings and assembled two more plates to match the model that she had made at a moment when she could leave the stove. He chopped the squash and microwaved it while she measured the saffron and placed it on an ice cube in the bottom of the rice cooker. Next, he oiled the ramekins, placing a thin slice of ham in each one while she mixed the eggs, herbs and spinach. When the crème caramel came out of the oven, the ham baskets were ready to go in. He rinsed the rice, and after mixing it with the right amount of water, some rose essence and the saffron, started the cooker. She prepared the fish as he was dealing with the broccoli and the squash.

While Cash helped Karel to the table, she ensured that the ice water and a bottle of properly chilled de-alcoholized white wine were correctly placed. She served the ham baskets and offered sesame bread sticks in a long silver server. A tiny dish of softened butter was stationed at each setting. When she rose to complete the first remove, the rice was ready, the fish cooked to a turn, the squash was smooth and sweet from the apples and the broccoli, still firm but bright green. On plates warmed by the oven vent, she arranged each serving. The men received theirs on the first trip. She served herself on the second. Karel fussed a bit about the wine but gave in when she pointed out that he had not had any for more than a month and that it was not a good idea to over do it on the first day at home.

After the second remove, she pulled the salads from the refrigerator and dotted them with a store-bought raspberry vinaigrette, hoping that Karel would not be critical. It seemed to pass unnoticed and soon she was clearing the table for dessert. She brewed a ginger tea and presented the entire plate of crème caramel as she knew that there would be requests for seconds.

They helped a satisfied Karel into his pajamas and settled him for the night after a song - a German lullaby that she remembered from her early voice training which exhorted the *Kinderlein* to go to sleep. He needed no such forceful urging. He had drifted off before she finished.

After hand-washing all the crystal, fine china and silverware and starting the dishwasher containing the remaining items, the couple stripped the table of the white linen cloth and replaced it with a brightly patterned cotton table covering in preparation for breakfast.

"Was it like this every day when you were married to him?" her husband asked as they slipped between cool linen sheets in the guest room.

"We ate out often, had dinner guests from time to time and went to concerts and parties but, yes, this is fairly typical of a day at home - if he didn't go into the office. Of course, when he was well, Karel helped in the kitchen, before and after meals, but he always insisted upon being waited on at table," she told him.

"I would have hit him!" her husband declared.

"Then it's a good thing you were never married to him, isn't it?" she shot back.

"It's a good thing that I'm married to you. No one else would do," he whispered tickling her behind the knee.

She kissed him and he pulled her closer, rubbing a foot down her leg - often an overture to intimacy. She pressed him gently but firmly away.

"I can't - not here," she whimpered.

"Talk to me, darlin'. Tell me what's troublin' you."

"I can't," she echoed herself as if repeating a mantra.

"Darlin', I'm tellin' you this for information not to pressure you ... you know I never would. I know something about how long it takes to rehabilitate muscles after the kind of inactivity and weight loss Karel has had from bein' so ill. It's goin' to take at least a month before he can get around enough that he can be left on his own, even for part of a day. Now, for you and for the love of you, I can take a month of cold showers - lit'rally or fig'ratively - whatever's needed. What can't be allowed is for that man or this place to come between us so you don't talk to me and share with me - so we can't keep close together emotionally. I'm here to support you but you best not shut me out. That I can't take ... and I know, in the long run, you can't either," he almost lectured.

"You are the most amazing man. Would you accept that I'm too worn out tonight to try to make any sense?" she asked with a half grin.

"I could," he told her solemnly.

"Would you trust me to talk tomorrow or the next day ... when I'm rested up?"

"You know I would but no longer than that, rested or not. After that we could be gettin' into a pattern we don't want to get started."

She laughed a little, cautiously, asking, "Is that more of your pop-psych?"

"Does it matter where it's from? It might be but there's no distraction allowed. I still want your word - two days but no more," he insisted.

"Okay, I promise," she swore.

"SWAK!" he interjected.

"What was that?" she puzzled.

"SWAK - sealed with a kiss. It used to go on love letters, pressed into sealing wax. You don't know that?" he teased.

She kissed him lightly, almost chastely, on the lips.

"It's a deal then. Could we just get some sleep now?" she begged.

"Can you stand my arm around you?" he probed.

"I guess so … but no monkey business!" she warned.

"None. Sleep well, darlin'. I love you, My Heart, My Joy, My Wife," he whispered as he curled his shoulder above hers and slipped his arm around her, finding comfort and reassurance in the rhythm of her breathing.

"I hope you sleep well, too, My Love, My Treasure, My Husband," she chimed back.

*****

In the morning, she rose, threw on cords and a pullover, and hurried out to start breakfast. As Karel was calling out for help, her husband pulled on a robe and went directly to the rescue.

"I want …" Karel began.

"I know what you want but she's busy makin' breakfast and she can't be in two places at once – least she couldn't last time I checked! Jus' settle down and take what you get and right now that's me," Cash scolded as Karel scowled.

"Wouldn't it be nice if she could be in two places? We could both be happy," Karel suggested.

"You'd best figure out some way to be happy without her," Cash replied.

"But if we could just clone her, would you agree to that?" Karel wondered.

"Karel, she's a wonderful woman but don't mistake her kindness for willingness to go back to you. Even if she could forgive you, she wouldn't ever trust you in that way again. Now, d'you want your robe or d'you want to get dressed for breakfast?" Cash asked.

"I need the water closet right away and I am not sure that I can sit down or get up safely without help. I never thought about having supports installed," Karel told him.

"Don't be frettin'. I'll help you now ... and the supports and the elevated seat are on order. As soon as they get here, I'll install 'em for you," came the reply.

Karel agreed that the rules could be bent to allow nightwear and robes at the breakfast table for just one day. The men had been seated only a fraction of a minute when fruit salad was delivered to each place. A coffee press and teapot were already on the table. While she took tea, the men opted for coffee. The aroma of oven-baked French toast teased their palates.

After clearing the fruit salad dishes, she brought a small pitcher of warmed maple syrup to the table. Born into Canadian sugar maple country, she could tolerate no inferior facsimiles. She also set a shaker of powdered sugar in front of Karel as he preferred his French toast the European way.

"This is delicious, *chou-chou*," Karel said, "*mais où sont mes fraises?*"

"They're out of season, Karel, and you never liked the frozen ones," she responded to Karel, soothingly, before turning to her clearly-annoyed husband to explain, "Karel just wanted to know about strawberries. There is no mystery here, darling."

"Karel, you got a lot of rules on how you like things done here and I admire your capability with languages ... I really do ... but where I come from it's jus' rude to leave one person out of the conversation at the table. Now, we can keep things cordial in a language I can understand or my wife and I can serve you in the dinin' room and take our meals in the kitchen. You state your pleasure," Cash explained with an amiable smile but a faintly menacing quality in his tone.

"*Chou-chou*?" Karel appealed, looking at her with puppy eyes.

"Don't look at me, Karel. You're such a stickler for etiquette and you've been caught out. As I told you, I will not referee," she insisted before adding, "It wouldn't bother me to eat in the kitchen, though."

"Please, *chou-chou*?" he pleaded.

"No, Karel. You gentlemen must work it out between you. I am not going to be drawn into this conflict."

"I would not like to eat alone. I hope you will both accept my apologies," Karel offered in conciliation. Both his ex-wife and her husband nodded in response. Murasaki did her best not to let Karel see how impressed she had been with her husband's suggestion.

"Thank you, Karel. I have some frozen blueberries that I could heat for you, if you wish," she suggested in the gentlest tone she could manage.

"No, no, *chou-chou*. You should enjoy your breakfast while it is hot," he urged, in order to show that he could be considerate.

The remainder of the meal passed in harmony.

*****

After breakfast, Cash helped Karel wash, shave and dress while Murasaki cleared the table and dealt with the dishes. She changed the tablecloth to white damask for luncheon and set the table. They arranged Karel in a comfortable chair with magazines, books, writing materials and a dinner bell within reach. His lap-rug was carefully tucked around him. The couple retreated to the guest bathroom to complete their own ablutions. In the shower, her husband scrubbed her hair energetically and soaped her skin tenderly. Kissing her ear, he reminded her that she had promised to talk to him.

"An' maybe *you* could convince Karel to accept a rollator. He won't take that suggestion from me."

"I'll do my best – though he's not ready to use one yet," she said as she applied soap to her husband's back.

"True but it takes a bit of time to arrange for an occupational therapist to figure out and order the right model. I'd like to have it here and let Karel stare at it – an' maybe even swear at it for a bit – before he's right ready to use it," her husband recommended.

She agreed and, as they rinsed the soap away, she began to unwind the mixture of raw emotions that had been lying in ambush for her when she had arrived at the apartment.

"First, I need your promise that you won't try to solve this. I know, my darling, that you are a take-charge-and-solve-problems kind of guy. These are not problems that can be solved by any action," she cautioned him before starting.

"Now, I can't promise that I won't make a suggestion or two but I understand the difference between my wife sharin' her feelings and my wife expectin' me to help out by doin' somethin'," he assured her with a Cheshire Cat grin. "I'm listenin', darlin'."

She described her memories and feelings of both shame and regret for having given up on her husband after his absence of fifteen years and, also, for marrying Karel; both anger and relief for Suzette and Karel's betrayal; frustration that the husband of her heart had taken ten months too long to escape and make his way home; sadness for Karel, who had been over the moon to have met his first real love not long after his sixty-fifth birthday, and yet more guilt that she had never loved Karel as much as she had loved and continued to love the lost one to whom she was once again married.

"I feel bad sometimes that my memory never come back soon enough to beat you an' Karel to the altar. There's not a thing can be done 'bout that neither."

"If I had waited just a little longer …" she lamented.

"Listen, darlin', I want you to know that, as difficult as it's bin, I wouldn't have wanted you to be on your own for life if I never was able to get back to you. Sometimes I wonder, though, how you could go for two such differ'nt guys. Karel's nothin' like me."

She laughed as she wrapped a towel around her wet hair.

"First, no one could replace you so I would never have wanted a pale imitation. It had to be someone different but with some non-negotiable points." she explained.

"Such as?" he demanded.

"Musical, intelligent, well-read, tender, kind, thoughtful, creative, mannerly ... which both of you are ... or can be. I also thought I was getting loyalty, honesty, respect ... and I thought I could trust Karel in the way that I have always known that I could trust you," she told her husband, finishing with a warm hug and a light kiss on his bare shoulder.

"I don't want to ... but I think we'd best get ourselves dressed and check on the patient," he suggested.

"I'm not really comfortable talking to you about Karel's good points ..."

"Darlin', as I told you before, we're the lucky ones. Sometimes I feel bad for Karel 'cause I got you an' he almost died from gettin' messed around by Suzette ... an', as much as I know you care for Karel, I got no doubts about the strength of your love for me. Now, what's your plan for lunch an' how can I help?"

"I'm doing chicken à la king in puff pastry shells. I bought the frozen pastry so that should save some time. We'll have a small serving of squash and apple soup - a plan-over from last evening - just thinned with a little commercial chicken broth and, of course, a salad plate. For dessert there's ice cream with the remaining pudding cake as a garnish," she detailed, counting off the items on her fingers.

"Why *are* meals such a production with Karel?" Cash asked rhetorically.

Still, she thought it important to answer.

"After the war, conditions were very bad in Europe for much longer than they were in North America, especially in the cities. He feels the need to draw a line between those times and now. It isn't enough that he has plenty to eat. He isn't interested in gorging now – though I think there was a time. He needs the elegance of many small courses, with a variety of foods, properly served. I would love it, too, if it weren't so much work to make it happen … Oh, and he'll expect us all to dress for dinner from now on … not full formal wear … but jackets and ties for the gentlemen …"

"Why would you go along with this?" he asked.

"It's his home. He makes the rules," she replied.

"We're not his servants … and I have one jacket and one tie."

"He knows we're not and, if he didn't, you made that clear at breakfast. He wants to help and it will be incentive for him to improve … and when he notices that you have only one jacket, he'll call his tailor for you, and put everything on his account," she told him.

Her husband grumbled something about not wanting to owe Karel anything.

"Sometimes I'm a little peeved with you, too, when you bait him," she confided.

"I don't think I bait him but you're entitled to express yourself. In fact, I'm right pleased to hear it. I like knowin' that you trust me enough to share even that with me. 'Course I don't mean to change how I deal with Karel just 'cause you have objections," he declared before planting a light kiss on the tip of her nose.

"You don't? I thought you liked to please me," she replied feigning a pout.

"I do. I made a lot of promises when I married you but I never promised to do everything your way. You are entitled to what you think and I am entitled to chose how I deal with Karel. Remember, you deserve better than a man who's got no mind of his own," he lectured, finishing with a light tug on her not-yet-dry hair.

"As if that would ever happen with you! Still, I think you have been wonderfully supportive and (*Dare I say it?*) co-operative," she praised with a cheeky smile.

"Just as long as you remember it's by choice!" he replied, winking.

They dressed quickly and, while she pinned up her still-damp hair, her cherished husband went out to discover that Karel had fallen asleep slumped in the chair.

*****

The days settled into a routine in which Karel's ex-wife prepared and cleaned up after meals composed of his favourite dishes while her husband assisted Karel in washing, dressing and moving from place to place, including attendance at physio and occupational therapy appointments. Cash took charge of monitoring and guiding Karel in his assigned physiotherapy exercises. Murasaki sang lullabies and held Karel's hand until he drifted off to sleep in the afternoons and evenings. At her insistence, they had hired a laundry service for household linens: sheets, table linen, dish towels and bath towels. Dinner clothing was also sent out. Casual daily clothing was handled in-house.

As Karel's strength increased, he began to help with small tasks in the kitchen such as cutting vegetables and tearing salad greens. Soon he was able to use the toilet alone, with the assistance of the elevated seat and the arm supports which Cash ("that man," as Karel still thought of him) had carefully installed.

At first, groceries were ordered by phone for delivery. Later, when Karel could manage access throughout the apartment, the couple were able to go out for brief grocery shopping trips. They accepted Karel's crabby outbursts and his impatience without comment so long as these were not personal slights nor linguistic exclusions.

The day came when Murasaki sent Cash out for a full day of sightseeing and shopping. Having lived in Basel with Karel, she knew the city well and was happy to afford her husband the opportunity to look around.

"You really will not come back to me?" Karel asked her when they were alone.

"Karel, you promised not to ask me while he is here."

"He is not here now. He is out," Karel replied with mischief in his grin.

"The answer is still the same … and you know it," she retorted.

"Actually, I am glad that he came. I could not have managed to attend my appointments without his help on the stairs and he knows just how far to push me with the exercises. I might have deceived *you* but I could not malinger with *him*," Karel admitted.

"He's more knowledgeable about healing and recovering strength than I am but you know better than to think that I'd put up with any of your tricks."

"Maybe that is so but you are still milder with me than he is. Cash is a good man and I can see that he is good for you," Karel admitted before begging, "Would you kiss me and sing to me?"

"I will gladly sing for you but any kisses will be on your forehead or cheek. Don't ask for what you can't have. Save your breath to cool your porridge!" she chided before placing a brief kiss just above one of his eyebrows.

"Will you sing 'Tell Me, Pretty Maiden, Are There Any More at Home Like You?'?" he wheedled.

"That's the original *Floradora* song. It's a duet. I don't think you're up to that, Karel. How about 'Pardon Me, Madame'? It's a similar vintage but I'll have to take it down a bit from where Jeanette MacDonald sang it," she suggested.

"Not my favourite," he sulked.

She suggested with a laugh, "I've got one for you. It's an Irving Berlin song called 'My Walking Stick'."

"Another of the comic selections in your repertoire? You know that I like your more classical pieces."

"Fine, we'll save that until my sweetheart is here. I have something classical and funny, too," she told him.

A spirited rendition of Flanders and Swann's "Ill Wind" followed. He was laughing as he asked if it was Mozart or Haydn.

"I think it's Mozart's ... the number four rondo. I'm sure that I had the whole horn concerto on vinyl when I was in high school. I can't believe you've never heard this version. You can search for it on the Internet. The originators are much funnier than I am."

"That would be difficult, *chou-chou*. You gave quite a performance. We enjoyed our life together, don't you think? You remember some things fondly? Please tell me that you do," he begged.

"Of course I do, Karel. If anything, that makes it more difficult to be here. Sometimes, when I have good memories of you and of this place, I feel disloyal ..."

"To *him*?" Karel demanded.

"Yes. It caused some friction when we first arrived but I think it's all worked out now," she explained.

"And still you stayed to take care of me?" he asked, waiting for her nod before he continued, "That was quite a sacrifice and I was a bit of a ... *Sheißkopf*? I'm sorry."

"As I said, it's fine now ... and I don't think I've ever heard you use that word. I know that it's milder in German than the translation is in English but I'm glad I don't need to translate that. My husband must surely have heard and, probably, used rough language in his working environments before I met him but I have never known him to tolerate it in my presence."

"You could have told him it meant 'poophead' as that would be close enough," Karel suggested with a smirk.

"I could have but he would have taken one look at your face and known that I was leaving something out and he would have liked *that* even less than the accurate translation."

*****

It was the full month plus a few days more before Karl could safely shower and dress himself entirely unassisted, get around the apartment with the use of his rollator, and put together a simple meal for himself. By then he could also, with determination, manage the stairs to and from the ground floor with just the handrail and his cane. To celebrate, they took him to the huge centrally located restaurant famous for its ice cream treats and its *Flammekueche*. He still needed help getting into and out of a taxi but he was becoming less testy about such struggles. This considerably soothed relations with the couple.

The problem remained that, though he could manage the stairs, he could not move the rollator down to the ground floor. Since he had grudgingly agreed that the contraption made getting around much safer, the couple suggested that he order a second one to be kept at the shop on the ground floor. He knew that this signalled their intent to prepare him for their departure. He sulked a little but, observing that this did not seem to discourage them, Karl gave up his performance.

*****

"We're going on to Italy in two weeks. You are doing so well now that you don't need us," Murasaki told Karel a week later.

"*Chou-chou*, can't you stay longer? I will miss you so very much - both of you," he pleaded.

"I think it's time, Karel. I'm sorry to desert you but I really think that we've been here long enough."

"Maybe I could come to Italy, too?" he suggested.

"Karel, Georges and his granddaughter are meeting us there. In fact, they may be there now. That means that the house will be full ... and I'm not at all sure how well Georges is going to react to seeing you again. He still considers you at least partly responsible for Suzette's leaving him ... and you need to know that she left Georges broken-hearted and his business in a financial mess. She disappeared with all the ready cash from their business and joint accounts just before the company's payday."

"Perhaps I could avoid Georges by getting a room at the little hotel nearby. Then you could visit me sometimes. Please say yes," Karel urged.

"Karel, if you want to arrange accommodation nearby, there is not a thing I or anyone else could do to stop you. If you want a warm welcome at the house ... that is more difficult to guarantee. I'm sure that my husband would like some time with me on our own schedule. He's been very accommodating to your needs and expectations. I wouldn't want to presume too much on his good nature."

"I don't want to be alone here, *mia amora*," Karel explained.

"Hire someone, then. You have the resources to get whatever help you need, Karel."

"Then I want to hire you," he retorted.

"I'm truly flattered and I will be happy to come for consultation from time to time if you want to pay the airfare for two but I do not want a regular full-time job. I'm mostly retired now."

"If I come to the hotel in two weeks, would you come and have breakfast or lunch with me sometimes - both of you, I mean. I don't mean you alone. I might like it but *that man* of yours would not - so both of you should come!"

"Ask him, Karel. That would be the polite thing to do," she acquiesced.

"And could we have a musical evening before you go?" he cajoled.

"I can almost guarantee that a musical evening would meet with approval. Who should be invited?"

"If we invite people, some of them may not speak English," Karel thought aloud.

"Then you will need to be courteous and translate, won't you, so that *no one* is left out?" she emphasized.

"Of course, *chou-chou* … and we will need to practise, too. It won't be too much work for you?"

"You will have to help … or we could have it catered," she suggested.

"We could … but maybe you would make something special for me?"

"That would be a reasonable compromise," she agreed, surprised that he would consider a caterer at all.

"What will you sing, *mia amora*?" he asked with hope shining in his eyes.

"I'm thinking *Rusalka*'s 'Song to the Moon' for my lost one's return. I haven't tried that for a long time."

"And something for me or with me? You and I could sing a duet."

"I don't think so, Karel," she objected.

"Just one song together. Our voices blend so well. Why not?" he argued.

"It would send the wrong message, Karel. I can't and I won't," she insisted.

"But you will sing something for me? Please?"

"Of course I will. What about 'Madamina' sung as a trouser role?" she asked, chuckling at the thought of a gender twist on the famous "catalogue song" normally intoned to a woman by Leporello, describing the legions of conquests his master, Don Giovanni, had accumulated.

"It was written for a baritone. Why ever would you ...?" he began, trailing off as he saw that she had an answer.

"As a cautionary tale ... and I think that I can adjust it to my range."

"You mean you want me to protect myself against the Suzettes of the world?" he teased.

"I want you to be more careful ... I do care for you, Karel. I want better for you. Georges and Suzette had a lifestyle different from mine and yours and that was their business ... but it had consequences that you were not prepared to accept," she reminded him.

"I will miss you, *chou-chou*. We work so well together."

"I'm relieved to know that you're well again, Karel, and that you're coming to accept the way things have to be. Don't let's make this anymore difficult than it needs to be," she admonished gently.

"I thought that the tenor was always the one who gets the girl," he groaned.

"First, I'm not a girl and second, this is life not opera," she contested.

He prepared his breath and began to sing "What'll I Do?" in a reedy voice, unlike his usual resonant tenor.

As the last note faded, she answered with the pneumonia love song - really an anti-love song. He laughed and nodded.

*****

A week later the couple put away the last dish and stored the sheet music in the piano bench following the musical soirée. As they prepared to retire for the night, Cash whispered, "You seem different tonight … more relaxed. More … I don't know, but I can see it and feel it."

"It always does me good to sing. I think the musical evening was a success," she agreed.

"Yes, but it was a lot of work for you – and Karel wasn't much help."

"You can't be disappointed if you don't expect too much," she responded. "Still, Karel is coming to accept how things are. He's stronger and more capable physically but he's also more settled in his mind. For a while he didn't seem to feel he had much to live for but now … well, he's even grateful for your help with his physio. He asked me not to tell you but …" she said, trailing off as she looked for a fresh nightgown.

"But that makes a difference to you … even though he wants to follow us to Italy? That makes me more than a little cross, you know," he complained.

"I know – but his acceptance that you're the one for me is a huge step in the right direction. He's still afraid and he clings to me because he knows that I wasn't waiting for him to die – that I encouraged him to live."

"It's a weight off you … I see that," he agreed, smoothing her long, loose hair.

"It is … and he knows that he can't stay with us. He'll be happy at the hotel as long as we visit him," she replied as she moved away to begin turning down the bed covers.

"You mean as long as *you* visit him," her husband corrected.

"He understands that I won't be visiting him alone – though sometimes I might take Yvette. Georges told me that she wants to be an architect and I think it would be good for her to talk to Karel about it and maybe even good for him to be a bit of a mentor," she explained.

"Great!" he retorted, making no effort to hide his sarcasm. "Then Karel would have two to flirt with!"

"It's just social flirting," she soothed.

"Not when he asks you to go back to him!" he argued.

"He never does that in front of anyone," she countered.

"That just proves he knows he's doin' wrong if he doesn't want witnesses!" Cash objected.

"Easy, my treasure. You know you don't need to worry," she assured.

"Yeah, I know. How old is Georges' granddaughter, anyway?"

"Maybe sixteen or seventeen."

"Far too young for Karel to mess with."

"And he won't … but not too young to enjoy his charm at table," the wife teased.

"*At table*? That always sounds so snooty to me," he commented.

"I'm bi-classical," she joked.

"Is that even a word? And wouldn't it be 'bi-classist' or 'bi-classal'?" he chuckled as he unbuttoned and removed his shirt, tossing it accurately into the laundry basket. He raised his arms in celebration as if he had scored a basket in a game. He stood there in his snug jeans and smiled a sweetly wicked smile before asking, "So what do you think *my* chances are tonight, now that we've got the baby to sleep?"

"The 'baby' is older than either of us," she corrected.

"He's as demanding as an infant and I guess I'm just a little jealous. I miss havin' your full attention. Maybe it's for the best that there was no Zoë or Poindexter in our lives … so what about my chances?" he teased.

She plucked up a small decorative pillow from the bed and tossed it toward him. He caught it effortlessly, even though it was well short of the mark.

"I'm takin' that to mean 'good'," he retorted.

"I throw something at you and you take that as a positive sign?" she kidded.

"Darlin', that pillow was soft and small … and I know you got better aim than that if you really meant to hit me!" he appraised with a smirk.

"Just get yourself over here and kiss me, love of my life, and then we can talk about *our* chances tonight," she told him.

This had barely passed her lips when the sound of the bell Karel had been given to summon help interrupted them with an impatient tinkling. She opened the door a crack in time to hear Karel call out.

"I need a drink of water, please, *chou-chou*!" Karel called.

"How does he know!" Cash snarled. "I don't s'pose you'd consider ignoring him?"

She shook her head ever so slightly.

"Then I'll go," he insisted, gently smoothing stray hairs away from her face and tucking them behind her ears.

She nodded in tentative agreement as he slipped on a T-shirt.

"Karel's able to get it himself, now, so you know it's just manipulative!" he contested.

"I know but I'm not sure whether it's intentional or, maybe, he's unaware of what he's doing," she replied.

"Don't matter. Karel can have his water but he can't have you with it," her husband retorted.

"It's important to send the right message … but Karel may want me to sing to him," she suggested.

"He won't like it as much but I c'n do that, too. I can even rock him to sleep – the bigger the rocks, the better," he threatened.

"You don't mean that, darling," she objected.

"Don't tell me what I mean and don't mean," he argued with a grin and a wink, "but you're right ... just gives me satisfaction to say it, though."

*****

Cash returned - after providing the requested glass of water, supporting the patient to and from the toilet, tucking him into bed and singing a lullaby - to find his wife asleep. Her book lay on the on the floor where it had fallen. She was slumped against the headboard as she emitted a snore as light as a kitten's purr. He picked up the book and set it on the nightstand. Gently placing one arm beneath her knees and supporting her back and neck with the other, he turned her legs up onto the bed and shimmied her away from the headboard until he had guided her body into proper sleeping position on the bed. She still did not wake when he kissed her forehead. He tucked the blankets around her. Compressing his lips in irritation, he returned to Karel's door.

"She's out for the count, Karel ... jus' plain wore out," Cash complained. "It seems like you want to show her that you can't manage on your own an' you want to come to Italy. I'm not real pleased about that but ... well, I'll make you a deal."

"A deal? What kind -" Karel began skeptically but was interrupted.

"You ride with us to Italy. We settle you into that little hotel an' you stay there an' pay the hotel staff to take care of you while I take my wife off for a real holiday at one of your cottages - you got one in Greece an' in the south uh France an' I forget where else. I get that you don't want to be here alone but my duty is to my wife an' she won't be at ease if she thinks you need her help ... an' I'm about fresh out of patience with your ... nonsense," he concluded, selecting a polite but descriptive word instead of what first came to mind.

*****

He stuffed the gaping hole in his pride with the knowledge that his wife would be delighted with the arrangements. Although he agreed that she deserved more than a self-catered stay at one of Karel's pieds-à-terre, it galled him to accept Karel's generosity. The couple would stay near Stephansplatz in Vienna at a small family-owned hotel that was the right balance between elegance and extravagance. Cash knew it was one of his wife's favourite European capitals. Tickets to hear the *Wiener Sängerknaben* (Vienna Boys' Choir) and to see a performance of the famous Royal Lipizzaner horses would await them at check-in. Karel would provide vouchers for museum visits, tours and other enjoyments that showed his acquaintance with his ex-wife's taste. Walks among the architectural pleasures of the city and leisurely stops for *Torten und Tee* (tea and fancy cakes) promised time for relaxation and the long talks the couple had been missing. Cash slipped into bed, curled his shoulder protectively around hers and kissed her hair. Then he smiled as he faintly hummed an old song – "My Girl Bill". It seemed like the right song for the moment. He smiled, remembering that it was important to send the right message.

Dust and Embers

The spinning loop of the lasso dropped neatly over her shoulders and pulled snuggly just above her elbows, arresting her in mid-motion as she was about to apply her dainty boot to the bulge in the neck of the man who was lying in the dust and moaning with pain. After securing the braided line to the pommel of his saddle, the rider slipped to the ground while the well-schooled cowpony maintained the tautness of the rope, thus immobilizing the woman.

Cookie's short legs bore him surprisingly rapidly toward the cloud of dust and the just-dismounted rider. The intent to scold the rider was printed on the old cook's face. No one should dare kick up dust in his camp. He slowed and allowed some of the ill temper to fall from his face as he saw that the boss was the rider. Eyes flitting from one to another of the figures in the tableau before him, he wisely held his tongue.

"If you was a man, I'd leave you in the next town!" Delbert Allen Townrow, the trail boss, almost spat at the woman. He was a tall, lanky Texan with striking amber eyes – now ablaze with anger.

"If I were a man, I just might agree to stay there," she spat back, uncowed by his tone and smug in her correction of his grammar. The subjunctive was not losing ground among the educated in his time, though it was in hers.

"Ah tol' yuh when Ah agreed you could come along, no fightin' amongst muh crew an' no exceptions even for a lady - but it ain't ladylike tryin' tuh kill one of muh men," the boss growled, lapsing into the dialect of his youth.

"I might not have killed him but he would have been whispering for a while," she retorted. "At least then it would be unnecessary to listen to him."

Joe continued to howl and moan inarticulately. Cookie moved in to check on the "victim" before turning to the woman with his brows up in question.

"A strategically placed knee!" she responded just above a whisper. "No hatpins with a 'John B.'," she explained, "else he certainly *would* be dead."

Cookie understood both references. He wondered what the dover's transgression had been to provoke the lady enough to knee him in the groin. As for hatpins, the lady, when first introduced to the cook, had been very properly attired in a fashionable - for the time - two-piece dress with a fine matching example of the milliner's art firmly attached with long hatpins to her carefully wrapped and pinned hair. In her own time, she used hatpins as a matter of convenience. For Victorian women, the long pins were not just for fashion but also for self-defence. On the trail, the lady dressed as the drovers did - in trousers, shirt, and a western style "cowboy hat", properly called a John B. Her foundation garments, however, she had constructed herself with period-appropriate materials both to maintain her modesty and to allow freer movement than the corseting normally worn with ladylike dress of the day.

When Cookie indicated that the victim would recover, the boss signalled his horse to slacken the restraint but made no move to release the lady. Cookie trotted over to do so.

"Why?" the cook whispered softly as he loosened the lasso.

"Long story ... later," she whispered back.

"Silver, you gyit back tuh work soon as yer up to it," the boss ordered the man who continued to lie in the dust, "an' stay away from her. She jus' might succeed in killin' yuh nex' time.

"Boss, I ..." the man struggled to say.

"Jus' back tuh work!" he commanded, cutting off any discussion before turning to the newly released woman.

"An' you," he began, reining in his rage like an overly spirited steed, "stay with Cookie - you ride in the wagon, you he'p with the cookin' an' you stay outta evibuddy's way. I'm tellin' Pony not tuh let yuh saddle up for a few days 'til I think on this."

"That man goes back to work and I'm confined to barracks?" she challenged.

"Enough! I tol' yuh," he said, gathering his lariat and moving to his horse to mount up.

Silver whistled for the horse that bore his saddle. (Drovers owned their saddles but the horses belonged to the drive.) Silver Joe, or sometimes just Silver, was named for the intricate silver detailing, so popular with Spanish riders, which decorated his saddle. He thought of himself as superior to Cinquo and Pancho, the other Spanish speakers on the drive, because Silver saw himself as Spanish rather than Mexican. He had the Castilian pale skin which contrasted with the stronger pigmentation of both Cinquo and Pancho's complexions. This sense of superiority in no way improved his disposition, she had thought on several occasions.

The black steed ambled over, head down in curiosity at Silver's position in the dust. The mare nickered and nudged the drover gently. Silver struggled to his feet, patted the horse affectionately and cautiously placed his foot in the stirrup. He was rightly concerned that sitting in a saddle after such an injury would be a punishment, intentional or not.

The boss, who was facing toward the cook and the lady but away from "the victim", saw neither Silver's longing gaze at the boss nor hostile scowl at the lady. The lady caught both. These explained the attack but revealed something that could never be spoken in his time. She turned to the boss, opening her mouth to complain of her treatment, but was warned off by a very subtle shake of Cookie's head.

Cookie's real name, she had learned but was cautioned never to repeat unless she wanted to be unable to sit for a month, was Leander Evelyn Beverly Cook. Cookie was not only the cook but also supply manager, medical man, tailor and harness mender, barber and sometime farrier - not blacksmith, which was a more general trade, but, rather, the person who shoes horses. His advice, even unspoken, was gold to anyone with even a modicum of sense.

After the meal, Cookie put away the supplies and equipment while the lady, a small but feisty woman, whose hair had mostly faded from a deep rusty red to luminous grey, washed the tin plates and cutlery. She - Almiretta Hendry by name - grumbled away to herself while Cookie waited for an opportunity to ask about the event that had all the men talking. She wondered how it had spread through the entire camp when the only witnesses were Cookie and Almiretta (who had barely spoken of that or anything else in the rush to prepare and serve up the meal); the boss, who was known to keep his own counsel; and Silver Joe, who should have been silenced by embarrassment from the fact that he had been bested in a fight by a woman. Cookie was sure that, had he been Silver, he would have held back. The snippets Almiretta had overheard bore little or no relationship to the facts as she remembered them. She smiled at the memory of a comedian from her time joking about "an unbiased account of the Civil War from the South's point of view". In her time, at a distance of over 150 years, the comment evoked laughter but here, less than a quarter century removed from the war itself, it could still provoke violence. Some on the drive, including the boss and Cookie, had served on opposing sides. Feelings were often still raw.

As incredible as the story sounded, Cookie believed Almiretta when she said that Silver had tried to push her face into the fire. The cook could see that the horror on her face was genuine.

"Why would he want to do that?" the cook wondered aloud.

"No guess that I could make would be flattering and I am reluctant to speculate in the absence of facts," she replied with just the right amount of ambiguousness in her tone.

The boss sauntered in just as Cookie asked her whether Silver had made improper advances upon her. Almiretta averted her gaze and let the two men think that it was a possibility. She had not been averse to stamping the life out of Silver in response to his attack on her. In her mind, that was self-defence and was justified. However, she would not reveal Silver's secret longing or, perhaps, lust for the boss. Her twenty-first century values would be appalled at the nineteenth century consequences for a revelation of any alternate sexual orientation. She supposed that Silver might be equally dead in either case. Still, it was not the same to her.

"Yuh coulduh called fuh help. Cookie was near an' woulda come runnin'," the boss scolded her.

"Yes, and Cookie could have helped me then but what would happen in the future if I had no one around. That would just have shown that I'm not able to take care of myself and that anyone who wants to hurt me should wait for a better opportunity," she argued.

"You coulduh got yussef hurt or killed!" the boss disagreed.

"As I recall, Silver was the one who needed rescuing! And while waiting to be saved, I could have had my face damaged in the fire. It may not be beautiful but its mine and I'm kind of partial to it."

"You got an answer fuh evithing!" he huffed.

"It's easy when it's the truth!" she shot back.

"What'm Ah goin' tuh do with you?" the boss asked himself aloud.

"With me? I defy you to look me in the face and tell me that *you* would just call for help if someone tried to throw *you* face-first into a fire," she bristled.

"Well, you *defy me* sure 'nough!" He almost chuckled. "Fahn, Ah'll speak tuh Silver. Ah'll tell him there best be no more uh this … else Ah'll let you loose on him and tell thuh crew that uh little lady beat his - Ah mean, got the best uh him in uh fight. But, ma'am, rules is rules. No fightin' in muh crew!"

"I won't start anything but I will not sit still if someone else starts. I promise you that," Almiretta declared. At almost sixty (but not looking it), she was long past submitting passively to unfairness.

The image of a wet hen came to mind but he dismissed it. There was something admirable in her determination and her boldness. He worked on suppressing a smile.

"Cookie, the lady rahdz with you fuh three days. Ah gotta let thuh crew know they can't be fightin' … but fuh three days aftuh that, Silver's yuh helper an' thuh lady rides with me … an' Lucky or Willow."

"Yes, sir," Cookie responded respectfully. He preferred Almiretta's help and company to Silver's but would not argue the point with the trail boss.

"That suit yuh sense uh fairness, ma'am?" he challenged.

"For justice to be done, it must be seen to be done," she quoted from a modern source, thinking it came from antiquity. Glowing with satisfaction, she concluded with a biblical referent, "And even Solomon could have done no better."

The boss found a spot to sit where he could watch her work. It always felt good to find a fair solution to any of the problems that cropped up on the trail. All the lives of the crew might depend upon such harmonious outcomes. He was surprised to notice that Almiretta's words of praise gave him an especially warm feeling.

No, he determined, *just ain't possible.*

He fingered the spot where, under his shirt, there dangled a locket containing a bit of hair and a miniature painting of his late wife, gone almost twenty years and still actively mourned. He remembered her reverently as a beautiful, sweet-tempered, mild, respectful woman who was skilled in the homely arts. Prudence would neither have found nor have wanted to find any place on a cattle drive. Though he did not consider Almiretta a shrew, she had none of these wifely qualities and she was quite clearly untameable. She was more than passable at camp cooking - give her that - and she was getting better at riding drag, the collecting of lost and lagging members of the herd.

Almiretta cast a glance at the boss as he walked away. She thought that the late nineteenth century was "a nice place to visit". However, she knew would not want to live here forever. Would it be as easy to pass back through the portal as it had been to get here? Her thoughts drifted until she wondered how the boss would cope in the twenty-first century. She could not imagine his liking it. A little smile crossed her face at the thought of him there.

No. It just wouldn't work, she decided. A fragmented image of his name on a document flitted across her memory but she was unable to bring it into focus nor remember the context.

Silver Joe glared at the Almiretta. He realized that it had been foolish to act out his jealousy instead of just holding it in. How, he wondered, would he have explained away her burns if he had succeeded in pushing her into the embers?

Because she not been as weak and vulnerable as he had expected, he was now in misery. The boss had had harsh words about fighting and, if anything, seemed supportive of the hated woman.

What did it get me? Just a lot of pain and three days of punishment helping the cranky old cook, he thought to himself. *I'm jus' loco to think it could ever be.*

The boss smiled to himself. The image of Almiretta, caught in his lasso, with her boot poised over Silver Joe's throat, would, he was sure, stay with him if he lived to be a hundred.

"But, no, it just ain't possible," he concluded.

Last Rodeo

Part the Second: A Sandwich with Meat So's Yuh Knows It's There

They had seated themselves in the lobby after tea, agreeing that they would meet there again the next day and that, though two o'clock was later than normal for lunch, it was a memorable, and perhaps even auspicious, time for them.

She had asked him about his food likes and dislikes. He explained that for most of his life he had had to eat what was put in front of him so he had never become a fussy eater. It turned out that he shared one of her passionate dislikes, lima beans, and that he was "not real fond of Brussels sprouts," either. She guaranteed that neither would be served. He also told her that he thought that a real sandwich (not the pretty tea versions which had their place) had meat "so's yuh knows it's there". It was fine to add cheese and other things but not so much that the meat was lost. It also became plain that he believed that meat meant red meat - chicken was "fowl" and more suited to "lady food". She had laughed at that and had asked if he believed that quiche was something that "real men" would never eat. He had chuckled, having heard of the book, too. He promised to eat and enjoy whatever she brought as long as it was neither lima beans nor Brussels sprouts.

At this point he had offered to escort her to wherever she was staying. Peridot insisted that she was not ready to allow him to have that information just yet. She told him that she would sit in the lobby until she finished her post cards and letters, at which time the concierge would arrange trustworthy transport for her. Stuart conceded that this was a safe plan and promised that he would not try to follow her. She knew that he was disappointed that she did not trust him to that extent. Still, it was clear to her from his little bow as he took his leave that he would be respectful of her wishes.

At dinnertime, Stuart returned to the diner for coffee, soup, and toast - enough to hold him through the evening. He felt that after the tea array, he needed only a light evening meal. Naomi was eager for a report of the event and Stuart supplied a condensed version. He used the washroom to change back into his regular clothes and acceded, with only a gesture toward an argument, to Naomi's urging that he allow her to launder and press the shirt and trousers and keep the tie and jacket smoke free as well. She listened to his joy at the picnic arrangements and his disappointment that the lady had declined his offer to escort her home.

"What's her name? I'm hoping you got that this time?" Naomi asked with a cheeky smile.

"Ah did … Peridot, uh big fancy name fuh uh sweet little lady - fahv foot an' hardly nothin' - an' hundert an' mehbe ten, mehbe fifteen pounds soakin' wet. Ah want tuh cawl huh 'Dot' but she's real careful tuh cawl me what Ah lahke tuh be cawled so …" he replied drifting off as Naomi seemed to have something else to say.

"Don't be offended that she's careful, Stuart. You're a big guy and the world is full of stalkers and scary dudes. I bet if you had a daughter or a sister, you'd want her to be real careful."

"Ah guess … yes," he agreed thoughtfully.

"And this lady could have had a bad experience in the past," Naomi speculated.

"Ah know yuh right, Naomi. It's jus' ... well, mah mamma tol' me uh fellah otta see uh lady safely home," he explained.

"That would be fine if we still lived in your mamma's time and if we all knew each other's families."

"Peridot's on holiday from thuh east - somewheres in Ontario. Way east uh here, anyway."

"Patience, fellah!" Naomi admonished. "Just be happy she's willing to meet you again."

"Ah am, Naomi ... an' Ah'm well an' truly grateful fuh awl yuh he'p an' good advahs."

"I'm glad to help, Stuart."

"Jes' one thing. Yuh figyuh Ah otta take muh guitar tuh thuh picnic?" he wondered.

"Are you any good?" Naomi challenged. "And is she going to like your kind of music?"

"We talked 'bout music. Safe topic. Ah c'n play lots she'd lahk ... an' Ah otta play fuh you so's you c'n d'sahd fuh yuhse'f - though muh voice ain't thuh best, f'Ah tell thuh truth."

"Come by for breakfast about ten thirty. It should be quiet by then," Naomi recommended.

*****

Alone in the room he shared with his three absent friends, he replayed the afternoon over in his mind. It had been the right first date for this lady. He smiled to himself at the idea of the "first" date and the plan for the second. This was new to him. He drifted and he had avoided getting involved with anyone as far as a commitment for a second date. He considered the music that Peridot liked and concluded that this put her age somewhere between thirty-eight and forty-five - near enough to his thirty-nine. It seemed surprising to him that someone who must have come of age in the late sixties or into the seventies would be so reticent - that was a good word though not one he was likely to say around his roommates - yes, so *reticent* to be touched. She had not shaken hands, she had not taken his arm and she had stayed out of reach when he had said good-bye. He considered that he had better manners than to try to kiss her - even chastely on the cheek - in the lobby with everyone watching. Still, he had thought that she might have clasped his hand briefly. They had talked easily and she had suggested the picnic so he was sure that she liked him. And that smile ... she was not just being polite.

"Well," he said to himself, "it's got tuh be on huh tahm."

*****

Peridot examined her memories of the afternoon carefully. She had to admit that she had been charmed by his efforts to transform his wardrobe for the occasion. She knew from the careful manner in which he had observed and followed her lead that afternoon tea was unfamiliar territory. (Fred's speculation had been confirmed on that point.) Given this, Peridot felt that Stuart's composure and grace had been impressive. He had dealt with her resistance to taking his arm smoothly and without complaint. While she considered that it had been a sweetly chivalrous offer, she simply could not place her arm on his. She hoped that her comments on the movie environment had impressed upon him that she did not want to be touched - at least not yet. Touch was, for her, at worst, oppressive and potentially dangerous and, at best, confusing. She could not move from being a total touch-me-not to accepting his arm and certainly not to handholding at the second meeting. She needed her wits about her. It frightened her that she both liked him and felt inclined to trust him so soon.

He had talked about his travels and had asked insightful questions about hers. He seemed to have read books on diverse topics. This suggested that he had a quick and inquiring mind. He had appeared genuinely interested when she had talked about her three major career shifts. Some anxiety played across his face when he learned that she taught English as a Second Language. It had been necessary to reassure him that she was charmed by his dialect and that she would not be monitoring his grammar.

"Ah worked so many places with fellah's from jus' 'bout evi'where Ah don't talk pure Texan no more … Ah mean, anihmore," he had explained, self-correcting.

He knew when to talk and when to listen. On top of this, he had arrived without a trace of tobacco smoke on his clothes or his breath. Also, he was, as the expression goes, sober as a judge. So far, he *was* a man of his word. She smiled at this and enjoyed the thought before calling Fred to bring him up-to-date. Fred had chided her good naturedly on her initial resistance to going to tea.

"A woman needs a man like a fish needs a bicycle!" she retorted.

"Perri, that old feminist chestnut is only true for lesbians and my gay-dar detects them as well. You are *not* a dy—"

"No rude words for our lesbian sisters, Fred!" Peridot interrupted sharply.

"I do so love to shock you, Perri. Even the possibility makes you bristle. I can almost see your nose wrinkling and your lips compressing," he chuckled.

*****

Stuart ordered fried eggs, sunny-side up, with bacon, toast, and coffee at the diner the next morning. He tucked into his meal as Naomi cashed out the thinning breakfast crowd. When the used dishes had been born away - except for his coffee cup - which Naomi refilled, Stuart opened his guitar case, tuned up and treated her to a couple of old Jimmy Rodgers favourites, Jim Croce's "Workin' in the Car Wash Blues" and "Big Bad John," which Jimmy Dean had made famous. Naomi joked about whether he had anything in his repertoire not by a Jim so he played "You Were on My Mind" by Sylvia Fricker Tyson. Then he showed off a bit with some finger picking - instrumental only, no singing.

"Oh, Stuart, how did you get to be so good?" Naomi asked and praised in the same sentence.

"Natch'ral talent!" Stuart quipped with cheeky grin. "No, ma'am, jus' lots uh nothin' tuh do in thuh ev'nin's 'til thuh week's done an' we gyit paid. Ah bin at it uh long tahm, too. Stahted in hah school."

The cook-owner came out from the back and told Stuart that, if he could do "The Reverend Mr. Black," his money would be no good for the breakfast.

"Ah pay muh way, suh!" Stuart protested.

"You play my request and I'll call it even," the aproned man insisted.

Stuart played and sang/recited the song. The cook joined in on the chorus. Stuart went on to "Ring of Fire" and "Folsom Prison Blues" - both Johnny Cash hits, as was the requested song.

*****

Peridot made an early start in the morning. She had a long shopping list and she wanted to return in time to shower and change. She found a sturdy basket, blue cloth serviettes, a small blue gingham tablecloth, cutlery, and a box of zipper-closure freezer bags in a discount store. At Eaton's, remembering how her father hated eating from paper or plastic plates, she bought a pair of china luncheon plates, bread-and-butter plates and almost-matching mugs from the sale bin. She returned to her room with this haul.

With the basket primed with a freezer bag of ice from the hotel's ice machine, she went off to the deli counter of the grocery store. Envelopes of sliced roast beef, sliced ham, shaved turkey and hand-cut cheese - cheddar chunks and Swiss slices - were prepared and marked with weight and price by the young deli attendant. Containers of coleslaw, potato salad and orange-and-almond salad were packed with a smile. Individual bubbles of butter and plastic envelopes of mayonnaise, horseradish and mustard completed the deli portion of the tour. The bakery counter supplied half a dozen large bread rolls and two pies - one apple and one cherry. The only remaining problem was what to drink. From the refrigerated cases, she selected a bottle of lemonade and one of iced tea. She had thought about doilies and serving trays but reconsidered. The afternoon tea the day before had been arranged for her taste. This day's event was to be a picnic for a man.

Back at the hotel, she packed two more ice packs to ensure that the meat and salads were well insulated against the forecasted heat. She found a marker, lying abandoned at the bottom of her purse following the end of the term, and used it to cover the prices of the food. She did not want him ambushed by the cost of the luncheon - especially since he had been so careful to protect her sensibilities at tea. When she finished arranging the food safely, she tucked in the remaining items, placing the pies carefully on top. She then covered the whole thing with the tablecloth and serviettes - still in their plastic covers.

Peridot chose her ankle-length denim skirt, a long-sleeved floral shirt and a crocheted cotton bucket hat, laying them, and the necessary" inner fashions", out on the bed. She then showered, fixed her hair and dressed. She had thought she was on schedule to beat Stuart to the lobby when she discovered that she could barely lift the filled basket. She dithered about whether to phone the desk for assistance but concluded that she would just grit her teeth and get it to the elevator. In the lobby, the bell captain assisted her to her favourite chair. She was just catching her breath when Stuart strode in the door with guitar case in hand.

"I hope you've had your Wheaties this morning, Mr. Cowton! It took all my strength to get this basket here," she greeted him, eyes asparkle.

"Bacon an' eggs otta do near thuh same job, Ms. Stone," he bantered back with a smile and a half wink. "An' Ah got tuh say yuh dress down real nahs, too, darlin'."

"Thank you, Mr. Cowton," she replied.

*****

When he had finished his last bite of pie, he helped her pack the remaining food and dirty dishes away.

"Thank yuh, darlin'. That was uh meal … uh real fahn picnic! An' now Ah mean tuh make use uh this ole guitar. What would yuh lahk tuh heah? Ah need no 'pologies fuh muh playin' but muh singin' voice is anuthuh mattah," he told her with a broad smile.

She hesitated.

"Jus' don't ask fuh 'Stairway tuh Heaven' now," he cautioned.

"Why? Don't you know it?" she asked innocently.

"Ah do … but anyone who plays at awl is sick tuh death uhvit."

"Then you choose," she urged.

He played "The Yellow Rose of Texas" and finished by saying, "Fuget thuh yellow rose, darlin', *you* ahr thuh only lady fuh me."

He followed with the Green Beret song, telling her that it was the first song he had learned. Next, she heard the distinctive chords of the Seekers' "I Know I'll Never Find Another You."

"Sing with me," he invited. She did - in a sweet well-controlled soprano.

"Oh, darlin', yuh put me tuh shame. That's uh real fahn voice yuh got there," he told her when they finished and then asked, "Yuh know 'Summuh Wahn'?"

"Just the chorus," she admitted.

"That's thuh woman's part. Ah'll gyit thuh rest," he said as the introduction finished and she began to sing. Instead of the sultry, seductive style he remembered from the popular recording, her approach was pure and sweet. He figured he would have willingly handed over the spurs were he confronted with such sincerity.

Next, he played "Remember the Alamo." She just listened to the words since she remembered it only vaguely from childhood.

"Mehbeh yuh'd lahk uh little Canadian content," he suggested, bridging into Ian and Sylvia's "Four Strong Winds." She sang along.

"I love that song but it's so sad it almost always makes me cry. You know he's never coming back and she won't be going there," Peridot told Stuart after the last word.

"Let's have sumpthin' happier then. British Invasion fahn with you?" Stuart asked and Peridot nodded.

"Woke up this mornin' feelin' fahn ..." he began and she recognized "Something Tells Me I'm into Something Good." She sang back-up and harmonized as required. They laughed when he changed "next week" to "next day".

"Now Ah got muh fingers limbahd up Ah'd lahk tuh show yuh some finger pickin'. Some folks think this song otta be thuh national anthem uh Texas," he told her as he began to pick. She chuckled.

"Oh, darlin', you nevah knew Texas was uh country uvit's own 'fore it joined thuh republic? Some think it otta still be. Ah got no dog in that faht. Ah just bin driftin'. Still, some parts uh Texas ifuh Texan gyits uh request fuh this song an' don't know it ... 't's big trouble. Ah jus' lahk it 'cause it's tuneful an' it shows off muh pickin' real fahn."

"Well, Ah'm uh good ole rebel an' that's jus' what Ah am. An fuh yuh grand republic Ah do not give uh ..." He broke off singing.

"Those ain't words tuh sing in front ovuh lady," he explained and went on picking without singing. "This next one is fuh uh lady's voice. 'F you know it, you best sing it. It's 'Someday Soon'."

She sang and he spoke corrections for the information in the lyrics, substituting old man for young, changing the age from twenty-one to thirty-nine, saying Montana for Colorado, and explaining that he did not like any rodeo - or anything else - as much as he liked her. He harmonized with her on the closing refrain by which time she was struggling to keep from laughing. When they finished, he reached his hand out toward her shoulder perhaps in congratulations for her singing or perhaps to steady her against the laughter which was overtaking her.

She cringed - actually cringed, he noted - before collecting herself enough to move out of his reach. He reacted, feeling deeply and immediately offended.

"Ms. Stone, Ah'm real taken with yuh but 'f' you don't fancy me an' yuh can't trust me, yuh got tuh know Ah nevah would force muh comp'ny on uh lady ... an' 'specially not on you."

Her lips pursed and her brows pulled together. With effort, she settled herself before dropping her gaze to the ground, ensuring that he could not make eye contact while she spoke.

"Mr. Cowton, that's just the problem. I do fancy you and I'm too inclined to trust you … but I know it's much too soon. This is far too fast for me," she explained.

He remembered a mutt he had tried to befriend in a war zone. The poor thing would cower as it inched closer and closer. It desperately wanted the affection and needed the food he offered but its wounds were evidence that it had been tormented and beaten. It could not trust the kind hand that Stuart had extended.

He shook his head as if to dispatch the mental image. He could not reconcile this outspoken woman with … well, he did not want to think of Peridot in the context of that broken creature. He figured, however, that there was something to be learned from the memory.

"Ah 'pologahz, darlin'. Take awl thuh tahm yuh want … an' need. Unless an' until yuh tell me yuh nevah want tuh see me agyin, Ah'll be waitin. Ah ain't goin' nowhere … an' Ah need both hands tuh play this guitah so yuh maht jes' well tell me sumpthin' yuh'd lahk tuh heah."

"How about 'Where Have All the Flowers Gone?'." she suggested.

"Well, we heard from thuh Green Berets so now yuh want tuh give thuh pacifists uh chance? Awlraht, darlin'," he agreed with a grin. He played the chords and harmonized with her as she sang lead.

"Some Gordon Lightfoot, if you know any?" she asked next and he responded with "The Minstrel of the Dawn" into which he inserted some finger picking and some harmonizing back-up as she sang. He reminded her of the words a couple of times when she hesitated.

"Ah lahk 'Bitter Green' but it's jus' too sad fuh this comp'ny," Stuart told her.

"Murray McLauchlan?" Peridot asked hesitantly.

"What d'yuh have in mahnd, darlin'? 'Farmer's Song'?" he asked.

"I'm sure you don't know 'Sweeping the Spotlight Away'," she said with a sigh.

"Ah do – not awl thuh words, though," he countered as he began playing the introduction.

She was surprised and asked him about it after they had finished singing. He explained that anytime a group of drifting ranch or rodeo hands spent an evening together before payday, they swapped songs.

"What about Stan Rogers?" she asked.

"Now yuh jes' trahn tuh stump me! Well, yuh won't with Stan. You tell me what yuh want tuh heah," he said with his slyest smile.

"How about 'The Flowers of Bermuda'?" she challenged.

"Ah know that one an' 'Thuh Idiot' an' 'Thuh Field B'hahnd thuh Plow' an' 'Thuh Mary Ellen Cahtuh' … muh new fayv'rit's 'Forty-fahv Yeahs from Now' an' Ah know one uh two more," he told her in understatement.

"Well maybe 'The Idiot' and then 'Forty-five Years from Now' if you like," she requested, deeply impressed.

They sang each song together. As they finished the second one, he remarked on the gathering clouds. He did a few bars of Roy Rogers and Dale Evans' show closer, "Happy Trails" before packing up his instrument and asking her if she would see him the next afternoon at the same time and meeting place. She agreed, reminding him of his promise that he would not hurry her into anything for which she was unready.

"Ah don't s'pose yuh brought 'n umbrella, darlin'?" he concluded.

"I was focusing on the food. I –" she admitted.

"No 'pology needed, darlin', but we'd best gyit insahd," he urged. Grabbing the basket and handing her the lighter burden of the guitar case, he explained, "Ah'm fahn but Ah got tuh keep thuh guitar drah … an' you, too, uh course."

They sprinted to the nearest doorway and gained access just before the shower began.

"You and Me and Rain on the Roof …" she sang softly before adding, "I don't remember the rest, though."

"Lots'uh good songs 'bout rain – 'In thuh Early Mornin' Rain' an' 'Have You Evah Seen thuh Rain' an' 'Listen to thuh Fallin' Rain' …" he listed.

"… and 'Rainy Day People'!" she contributed.

"Older but good, too, 'Singin' in thuh Rain' …" he countered.

"That would be my favourite. Gene Kelly was amazing in that," she declared.

"Yuh lahk tuh dance, Peridot?" he asked.

Worry crossed her face before she admitted that she liked to watch dancing and to dream about it but as it involved touching …

"F'yuh let me, Ah'll teach yuh sumpthin'. No touchin', Ah promise," he assured her. "T's cawled thuh Cowboy Hustle but it ain't no cowboy dance Ah evuh did see. Still, 't's gyitin' real pop'lar in bars an' even at thuh Stampede this yeah."

There was a man at the security/reception desk near the elevators who watched with amusement as Stuart used the spacious lobby to show Peridot how to line dance.

"Thaht's raht, darlin' … now heel, toe … heel, toe … kick an' quahtuh turn … Yuh got it!" he announced proudly. She smiled and he had to suppress the urge to give her a hug.

Before she left, Stuart had slipped out to buy two plastic raincoats from a street vendor – one to cover his guitar and one for Peridot – while she guarded the instrument and the picnic basket. He had been able to wrap the guitar case well enough to keep the instrument dry. However, Peridot had not done as well. The sky had opened up again just before she reached the hotel and the deluge had soaked her hair from which miniature rivers had run down her neck to dampen her clothes. She thought of a great uncle who used to say, "It's raining cats and dogs – I can see the poodles on the street!"

Back in her room, she changed into warm, dry clothes and towelled the moisture from her hair. She had rescued the remains of the orange-and-almond salad before sending the rest of the leftovers with Stuart. (He had clearly liked it least of the salads she had brought and it was her favourite of the three. It would, with some additions from the vending machine, be sufficient for a light supper.) He had correctly observed that she could move faster unencumbered so he had offered to take the basket and had also promised to wash the dishes and return everything but the leftover food to her the following day.

*****

The "fellahs" had not yet gone out for the evening when Stuart returned to the room so he shared the contents of the basket with them. They made jokes about his "fancy lady" and about how he must be seeing her again if she had sent the basket back with him. When it came to the food, they were appreciative, though. There had even been a sliver of apple pie with a bit of cheese for each of them.

"Stretch, yuh best watch yuhsef. Yuh losin' yuh mahnd 'cause uh that woman. Yuh stopped drinkin', yuh stopped smokin' and yuh don't go out in th' ev'nin's. She got some kahnd uh spell on you?" demanded one of the roommates.

"Shorty, you best mahnd yuh bizness," Stuart replied with narrowed eyes before adding, "Yuh eat thuh food she sent so yuh otta show some respect."

"Don't mean nothin' by it, Stretch," replied Shorty, backpedalling. "Never know'd yuh tuh be so touchy!"

Perspective

The tree was a pretty birch. Its main trunk was large but it split into three artistic prongs, each with smaller bare branches spread out as if they were the languid fingers of a huge hand. The grey and black markings on the bark stood out against the bright white of the snow which reflected back Greta's headlights. Greta had intended to crash her car at high speed into the trunk of the tree. She had chosen the birch, a well known and popular sight, because someone would surely notice. It was not her intention to force police and neighbours into a lengthy and stressful search. Greta did not feel that she was worth that. However, what she had seen when she had turned her car toward the tree had changed her mind.

*****

Peggy had been preparing her Christmas messages on cassette tapes for her nieces and nephews when the care worker had arrived for Peggy's weekly bath. Dhoullie had laughed and told Peggy that no one had cassette players anymore. Until that moment, Peggy had thought herself valuable and capable – with only a small fear that she might fall from having a weak turn in the bathtub. After bathing, she normally dressed herself while Dhoullie sat quietly watching, just in case. For the first time, Peggy sat slumped while Dhoullie did the honours.

The nieces and nephews always cashed the cheques that Peggy sent with the cassettes. She had never before let herself dwell upon the fact that they never referred to the recorded messages during their rare but treasured telephone conversations. She glanced at the four stacks of boxes, carefully packed and labelled: the creamy Rosenthal dinner set for Don, the gold-trimmed Minton for Linda, the bridal wreath Limoges for Miranda, and the turquoise serpentine Wedgewood for Daniel. They claimed to want the dishes but the boxes were beginning to buckle from waiting. Peggy, having inherited the fine china from childless great aunts and having taken supreme pleasure in selecting just the right set for each of her famous dinner parties, had hoped that the china would be treasured by the next generation.

After Dhoullie had left, Peggy used white medical tape to secure her birth certificate to her back under a gauze bandage. She put on her best coat and hat. Her boots left little prints in the fresh snow, which, in the wispy breeze, was dancing a stately quadrille to the ground. It was a bit of a hike out of town. Peggy was tired when she settled herself under the tree. A Russian short story she had read told of an old couple feeling warm before they froze to death. Peggy did not want to spoil her house for others by dying in it. The sun set. Peggy's thoughts drifted.

*****

A young woman wearing multiple piercings on her face and ears and dressed in black stood in a halo of light.

"Are you an angel?" asked Peggy drowsily.

"Of course not," Greta refuted sharply. "You must have some weird kind of faith if you think that!"

"When I was a child, I was told that God was a kind, loving father. As a young adult, I thought God was all-powerful but indifferent to our troubles and now I know that

He is a nasty man with a cruel sense of humour," exclaimed Peggy. "I should be dead now but it's too warm."

"There's a wind from the south. The temperature has climbed fifteen degrees ..." began Greta.

"See? A cruel sense of humour!"

"It's a miracle, lady. Come on. How 'bout getting a cup of tea to warm us up, my treat? Neither one of us is meant to die tonight!" declared Greta, as she helped Peggy into the car.

Never Forget the Words

She began rolling the handle-less blue-and-white teacups in the small red plastic basin of scalding water. She had ordered tea for two. Three cups always accompanied the service which included a large white pot of Chinese green tea. The scent of jasmine floating from the teapot spout coaxed memories both sweet and painful.

The server was Malay, which was a bit unusual in a low-end Chinese-Malaysian restaurant. His English was just barely equal to the task of taking her order. Her Malay did not extend past "*tandas*" - which would get her guidance to the nearest toilets. Her Mandarin was not much better - just greetings, introductions and thanks.

As she shook drops from the almost painfully hot cups, Ms. Pansy Pincombe wondered if Pan Li Pei would actually turn up and, if so, whether he would need to disguise himself in some way. She remembered other such meetings for tea in the past when they were free to move about comparatively unnoticed - except for the fact that she had been blonde then instead of grey and her western eyes and nose had contrasted glaringly with his delicately drawn Asian features. While the couple would have caused at least a stare or two, there had been no mobs of fans in his wake then. It had been she not he who had attracted attention.

She remembered his long, elegant fingers rolling other trios of cups in other plastic basins - sometimes cobalt blue and sometimes bright red - as he made a gallant performance of protecting her hands from the steaming water. The last time had been a decade before. Then she had still been in awe of him and more than a little on fire for him. This explained why the pictures and sensations in her mind remained so clear in detail and were so easily summoned even now. Memorable were the fragrance of jasmine tea slipping into the air like a ghost on a foggy night; the tiny beads of perspiration that trickled down her skin before being absorbed by the cotton undershirt which she wore in obedience to her long-dead grandmother's instructions; the oppressive heat modified only slightly by the blast of moist air from the oscillating fans under the veranda's eaves; the short-sleeved white cotton dress under the wrist-length turquoise linen jacket that she had worn to protect her pale skin from sunburn; and the beating against her cheeks of the stray hairs which had been teased by the fan from the tight bun she had pinned up that morning.

His shoulder-length baby-fine hair, which appeared black in interior light, revealed hints of chestnut and dark auburn highlights under the sun. That day he had worn a cerise linen shirt which she had bought him in an effort to expand his mostly black and white wardrobe, relieved only occasionally by brown and beige pieces. He had winked and lightly brushed her short, pale fingers with his long, burnished forefinger. Even now she had to suppress the electric shiver that this memory provoked.

She smiled at the thought that his story was the opposite of most rock stars. Rather than becoming a success and, with the sudden disposable income, being seduced into drug problems, he had beaten - with her support - all his bad-boy habits before striking it rich. Pansy had been well aware, from careful research, that there was a chance that he would lose interest in her when he became clean. It had not come all at once during his recovery. In fact, there had been a handful of years when she had made friends with her travel agent in negotiations to get the best-fitting tickets for every opportunity that either she or Li could snatch to visit the other's country. The low international value of his country's currency combined with a lack of remunerative job opportunities for him had meant that, whichever of them travelled, the tickets and most of the expensive phone calls to arrange details came from her diminishing savings. Eventually, they had each started new and better jobs, resulting in over a year of reduced flexibility. His music was just beginning to be in demand and his day job still allowed no chance for travel when she had called to say that she had earned the right to two weeks holidays in the coming July. She had asked about suitable dates and he had hesitated.

"Maybe it's not such a good time to come. I'm working hard every day and I have a few gigs in the evenings ..." Li had told her.

"You know that I love to hear you sing. I could come with you in the evenings and I'm quite able to amuse myself safely in the daytime. We could stay at Mid-Valley. It's more convenient to your office and it can't be worse than your family's place for getting to your gigs," she had assured him, thinking of the multi-generational home in a suburb of K-L where he lived with his mother, three sisters, a brother-in-law and an assortment of nieces and nephews, as well as a baby grandnephew. It had always been a delight to Pansy that Li's mother approved of the relationship.

Li's response to her proposed visit had not been enthusiastic. There had been a pause of seconds that seemed an eternity. A stab in the chest could not have robbed her of her breath more effectively.

"We'll wait and see," he had said before ringing off.

Pansy, recognizing the death knell of the relationship, had raged and stamped her foot. She had howled and wept until it seemed that she had no tears left. She had fallen into a despair that took gallons of ice cream to relieve. Then she had had her hair cut short before sorting the clothes that he kept at her place. There were two piles. One had easily replaceable items and clothing that would never be needed in a hot country. These she had given to charity - including the pricey winter boots she had bought him during his last visit. He had been unwilling, she recalled with a half-smile, to be seen in any of the shoe store's affordable offerings available in his size.

The other pile included mementos, papers, a favourite shirt and other odds and ends. These, she had mailed by surface post to Malaysia. In her pique, she had not checked the papers piece by piece. As a result, poems that she had written - some inspired by their time together - had crept through time zones until they had arrived in Li's hands, without her realizing or intending this.

*****

She was marvelling at how quickly the Malaysian climate moisturized her normally dry skin when a strange man took a seat across from her at her table. Unlike her memory of Li's tall, lean elegance, this man was medium height and pudgy with a bad case of what a friend whose husband was a police office described as "cruiser butt." It resulted from sitting too much in cars or, perhaps in this case, in office chairs. The stranger also had a migrating hair line, dark aviator sunglasses and a costly straw-coloured linen suit. Completing the outfit was a cream silk shirt with a stand-up Chinese-style collar which obviated the need for a necktie.

In response to her blatant recoil and glance around for a safe and graceful egress, he slid a business card across the table toward her. It proclaimed his association with a firm of barristers and solicitors. She smiled but not warmly.

"I expected to see him, not attend a meeting with a lawyer. I would have brought my own representative and would have suggested a chic little tea and cake shop or a trendy cafe had I known this would happen. When he was out of work, we would sometimes meet in a place like this one so that he could afford to pay if he wanted to offer to treat. Even when he was low on money, he still had his male pride," she told the man, enunciating in such a clear manner that it made it seem that she had a bad taste in her mouth.

"He wants to know what you want and why you come back after all these years," the lawyer tossed back.

"Then he should have the courtesy to ask me - not send a … messenger," she replied, pausing before the noun to show that she was choosing carefully. She had considered using "lackey" instead of messenger but preferred to deliver the insult by implication.

"He doesn't meet people in public places," the lawyer began.

She could tell that he meant to go on. A recollection of Jean Hagen in *Singin in the Rain* sputtering, "People, I ain't people!" flashed through Pansy's mind. The thought inspired a wicked little grin.

"I don't meet strange men in public places - or private ones either, for that matter. Li and I meant something to each other once. We had a relationship that lasted ten years and spanned two continents and three countries. I had hoped that he would have the decency … the respect to come here himself, considering that he accepted my invitation and -"

"He wants -" the lawyer tried to interrupt.

"- AND," she interjected, taking back control with greater volume, "considering that I am his uncredited lyricist."

"Now we are getting somewhere!" he uttered triumphantly.

"No, Mr. Chan, we are getting nowhere. I'm leaving now. Please enjoy the tea. I will settle the account on the way out. I'm staying at the place I stayed on my first trip to Malaysia - when Li and I met. He knows where that is if he wishes to leave a message for me. I will be sightseeing in K-L. Notify him that I would have been happy to come to some agreement over tea today but now it will cost him a dinner at The Pan Pacific - where I am not staying - and I might just find it necessary to call the press so that there's a nice picture in the media for him to explain ..."

"You wouldn't ..." the lawyer started.

"It would never have entered my mind if he had turned up here as agreed," she responded icily.

"His wife is very concerned about your visit here," Mr. Chan explained.

"I saw her picture on the Internet. She's less than half my age and she seems like she has an entourage to keep her looking beautiful. I can't imagine that I could pose any threat to her. Li had moved on when it ended between us - ten years ago. It took me a little more time but I have no interest in trying to rekindle that fire. It's ancient history, now," Pansy explained with a serene face. It belied the hurt she still felt - or was it just the memory of hurt. After the anger had faded, she had felt wounded. Even when this was no longer raw, she had decided she would never allow herself to be that vulnerable again. Now, conflict, like so many other things, exhausted her. It was essential to disguise this as she wanted no one to know.

"Besides, I'm happier and more centred when I'm on my own than I have ever been with any man," she spat, rising and turning her back on the lawyer. When she caught the waiter's attention, she twirled her index finger in the air to indicate, as per local custom, that she wanted to settle the bill. The bank note she handed him exceeded the account by much more than the few cents that it was customary to leave when satisfied with the service but she waved him away when he tried to run after her with the change. Tipping in the way of western culture had not existed in Malaysia ten years before. Evidently that had not changed.

To ensure that she was unavailable (and, therefore, could not appear overly eager), she travelled to the Central Market. Instead of the stiflingly hot building she remembered, she found a renovated shell with tinted glass and an air-conditioned interior. She bought gifts of miniature carved and painted masks, batik shirts and scarves, and *songket* table runners for friends, paying the price quoted without argument.

She remembered Li's amused response when he discovered that she had done this on her first visit to the Market. When she had expressed an interest in making a subsequent visit, he had insisted upon going with her. Whenever she found something that she liked and asked the price, she would wait for the seller's quote and then look toward Li. Invariably the price would be too high in his estimation and he would shake his head. The seller would respond with, "But for you ..." and fill in a lower price. She learned to feel only marginally uncomfortable with the bargaining culture. Where she came from, the price was the price and the customer either wanted the product at that amount or left the item in the store.

*****

Although, on principle, she preferred the old scorching, dusty, sweaty form of the market, she was thankful for the strength-preserving modern facility. It was necessary to measure out her power through the day so that her true condition would not be written large across her face and in her every motion. Pansy stopped for a restorative break in the upstairs tearoom, where she ordered a mango lassi. It was not ice cold when it arrived but it was as sweet and fragrant as expected and it bought her time in a chair and away from the push and shove of other shoppers. When she caught her second wind, she gathered her purchases and returned to the hotel.

She splurged on dinner in the hotel's extravagant Chinese restaurant. It was richly decorated in reds and golds with sentries of reproduction terra-cotta warriors at the gate. After her meal, a stop at the desk to check for messages yielded a polite assurance that nothing had come for her. When she turned to leave, a smile on the face of a tall man lounging in a deep lobby chair arrested her attention. He wore dark tinted glasses, a baseball cap, jeans and a faded cerise shirt that had been in fashion ten years before but now looked a bit worse for wear. He stood up, clasped her arm tightly and said through his teeth, "Don't say my name!"

The bell captain moved swiftly toward her, intending to protect the foreign lady from the stranger.

"Thank you for your kindness but it's quite all right. I know the gentleman and I have been expecting a message from him. I'm a little surprised to find him waiting for me but there is no reason for concern," Pansy assured her uniformed guardian before asking, "Is there a café or tearoom in the mall?"

"Certainly, madam," he replied, giving her directions.

She eased a five ringgit note discreetly into his hand.

"That was too much," insisted Li when they were out of earshot.

"It's what I had handy and I like knowing that someone is looking out for me," she argued.

"We could go to your room," Li suggested.

"Are you daft?" she volleyed.

"We need to talk and I can't risk being recognized,"

"You should have turned up at tea," she admonished.

"I'm sorry about that. I was advised not to," Li replied.

She laughed before reminding him that she had never before known him to accept advice willingly.

"Would you ride in the car with me or do you not trust me there either?" he returned.

"First, how anonymous is your car? Second, do you really want to have this conversation in a traffic jam?" Pansy bantered.

"Did I leave you because you were too smart for me?" he needled.

"No, I thought you left me because we'd spent all my savings," she countered.

"Oh, that was nasty!" Li shot back.

"Yes, it was but the truth was nastier. I think you had already met someone - your current wife or someone in between?"

"Did we ever love each other?" Li wondered aloud.

"I can't speak for *you*," she retorted and, realizing that they were standing in the middle of an arm of the mall, added, "Let's go to the coffee shop for a chai latte or, better, to a place where we can get some wonderful Malaysian cold drinks. This is the best country I know for interesting alcohol-free drinks. Maybe we can find a quiet corner."

"Give me your room key," he said slipping her a fifty ringgit note with one of his hands while holding the other out to receive the key card. When she glared at him, he clarified, "You get the drinks to take away and we can talk in your room in guaranteed privacy."

"No matter what I say we always end up doing things your way - but I warn you, if we talk where you want, I expect you to be generous in your negotiations. Think on that while you're waiting for me!" Pansy insisted before surrendering the card. She was thankful that she had kept her medication in the room safe so that no matter where he snooped, he could not invade her privacy in that, at least.

She returned with two takeaway cups dripping condensation from the meeting of the icy drinks within and the hot air without. She recalled the challenges of trying to sip takeout drinks through straws stuck into plastic bags knotted at the top. That Malaysian custom went back to her first trip to the country. Instead, the drinks she held now were served in the same lidded plastic containers as might be found in her home country. The contents of one cup appeared opaque pink - the iced rose lassi - and the other was transparent green - the apple *katsuri,* a favourite from the shop's menu.

"Lassi? Really? That's traditional," he observed with disbelief and not quite contempt.

"It doesn't matter to me. Take whichever you want," Pansy conceded yet again, holding out one in each hand.

"No, you always preferred the *katsuri.* Take it. You're only here a short time," he offered generously. He curled his fingers around the bottom of the pink drink, careful not to touch her fingers but tempted to elicit the reaction that would have followed such an action.

"You know the one I could never learn to like? What's it called?" she asked with the sour expression the taste would have provoked. "Do people still drink that here?"

He nodded, naming the locally popular malt beverage and smiling at the memory of her efforts to be polite when his mother had treated Pansy to the concoction.

She struggled to pull his change out of her pocket.

"Keep it! I should be taking you out for dinner but it's not that easy for me these days and Elke wouldn't like it," Li apologized. They paused a moment to take long draws on their respective drinks. She smiled with satisfaction at the sweet-tart taste. He nodded to acknowledge her pleasure.

"It's fine. I just didn't like your Mr. Chan … and would Elke like it any better if she knew you were in my hotel room?"

"Probably not. Are you going to tell her?" Li asked raising his fine eyebrows and the corners of his lips in unison - as a choir rising to sing an anthem. He looked her over and noted that, though a little more snug, the ankle-length local store-brand denim skirt they had bought together in this very mall more than ten years before still looked good on her. In fact, the effect was more to his taste. She had been inclined to wear her clothes on the baggy side then.

"I don't want to cause problems in your marriage. I just want you to treat me fairly. You knew where I was all this time. You should have contacted me," Pansy admonished.

"I should have. I was a little ashamed of how things ended between us."

"So you just thought you'd compound the crime by using my words without giving me credit - or compensation," she accused, putting no effort into softening the sarcasm.

"Sorry. Did you ever get your little pied-à-terre in France or was it Italy? That was your retirement dream, wasn't it?" he asked hoping for a safer subject.

"No, everything I had saved for that purpose went on airline tickets and hotel rooms and dining out so that we could see each other ... and then real estate prices went up ... and I'm still working - one more term and I'll retire. I don't ever expect to be in a position to make *that* dream a reality."

"I'm sorry. I never realized that you didn't have an unlimited source of funds. Compared to my upbringing you seemed to be so very rich," Li replied with a wry smile.

"The old myth that all foreigners must be rich ..." Pansy interjected in a cynical tone.

"Especially blond-haired white ladies ..." Li chuckled.

"Just think about it. It has the same validity as the Malay *Bumiputra* belief that all Chinese Malaysians must be rich. Still, after you'd seen my house and how hard I worked ... and how much more expensive it was to live in Canada, you should have figured it out," she lectured, taking a final swig of the *katsura* and punctuating it with a noisy draw on the empty straw.

He laughed brightly at her uncharacteristic noise, becoming serious before his response.

"Even when I got clean, I didn't pay enough attention to you. Addicts are selfish but I don't have any excuse for afterwards. Is that why you left me?"

"I didn't leave you – though I should have. I look back now and wonder how I could have been such an idiot to put up with less than your best for so long," Pansy lamented.

"So, after all these years, why come back now?" Li asked.

"I'm in the winter of my life, Li, and I have a few things to tidy up. Imagine my surprise last month when I put on the local pop station to get a weather report and I hear *your* voice and *my* words!"

"You hadn't heard me before that? I'm offended!" he huffed.

"I figure 'Panda Eyes' has to be a huge international hit if I'm hearing a Malaysian artist on my local station. Imagine how much more air play you could have had in Canada if you had met even part of the Canadian content MAPL designation by crediting a Canadian lyricist," Pansy needled.

"You *gave* me that poem!" he shot back.

"If I had given you a painting, would you have had the gall to say you painted it?" she returned in a mocking tone.

"Mmm," he considered, "maybe not. It would have been a comedown. After all, I'm better with oil and canvas than you."

"No, you're a better copyist than I am," she challenged, "and I've never known you to produce an original work on canvas."

"True, true. So it's money you're after? You could never stand it if you were shortchanged." He shook his head at the memory, as if it could be dispatched by the gesture.

"You know me better than that. I always returned the overage if someone gave me too much change. It's fairness I'm after," she sniffed, "and I've done my research. You - Pixieman and the Gr8 Panda Band - had two other charting songs with my lyrics —'The Eternal-Summer Boy'— which I wrote about you but don't remember giving to you - and 'When You Feel Like *Hmm*, You Have to Look Like Gold.' In Malaysia, you used 'lead' and in the US the word is the rude *s*-word for excrement and in most other places it's issued as what I originally wrote, 'When You Feel Like Crap, You Have to Look Like Gold.' I rather like the Malaysian version - it makes more literary sense. I *know* that I never gave *that* to you. I started it before I met you. It's about the aftermath of a previous relationship. How did you get it?"

"I think you must have left a copy here or, maybe, when you were angry and sent all my clothes and odds and sods back to me, one poem, or maybe both, was in the package. I don't really remember. Does it matter?" he said by way of admission.

"Not really - as long as I don't need to deal with Mr. Chan again and as long as I get satisfaction."

"My wife might have something to say ..." Li began with an evil chuckle.

"Don't flatter yourself. I don't mean that kind of satisfaction and you know it," Pansy snapped.

"I know - but, Pansy, I can still get some pleasure out of twisting your ears," he retorted with a grin. He walked over to the chair she occupied, placed his exquisite hands firmly on either side of her face and bent down to kiss her lips. She kept her teeth clamped together and her lips firmly compressed. It was a struggle for her to show no response but she was determined that he should not know how much this revived old feelings - and especially old hurts.

He was almost fifty now but still slender and elegant. There were a few lines on his face but, if anything, they added character. His forehead seemed fractionally longer but his hair still provided full coverage on the top, sides and back. A dusting of silver hairs gleamed amongst the dark. He no longer pulled the pigmentationally challenged ones out as he had done when they had been together. In those days she had looked so much younger than her years that no one could have guessed at the ten-year age difference between them. This was no longer the case. She looked all of her sixty years. She had earned every white hair and each wrinkle but she carried them with as much poise and confidence as her current life force allowed. This, and her still-lively eyes, allowed her a certain attractiveness.

"I have no effect on you?" he asked with a note of disappointment as he returned to his place on the room's only other chair.

"Li, I'm long past being angry over our breakup but I don't expect that I will ever completely recover from the hurt. In fact, I don't work at it anymore. The hurt is what keeps me safe. As long as I hurt so much over you, I will never be tempted to trust anyone romantically again. Please don't toy with me. I can hire lawyers, too, but I don't want to. I want you to come up with a fair and reasonable offer. That way we both avoid expense and public humiliation."

There was a period of silence during which she mentally started marshalling arguments she had hoped not to need. She could see from the crease between his brows that he was deep in thought.

"How would I explain the fact that I failed to credit you before now?" he asked.

This was not what she had expected. It triggered a sharp puff of air through her nose, which, had she given it voice, might have come out as a snort. It was fuelled by surprise not derision, however.

"Just say that you found the poems but you have just discovered that I was the poet and, now that you know, you want to make sure that I am properly credited - decent person that you are!" Pansy recommended with a cheeky grin.

"I've been invited to perform and make a presentation at a music awards thing in the States next year. I liked it better when I was receiving awards, I must say … but I could fly you down and bring you up on stage and make the announcement then. What do you say?"

"There are some things going on and I'm not sure that I'll be available much next year. I was hoping for something a little sooner," she replied lightly, concerned that her inner struggle to sound casual would become evident to him.

"'I have a 'Best of' album coming out. In fact, I have studio time booked this week to put down a couple of bonus tracks. You could come and hang out," he offered.

"Will Elke be there?" Pansy asked cautiously.

"I really don't know," he replied, hinting at the exasperation he felt on the subject. "Things aren't great between us right now. She says she's picked out a lawyer to … well, you can guess … but I really don't want to lose my kids. Helly - she's the baby, just two years old - she's got my hair and Elke's nose but she has green eyes, kind of like yours. She's smart and pretty. Arthur -"

"- Arthur?" interjected Pansy in disbelief.

"Yes, Arthur, after The Beatles' haircuts … Arthur's nine - almost ten - and not so pretty to look at but he has perfect pitch. Man, can that kid play guitar and draw and … I wish you could meet them but that would really put a twist Elke's knickers," Li enthused.

"Then what are you doing here, Li?" Pansy asked softly, concerned for him.

He slid to the edge of his chair and reached for one of Pansy's hands, which were resting just above her knees. He enclosed the captured hand in both of his and tried to hold her gaze but she looked away.

"Elke's young and blonde and gorgeous. She likes my looks and my success ... and the money ... and being part of a celebrity couple. All of those can disappear. I know that now. I'm not sure she likes the things about me that can't disappear. I'm not sure she loves *me.* My mother always told me that *you* loved *me,*" Li told her earnestly.

"It's a little late to figure this out now, Li," Pansy replied, patting his hands with her free one in the manner that one pats a distressed child on the head. The gesture said, *"I care for you but you have to sort this out for yourself."*

"Tell me that you love me. Show me that you love me. I'm so hungry for a truly loving touch," he moaned.

The thought of lying in familiar arms tore at her. She considered that this might be her last chance for such comfort. That, however, was all that she wanted and she knew that it would not stop there. Li would see it as a train going off onto a siding. The engineer could not put just part of the train onto the siding. It would have to be all.

"Li, even if I were willing to gamble that my own heart might not be ripped to shreds again, what good would this do you? Women know. Elke would know and you and your kids would be the losers. I should not ... could not ... would not want to be responsible for that. I need what's best for *me* and I still want what is best for *you.* Nothing that can happen in this room, except a fair and just agreement concerning authorship of the lyrics, can be good for both of us or, in fact, *either* of us ... and don't worry about money, I'm not greedy, Li."

*****

On the last day of her life, Pansy Pincombe left her tiny but pretty pied-à-terre in the historic centre of Strasbourg, France. Li had willingly bought the bright retreat for her in lieu of royalties. For the first few months, she had been able to enjoy walking and shopping in the old city. She had made almost daily visits to the stunning thousand-year-old cathedral where she meditated or prayed depending upon her mood and the strength of her faith on that particular day. More recently, the distance was too great and her energy too low to go beyond a few steps from her door.

This last day, she tottered, a bit unsteadily, to the café which was but a few metres from her startlingly purple front door. She gloried in the taste and texture of a *pain au chocolat* presented on an icing-sugar dusted plate, garnished with a cut and fanned juicy red strawberry. She inhaled the aroma of a honeyed-pear-and-cherry tisane as she waited for it to cool enough that it would be gentle on the sensitive lining of her mouth.

She exchanged a lively banter in English with a former student, passed a few words in Italian with the immigrant server who brought her order, and made the café owner smile with her distinctive mixture of high school French and the rural Québecois *joual* learned in her youth during a summer homestay in La Belle Province.

When she returned to her little place, she loaded the review copy of the CD, *The Best of Plus: Pan Li Pei – Pixieman and the Gr8 Panda Band,* that had arrived by courier earlier that week. She cued it up and, as the first song, "Panda Eyes" began to play, she studied the credits:

Music by Pan Li Pei
Lyrics by Pansy Pincombe

Three more of the twelve songs had the same designation. The lyrics to "Case by Case" had been handed to Li in the chauffeur-driven car on the way to the airport ten months before. This last song was performed by Li alone with just his guitar. The words detailed certain legal situations and the refrain to each verse commented upon whether a lawyer should be called.

The first stanza described an impending divorce and closed with the refrain:

> If it's been all about greed
> And not at all about need
> Better call your lawyer!

Pansy was weakening but she smiled as she heard the words:

> When she's been honest and fair
> And you know you took her share,
> Never send your lawyer!
> (Man, it will just make her mad!) – an ad lib spoken in the background.

The note that had come with the CD was handwritten:

> Pansy,
>
> Hope you like this. Even though you won't say it, I know that you love me because you won't agree to do anything that's bad for me!
>
> Love Always,
> Li – your Pixieman

She had decided not to take her medication that morning. There was little time left for her anyway and, though she knew the prescriptions kept her alive, they also made her sick to her stomach and left her feeling lethargic and deeply depressed. She had wanted just one good day or even part of one.

She thought she heard Li say, "Are you satisfied now?"

She thought she replied, "Yes, completely." She might have smiled again but her heart had already stopped beating.

Last Rodeo: Epilogue

In the days that followed the picnic, Stuart took Peridot to the diner to meet Naomi, who begged Peridot not to hurt him. She took Stuart to lunch at The Palliser where they dined with Fred. Stuart received Fred's approval. In the hotel's business centre, she set Stuart up with an email account and taught him how to use MSN instant messaging so that they could keep in contact after her return home.

She was startled and amused to discover that, though he spoke in dialect, he wrote in standard English.

"Military didn't cyeh fuh reports written in muh way uh speakin'," he explained, "an' b'sahds, they teach us thuh Northern kahnd uh wrahtin' in school."

Every day, he was a man with a plan for a free or inexpensive activity around the city and everyday she had an amendment. He learned to take these with good humour.

In a public garden, the day before her flight home, he asked if he had proven himself enough that she would allow him to continue his courtship in the area of her residence.

"What will happen if I say no?" she had asked.

He looked a little discouraged but shot back, "Then Ah guess Ah'd ask yuh tuh meet me in uh neutral place ... in uh month's tahm ... so's yuh'd have tahm tuh miss me! Jus' so's yuh know Ah'm serious but Ah'm not meanin' tuh hurry yuh none."

She had given his hand a brief squeeze then and his battered face had erupted into a smile of such delight that the sadness at leaving so soon had ambushed her.

"As always, I have a counteroffer," she told him playfully, after she had blotted a few escaping tears.

"Jus' tell me, darlin' Dot. Ah'm not sure Ah c'n stand thuh suspense," he teased.

"Toronto is no longer my home but I know it well. I would be willing to meet you there in two weeks if you think you could find a way to get there on such short notice."

"Ah b'lieve Ah cyan – 'f'Ah got tuh move heaven an' earth," he proclaimed.

"Besides, I think a month might be too long to be without your kind attentions," she added with a lilt in her voice and a sparkle in her eyes. With just a short and feisty but not hostile exchange, they were able to come to an agreement on a meeting place.

The next morning, he found her as she waited to board the airport shuttle.

"Mr. Cowton, do you think it would be forward of me to kiss you at this early stage in our relationship?" she asked solemnly.

"No, ma'am!" he answered immediately, concerned that she might revoke the implied offer.

"Just a little one, mind!" she told him firmly, narrowing her eyes in warning.

He bent close to her ear and softly began to sing the lovely old standard, "A Kiss to Build a Dream On." When he reached the end of the fourth line, she turned and kissed him quickly and lightly on the lips before grasping her bags and heading for the shuttle's open door.

"I'll wait for you in two weeks," she called as she boarded.

"No yuh won't, darlin'. Ah mean tuh gyit there first!" he bantered just before the bus door closed. He beamed, pleased, for once, to have the last word.

www.ingramcontent.com/pod-product-compliance
Lightning Source LLC
LaVergne TN
LVHW090222010725
815114LV00007B/173